THE SEVEN SISTERS

Alex Wheatle is the author of *East of Acre Lane*, which won the 1999 London Arts Board Writers' Award. He spent most of his childhood in care homes and foster families. He has worked with the Book Trust and the London Arts Board to promote literature. He lives in South London with his wife and three children.

by the same author

Brixton Rock
East of Acre Lane

THE SEVEN SISTERS

ALEX WHEATLE

FOURTH ESTATE • *London*

First published in Great Britain in 2002 by
Fourth Estate
A Division of HarperCollins*Publishers*
77–85 Fulham Palace Road,
London W6 8JB
www.4thestate.com

10 9 8 7 6 5 4 3 2 1

A catalogue record for this book is available from
the British Library

ISBN 0-00-713584-X

Typeset by Palimpsest Book Production Limited,
Polmont, Stirlingshire
Printed in Great Britain by Clays
Clays Ltd, St Ives, plc

For Carol, Tony and the Donnelly family

Acknowledgements

Thanks to Chris Holley (counsellor) for your advice, support and encouragement and my deepest gratitude to WPC Debbie Carson and the rest of her team who vigorously worked alongside CHILE, who have dedicated many months and years to the Operation Middleton investigation. Thanks to Chris, Lee, Kim and the rest of the gang at Book Trust.

'Oh children weep no more
Oh my sycamore tree, saw the freedom tree . . .'
Bob Marley

THE SEVEN SISTERS

Prologue

It had been the third suicide of one of Curvis Butler's junior class mates within five years. In 1980, Samantha Redding strangled the life out of her three-month-old baby, then, with the dead infant in the passenger seat, she drove at high speed, smashing head-on into a concrete pillar. During the summer of 1982, Mark Kelly had launched himself from a platform and met death in front of a Northern Line tube train. A few weeks ago, Elvin Walker had flung himself off a motorway bridge and died instantly under the thigh-high wheels of a truck. Following the Samantha Redding funeral, Curvis vowed never to attend another one. But he felt obliged to pay his respects for Elvin in some form or other.

A strange sense of apathy troubled Curvis as he approached the house. Flowers and cards of sorrow displayed how popular Elvin was. Somehow, Curvis felt numb to his friend's death;

when he had heard the bad news he couldn't produce any tears and he rebuked himself for not being surprised upon hearing of Elvin's abrupt end.

Curvis wiped his forehead clean of the rainwater as he entered the lounge. Noting the teak-armed furniture, he wondered if he had wiped his feet on entry into the house as his soaked moccasins sank into the deep carpet. He surveyed the room and picked a glass of apple juice. The framed picture of a leopard in the African wild, hanging above the mantelpiece, caught his attention and he stood, trapped in its gaze. Elvin's wife, Michelle, who was circulating the room, accepting hugs and kind words, noted the thought-lines in his forehead which seemed too deep for someone still in their twenties. He had the eyes of a man who had witnessed many things, good and bad, she thought, yet there was a strange calm in his face that Michelle thought bordered on indifference. She noticed the way he hung his head when he walked, almost staring at his feet. His goatish beard grew freely, suggesting to Michelle that Curvis didn't care what people said about him. He was of slim build but a powerful presence, something between a 800-metre runner and a lightweight boxer. Dressed in an old mac and flared trousers that were in fashion ten years ago, he was scanning the room as if he had to write an essay about it.

She approached him quietly. 'Why did Elvin kill himself, Curvis?' Michelle suddenly asked. He jolted, shocked out of his indifference. 'I know you wasn't best friends with Elvin but you did grow up with him in *that* home. You knew him better than most.'

Curvis fingered his shoulder-length, brown locks, a glass of apple juice shaking in his other hand. He felt that Michelle deserved the truth, but he had been avoiding the truth, blocking it out of his everyday life, since the age of sixteen. For Curvis, only when death occurred did truth return to invade his life. Besides, he was sworn to lifelong secrecy. He

2

glanced at the framed wedding photos of Elvin and Michelle resting on the mantelpiece. It was only now that the cold reality of Elvin's death smacked him in the skull. 'Why am I feeling this way?' he asked himself. He closed his eyes as an image of Elvin grew before him. 'It's hard to explain what he went through in the home,' he answered finally.

'I thought he got over all that,' Michelle responded. 'The last three years were the happiest of his life. He had a decent job, good prospects and someone who loved him.'

'But all that couldn't wipe out the memories,' Curvis replied coldly, training his eyes on the leopard.

'What memories?' Michelle raised her voice. 'What happened to him in the home? Why can't you or anyone else tell me what happened? I was his wife! Haven't I got the right to know?'

Curvis sipped his apple juice and met Michelle's eyes. His face remained still, blinking rarely as Michelle's gaze drilled into him. If neither he nor any of his peers could handle the past, then how could a poor widow, who could never understand or even begin to accept the unacceptable. 'He was picked on a lot, you know, beaten up by the people who were supposed to look after him.'

Michelle sat down beside Curvis on the sofa. 'Go on,' she urged, holding Curvis's gaze so it was impossible for him to look away.

'That is basically it. That's all we know. Every now and again his housefather would pick on him.'

'Everyone gets a walloping from their mum and dad now and again,' Michelle remarked, frustration evident in her voice. 'There must have been something else that went on.'

'Not that I know of.'

'Not that you know of? You're a liar! Just because people get picked on when they are kids, it doesn't mean they gotta kill themselves when they are adults!'

Michelle wiped her eyes as Curvis's discomfort spread

through his body. He shifted in his seat but he still kept control of his facial expression. 'Look, I'm doing more damage than good, maybe this wasn't a good idea.'

Michelle stood up, wiping her cheeks. 'I didn't mean to . . .'

'It's alright,' Curvis reassured her. 'It's natural to try and understand why Elvin took his own life. What we go through in our childhood shapes our whole life. Sometimes it can be a blessing, sometimes it can destroy you, no matter how successful you are as an adult.' Curvis got to his feet, collected his thoughts and prepared to leave.

Michelle watched him suspiciously. 'What destroyed Elvin's life, Curvis?' For a split second Michelle detected a rage within Curvis. It left as quickly as it had come. She tried to read his face. Curvis dropped his head, peering into the carpet. 'Why didn't you come to Elvin's funeral?' she asked. 'A lot of your old Pinewood Oaks friends were there.'

'Because I want to remember Elvin as someone who was happy, not someone in a coffin.'

Michelle shook her head. 'You homes people are weird, different to everybody else.'

'That's 'cos we were treated different to everyone else. Look, like I said before, I'm gutted for what happened to Elvin. I would like to show how sorry I am but I don't know how . . . Elvin was alright, a good mate, but he wouldn't want you to look in his past.'

Curvis bade his farewell and went out into the street. The rain had relented but had left its mark in small puddles along the kerb. He wondered whether he should have told Michelle the truth about what Elvin went through. But if Michelle was told the truth, she would remember Elvin as a victim, not as a husband, nor as a best friend who enjoyed adult life, but as a victim. Elvin wouldn't want that, Curvis told himself.

As he walked to the bus stop, images of his childhood in Pinewood Oaks flashed through his mind. He could see his

4

friends Bullet and Glenroy wrestling on the grass. He saw Carlton, his best pal, speeding by on his bike. Elvin came to life, giggling and hiding behind a bush. Lastly, Curvis saw himself, adventuring into the Pinewood Hills, running up and down between the trees and the foliage.

Curvis boarded the bus, and with his mind refusing to come back to the present, he muttered under his breath. He ran a quick check to see if there was anybody else on the top deck; there wasn't. A second later, he slammed his forehead against the perspex glass, wanting to give himself pain.

Wormwood Scrubs Prison, May 1985

A young man's head was tilting over the metal rail of the bed, his throat viced by strained fingers. The victim's eyes betrayed his fear as blood spilled out from his torn nostril, spotting the concrete floor.

'Don't fucking *dare* tea-leaf my bacco again, *right*?'

A right fist connected with the thief's cheekbone, sounding like a cricket ball hitting an advertising board. 'Do you hear me? You fucking tea-leaf. *Do* you fucking hear me!'

A black guy entered the cell, chewing a matchstick like a cow grinding grass. For a moment, he was strangely fascinated by the victim's petrified eyes and he wondered why the man never returned any blows. He was about to turn around and leave the thief to his sorry fate when he noticed the flecks of blood on the cold floor. In a calm but authoritative voice, he ordered, 'That's enough, Gravesey. I think he's got your hint.'

Gravesey released his grip, turned around and looked at the solid, coffin-shaped jaw, moving up and down and reducing the matchstick to pulp. 'You know I hate tea-leafs,' offered Gravesey.

Satisfied with the punishment inflicted, Gravesey left,

wiping his blood-stained fingers on his denim prison over-alls.

'Thanks, Carlton, you're a diamond,' the thief stuttered gratefully. 'A real mate.'

'And what makes you think I'm your mate?' Carlton replied coldly. 'I just don't like to see someone getting the shit kicked out of them just after dinner . . . You're new here, and you'd better learn that bacco is like fucking gold when you're doing bird.'

Before the man had a chance to say any more, Carlton about-turned and left. As he made his way to his own cell, he glanced down from the iron-railed balcony and surveyed his fellow inmates playing a variety of games – table tennis, cards and chess. A trio of screws were patrolling the stone walkways, each bearing enough keys to open any treasure chest.

Carlton could always work out who were the new arrivals. For, more often than not, they sat silently in isolation, their faces full of regret, pondering their stupid crimes while cautiously observing their surroundings. They always recoiled to the sound of heavy, metal doors slamming. Carlton liked to get to know the fresh intake, he knew he would receive their respect and they would look up to him.

Carlton found he had his cell to himself; his cellmate was frantically gambling downstairs to supplement his prison currency. The walls of his living quarters were partly decorated with pictures of topless women. The screws thought this normal, but what they deemed abnormal were the pictures and cut-outs of trees which surrounded Carlton's bunk. Fellow inmates never questioned him, but during lights-out, in whispered conversations, he was referred to as the 'tree man of Wormwood Scrubs'.

Sellotaped to the wall, just above his pillow, was the only clue to Carlton's life before prison. A black and white photograph of a twelve-year-old boy sitting on his bike, flanked by his friends: one with a spanner in his hand, one eating a chocolate bar and another with a comic war magazine jutting out from his back pocket.

Carlton parked himself on his bunk and thought about how much he loved his friends, and that rusty bike. He also remembered how much he respected the woman who took the photo. But ever since being incarcerated he had never once replied to any of her letters. These recollections had come to him every day since his imprisonment eight years ago when he was just sixteen. In the dead of the night, he could hear his friends' voices, backdropped by the gentle rustling of leaves in a calm wind. It was a soothing memory, a quiet natural moment far away from everything else that filled his past.

A tapping at the cell door jolted Carlton awake. Standing in the doorway was Smokey Davis, a friend of Carlton's since he had been relocated to Wormwood Scrubs from Wandsworth Prison two years ago.

'Ain't cha gonna play any table tennis, games time over soon?'

'Nah, don't feel like it. I'm bored with the fucking game.'

'Then how about a game of poker or something?'

'Nah, fuck that as well. Besides, I don't like losing.'

'So what cha gonna do, we only got twenty minutes left,' stated Smokey, trying to drag Carlton out of his melancholy.

'Read a book or something. And stop Gravesey from kicking the shit out of Wallace.'

'Wallace deserves all he gets. He's a fucking bacco tea-leaf.'

'Yeah, Wallace is a fucking loser and a tea-leaf; it's kinda surprising 'cos he's new and shit. But Gravesey ain't a fucking angel either. He's always beating up the new ones. I wouldn't give a shit but the screws kinda expect me to keep order in this wing . . . I don't wanna fuck up my leaving date.'

'Wallace should fight his own wars. What's he gonna do when you fuck off out of here in a few weeks.'

'Gravesey will probably kick the shit out of Wallace 'til it starts to come out from his fucking ear-holes. And if he don't start to fight back, Wallace will be easy meat for Jenkins and his shirt-lifting crew. He'll probably get his arse sperm-rinsed a few times a day.'

Smokey rolled a bacco joint. 'So what cha gonna do when you get out?'

Carlton looked towards the photo of his friends just above his pillow. 'I dunno, maybe do some joinery that I learnt. I'll be staying with an old friend when I get out. Then I'll try and find a gaff I s'pose. After that I might look for a whore to grind, if I've got enough money. Who knows, some liberal wanker might want to give me a fucking job.'

Smokey tossed the roll-up to Carlton and began to make his own. 'I've always wanted to ask, who are the other guys in the photo?'

'None of your fucking business, that's who they are.'

'Sure you don't want to play no table tennis?'

'You want me to make a fucking statement?'

'Yeah, alright. I get your drift.'

Smokey left, regretting he'd ever asked about the photo. As he made his way downstairs, he wondered why he could never work Carlton out. Carlton had saved his arse twice, literally, and rescued his hide once. In all the time he knew him, he couldn't sustain any conversation with Carlton about his past; it always ended with Carlton becoming aggressive, like a frightened child backed into a corner.

Carlton remained in his cell, staring intensely at the photo of his friends. He placed his roll-up underneath his pillow, saving it for the night. Glenroy, *where* the fuck are you? his mind questioned. Carlton spat out the remains of the matchstick and found a fresh one on his bunk. He inserted it into his mouth and proceeded to gnaw. The small muscles around his jaw bone bulged as the tissues within his eighteen and a half inch neck danced to the rhythm of chewing. His head sat on a body of perfect strength; within the prison he had plenty of admirers, though none of them were forthcoming with their praise.

The only thing that scared him was the prospect of being free of the prison walls. Being locked up, he didn't have to worry about paying rent or when his next meal would arrive. In prison he was king, the fittest of the fittest; even the screws respected him and invited him to 'deal' with the convicted perverts with just one rule; *don't* mark the face. But in the outside world, he would be a nobody, a back-marker in the rat race that he would have to join to survive.

Maybe he could brutalise a shirt-lifter to extend his sentence, Carlton suddenly thought. Fuck up his face. Or pick a fight with one of the screws, fist one of them for no reason. That's bound to cause an extension to his sentence. Nah, fuck that, he reasoned. Don't wanna do that isolation shit. Had enough of that already. He looked at the images of trees that surrounded his bunk and he still couldn't understand why they held such a fascination for him. He could never express it in words, but he felt that trees, especially at night, were more alive than people realised. They could even tell you to do things.

Toronto, Canada, May 1985

Bullet felt his guts sink and stay on the ground floor as the lift raced to the viewing platform of the CN Tower. A Korean tourist fretted in her own language, while an American kid, dressed in a Michael Jackson T-shirt, was singing 'Thriller'.

Monty, Bullet's one-and-a-half-year-old son, blinked wildly as the lift door opened and natural light flooded his eyes. His wife Linda touched Monty on the cheek before smiling at her husband, not letting on how much the speed of the lift had unnerved her.

Bullet's brown hair was cropped short as if he still wanted

9

people to know he was once in the army. His eyes were alert and seemed ready for confrontation at any moment. Brown freckles dotted his face, lessening his twenty-four years, and spread across his dented nose.

Bullet led his family to the large, angled windows that offered a view of the entire Toronto skyline and Lake Ontario. The buildings below looked like stepping stones for a giant, and the blue brilliance of the lake made Bullet's eyes squint as he looked around. The white sails of the yachts, seemingly motionless in the lake, pricked the calm waters like white bayonets.

Linda took her camera out and started taking snaps of Bullet and Monty. 'Well, smile then,' she said. 'At least pretend you're enjoying yourself.'

Bullet smiled weakly. Monty had no time for the camera. 'Let's get away from it all you said,' Linda snapped, but not loud enough to reach the ears of other tourists. 'You're about as miserable as when we were back home. What's the matter, Bullet?'

'Nothing.'

Bullet passed Monty to the arms of his wife and then looked out to the lake. It looked to him as if Lake Ontario might as well be an ocean. For a reason he couldn't comprehend, Bullet suddenly imagined himself looking out from the highest point of the Pinewood Hills. The first time Curvis had showed him the view of the Surrey countryside, Bullet had been ten years old and from that day he always wondered what went on in the outside world. A world away from Pinewood Oaks Children's Home.

Bullet, travelling with the army, had now seen many countries and many peoples. He felt that the evils that he thought were confined to Pinewood Oaks were everywhere – in Northern Ireland, the Middle East, Hong Kong – all places where he served with the army. The big losers in all this evil were children, he concluded.

10

Bullet turned around and looked at Monty and wondered why he had brought him into this world. He then thought of Glenroy, Carlton and Curvis, the only friends he really had. Perhaps the only friends he would ever have, he thought. His wife had made the first move on him, and in the army you are forced to get on with everybody. He knew his time in the army had been a cop-out to shield himself from the outside world. Now he had to face it. He smiled to himself, thinking that at least he and his friends had the memories of the Pinewood Hills. No evil could take that away, he thought. One moment of freedom in his life that nobody but his friends could understand.

'Did I tell you Carlton's coming out in a few weeks' time?' said Bullet.

Linda's smile died. 'How could I forget? It's all you talked about on the plane over here.'

'It's gonna be great,' enthused Bullet. 'We're gonna be together again . . . As soon as he gets out we should take him out for a meal.'

'When's the last time you took *me* out for a meal?' Linda glared.

'I took you on this holiday, didn't I!'

'Well, remember what I said last night. Me and Monty are *the* priority in your life now.'

Bullet didn't reply. He stared out to the horizon and saw a light aircraft gliding high over the lake. 'It's a shame Glenroy won't be there when Carlton gets out.'

Linda grimaced and took Monty a few yards away to look out in a different direction.

Bullet didn't even notice his wife walking away. He was lost in the past, his mind bombarded with image after image. Trees can't lie to you, he thought, and fields can't conceal nothing. The children's home lied to me, so did the army. Maybe my wife lies to me too?

Looking into the horizon, Bullet dwelt on his thoughts,

feeling as insecure as he'd ever been. He knew it was ines-
capable to return to thinking about his friends. 'Where the
fuck are you, Glenroy?' he whispered.

Carshalton, Surrey, May 1985

Glenroy felt a massive sense of achievement as he successfully
made himself a cup of tea. It had been two weeks since he
was discharged from the mental hospital and only now was
he beginning to think he might cope. But only if he could
remember to take his medication. He had to remember to
look for his nearest chemist for when his pills ran out.

A care in the community nurse was supposed to call on him
the day before but he never arrived. Even though he was in
the outside world, Glenroy felt like a suckling skylark who had
just watched his parents fly away and abandon him. Two days
ago his sworn enemy, Panic, found an entrance to his brain,
causing him to smash his head on the cold water tap in the
bathroom. He cut his scalp and ended up putting his head in
a bath full of cold water, holding his breath for as long as he
could before dunking again.

When Panic finally departed, he ate a dinner of cold
sardines and boiled lemonade and retired to his bed, fully
clothed, adopting the foetal position. He preferred to keep
his bedroom window wide open because the sounds of the
birds at dawn soothed him. Only now, two days later, did he
emerge from his sleeping place.

He was frightened of this outside world. The shopping
trip to the supermarket destabilised him. So many people,
all in a hurry and knowing where they're going, and when he
reached the cashier, he thought Panic might take hold of him
again. 'Eight pound fifty please,' the cashier said, looking at his
eighteen-stone frame and recoiling at his wild hair. Glenroy felt
his sweat sogging his eyebrows and dampening his untamed

12

beard. Should he give her the blue note or the brown one? It seemed like it took an eternity to decide. 'I ain't got all day you know,' the cashier snapped. Panic, Glenroy's shadow, was very near.

He gave her the brown note, and just as Glenroy expected a fierce rebuke, the cashier opened the till and gave him change of £1.50 and a receipt. Glenroy stood for a long second, smiling widely. Panic had to retreat. *Yes!* He congratulated himself.

Glenroy sat down in his kitchen, downing his over-milky tea and eating a Mars bar from the collection of sweets he kept in a fruit bowl. He thought back to the day he left the hospital. His eyes were sore from tears at leaving his friends behind. Everyone said he'd be alright and that he was better, that he would be OK to go home now. But the hospital was home, and he knew there what he had to do every day. Make your bed in the morning, breakfast followed by chores. After eleven was games time; Glenroy always hogged the table tennis table. Lunch at 12.30. Training in the afternoon, where he had to learn to cook, count money, read essential shopping lists and fill in various forms.

Dinner was at 5.30 followed by another games session. At 9 p.m., he would politely ask for his supper of a chocolate roll or fairy cakes, then he would watch a bit of telly; his favourite programme was *The Young Ones*. Ten p.m. was lights out.

In those quiet hours of darkness, Glenroy wondered about his life before coming to the hospital. He was told he had spent his childhood in an orphange. But that's all he knew. His pre-teenage memories were lost in a fog of tablets, injections, beatings and straitjackets. Almost every night he would dream about an enchanted forest, where the terrain was hilly, the trees were tall and where the long arrows of sunlight made your eyes squint. Now and again, a little girl would appear in these dreams. She looked very sickly but she had an abundance of energy as she danced in the woods, inviting Glenroy to play tag. She only ever spoke two words. Pinewood Hills. Glenroy assumed it was her name. But he knew he could only play with her when it was light, for when darkness came, she turned evil. From blonde, her hair would change to dazzling white and her eyes to a glowing green. She roamed the forest at night, blackbirds swirling around her head, looking for someone to kill. Tightly gripped in her right hand was a dolly's head, and protruding out of it was a three-inch nail.

PART ONE

Pinewood Oaks

Pinewood Oaks, April 1970

A nervous chimpanzee was performing a card trick to seven cynical gorillas when the nine-year-old Glenroy Richards opened his eyes and cleared his head from his day-dream. He focused and sneered at the maths equation taunting him from the blackboard and considered using the chalk to sketch a monkey's face on it. Glenroy smiled. He looked down at the wonky wooden desk above his knees and studied the black biro sketches of a matchstick mother holding the hand of a matchstick child.

On a table at the back of the classroom, textbooks formed a pillar; with one push they would tumble, but he would leave that for another day. Drawings of families at the beach were sellotaped on the cream-painted, brick walls. The ceiling of the classroom was high enough for three teachers to stand on each other's shoulders, and the large windows always teased Glenroy as an escape route.

He stared at the tiled wooden floor beneath him and wondered if he would ever visit the seaside with his own mother. But, he thought, maybe the horrible people in that place where his mum was living wouldn't let her go. He wondered if she ever had the same thought. Maybe if he asked Father Patrick, perhaps he could do something. He looked up at the stubborn classroom clock, willing the time to spring forward.

The rest of the class had been dismissed half an hour ago, leaving Glenroy to contemplate his misdemeanour. He thought he should not be the only one in detention; there were others who deserved the same punishment, especially Tommy Whittle, who had pulled a chair away from the soon-to-be-seated Claire Woodhouse. And then there was Billy Crawford, who had made funny faces behind the teacher's back.

Miffed, Glenroy stooped to pick up a pencil from the floor and noticed the chewed marks at one end of it. As he tapped the pencil on the desk and rocked in his chair the classroom door opened. 'Stop rocking on the chair and will you please stop making that irritating noise with your pencil,' rebuked a teacher.

Glenroy's tutor was stocky in appearance, formally dressed in a navy blazer, black trousers and a ridiculous black and yellow, polka-dot bow-tie. His eyebrows seemed to be as thick as a working end of a broom, angled towards the middle of his face where they almost overlapped. There were small red veins all over his face, as if someone had gone mad with a thin, red biro. His only hair, apart from the sproutings in his ears and nostrils, was at each side of his round head. Glenroy thought he looked like an aged goblin.

'Right, young boy,' he addressed, wagging his right index finger. 'I have phoned your housefather and I am sure that he will see that you are further punished for your behaviour in class this afternoon.' Glenroy flinched. 'You are at liberty to go.'

Glenroy's chair whined as he shot up, trying to suppress a smirk. As he approached the door, the teacher warned. 'Glenroy Richards, let this be a lesson to you that if you continue to disrupt my class with your teasing of other children, then you will continue to have my company after school has finished. Do you understand me, boy?'

'Yes, Mr Bowles.' I hope Father Patrick doesn't hear about this, he thought.

Normally he had to walk in file but now Glenroy sprinted along the empty corridor, his footsteps resounding from the wooden floor. As he turned a corner to depart out of the main school exit, he ran into Miss Worthington, his music teacher. 'How many times have I told you *not* to run in the corridors? *Walk.*'

'Sorry, Miss. I wanna catch up to my friends.'

Miss Worthington inspected Glenroy's clothes. His grey shirt was escaping his grey shorts. His black shoes were scuffed and his grey socks were nearer to his ankles than his knees. Miss Worthington noted a mischievous but sad look in his eyes. She felt a little sympathy for him. She had learned that Glenroy's mother was certified insane, but hadn't known the full story, just the cold fact that Glenroy owned a mad mother.

'You'd better do something to your hair before you get home. Your housemother will not tolerate that appearance. Try and borrow a comb from Carlton Henry if you catch up with him.'

'Yes, Miss.'

Glenroy trotted out of the main exit and into the children's playground, slowing down as he turned corners. He skipped around to see if any of his school friends were waiting for him like they had promised. The playground was empty. At least Carlton, his best mate, could've waited.

The school was a Victorian building with brownish-red brickwork and white painted window frames. Its gabled roofs and pointed arches gave the construction a Gothic feel, especially at night. All children up to the age of eleven, who lived in the Pinewood Oaks children's home complex, were educated here. From eleven upwards, the children would attend 'outside' comprehensives in nearby villages to allow the orphans to integrate into the local community. An unspoken rule was that no single secondary school would absorb all the children who had just left Pinewood Oaks junior school. Consequently, the headmasters of the local comprehensives had a nodding agreement that they would equally share the intake from Pinewood Oaks. Thus it was easier to deflect arguments from village parents.

A wooden brown rickety fence, about five foot high, circled the playground area. It was the northern boundary marker for Pinewood Oaks children's home complex. For seventy years or more, pupils of Pinewood Oaks junior school leaped up to grab a glimpse of the outside world. Glenroy approached this fence and jumped up, reaching out with his hands to grip the top of the barrier. He managed to get his head above the fence and scanned the recreation field which neighboured the school. He saw a team of boys playing football, using their pullovers and satchels for goalposts. Dogs were running freely, teenagers were smoking cigarettes under an oak tree and a couple were necking on the grass. In the distance, at the far end of the park, he could just make out the buildings of Ashburden comprehensive school. Beyond this was the village of Ashburden itself, full of avenues, semi-detached houses and middle-aged women walking small dogs.

Glenroy looked into the horizon and there, pricking the skyline, beyond the hills, was in his mind the Eiffel Tower. He had seen it in a book once and had promised himself to walk to France one day. He climbed down from the fence and ran out of the playground into a tree-lined road. At the bottom of this road was a seven-foot-high wooden gate with a huge padlock on it. Boys who were in their last year of junior education at

Pinewood primary and didn't care about the threat of a caning, dared each other to climb the gate and land on the winding gravel track that led to Ashburden. Opposite the school, on the other side of the Pinewood Oaks through-road, was the school's own playing field. Pupils of ten and eleven years old were practising gymnastics. The boys were dressed in white vests and black shorts, and the girls in white flannel T-shirts and short, pleated black skirts.

The noise of a confused amateur band coming from a building at the far end of the playing field hitched a lift on a freshening easterly breeze. All that practice and they still sound like a dying Dalek, Glenroy thought.

He scampered up the small incline of the road and when he crested the hill, he stopped and looked around. The road headed due south, where Glenroy could see the first of the Georgian cottages which accommodated up to fourteen kids each; all of these cottages had three-pointed gabled roofs sitting on a rectangle of brick forty-foot high. Large bay windows caught the sun and there wasn't a front door without a porch over it.

To Glenroy's right there was a thirty-yard-wide strip of grass about half a mile long, fringed by nettles, thorn bushes and hard-to-get-to berries. This acted as a border for the western side of the children's home. Beyond this were the lush and well-kept gardens of Pinewood village. No roads were curved or arched here. They were as straight as Pall Mall and covered in the same reddish-brown tarmac. This was the prized route for paperboys who worked for Fred Hawes newsagent's on the high street. A seventy-pound-haul 'Christmas box' wasn't unheard of when the lucky lad cycled around Pinewood village to collect his bonus. No boy from Pinewood Oaks had ever been given the honour. Refuse collectors, who took extreme care not to leave any stray rubbish lying around, were even more fortunate on their Christmas round.

On hot days, the kids of the orphanage would eavesdrop

and peep in at garden parties where salmon and champagne was served to women in wide hats and men in Bermuda shorts and Fred Perry T-shirts. The orphans would also mock and gesture rudely to the job-a-day cubs who, in the summer holidays, were spotted tidying back gardens, cleaning ponds and saluting every adult who came into their view.

Glenroy sensed a commotion coming from the grass expanse to his left. He strained his eyes and made out a rabble of young boys larking about in the hazy sunlight. Not wanting to miss out on any fun, he darted across the field, passing one of the imposing Georgian houses, before bolting through a deep, swerving dale. He could see the Pinewood Oaks water tower rising over the trees towards the east. Glenroy always compared the red and sky-blue brick building to a lighthouse.

The grass was recently cut, making him sneeze as he neared the pack of yelping schoolboys. The juniors had formed a ring, with a strapping, mixed-race boy, aged about eleven, in the middle. A smaller lad was being pushed into the ring against his wishes, blubbering at the thought of what was to come.

'Get in the ring, Bullet!' cried out a juvenile voice. 'You said that Osgood was a big head.'

A score of kids started to yell. 'In the ring! In the ring! In the ring!'

Osgood yanked Bullet's arm and lugged him into the centre of the circle. Osgood, who appeared to be more than his eleven years, was one of the few boys in long trousers. He smirked as he caught Bullet in a vice around the throat and began to check the power of his well-practised right hook. Bullet felt like a defenceless nail in the presence of an eager hammer. The schoolboy mob changed its chant. 'Kill him! Kill him! Kill him!'

Glenroy reached the mob of boys and caught sight of Carlton. He barged his way to Carlton's side and watched Bullet being hammered into the grass.

'What's he done?' asked Glenroy.

'He was calling Osgood names after Osgood tripped him up in school,' revealed Carlton, his eyes fixed on Bullet's face.

Meanwhile Bullet tried to fight back but it was useless. His spirited display only infuriated Osgood, who began kicking his wailing victim. When Osgood was satisfied he had inflicted enough damage, he strutted away with his friends and hangers on, who congratulated him on his latest victory.

Bullet wormed on the ground, silently sobbing, with his arms covering his swollen face. Glenroy ambled away from the scene. 'Come on, Carlton, let's go home.' Father Patrick would say, 'go forth and lend a helping hand' but Glenroy didn't want to get involved.

Carlton stood still, glancing at the sorry sight of Bullet, who was now sitting up, picking off grass and dry mud from his clothes. Carlton walked three strides towards Glenroy but curiosity got the better of him. He turned around and caught sight of Bullet peeping at him from under his arms. 'Let's see how he is.'

'Are you a divo?' charged Glenroy. 'Osgood will punch in your face to look like a rotten apple.'

Carlton strolled over to where Bullet was sitting, with a reluctant Glenroy following behind. Bullet warily moved his arms away from his face as Carlton studied him. 'You're mad. Why you wanna start calling Osgood names? He's the best fighter in the school. You must be a thicko.'

Glenroy stared at the boy, seeing a despondent bloodied face. Bullet's brown hair was flecked with grass.

Although Bullet had been at Pinewood Oaks for over two years, he had found it difficult to make friends. It seemed as if all the other pupils in his class had made a pact not to talk to him. He was suspicious that Carlton was looking at him. He never took any notice of me before, he thought.

'Come on. Get up,' said Carlton.

Glenroy appeared resentful as Bullet hauled himself up and

walked away with Carlton. He ran up to them and pulled Carlton aside and spoke urgently in a whisper. 'We can't walk with him! Everyone hates him! What if Osgood sees us? He's gonna beat us up. Didn't you see what he done to Jeremiah Collansk – that Jew boy? He still can't talk and he walks with a limp. Elvin told me one of his balls was crushed.'

'Osgood's gone home,' said Carlton, dismissing Glenroy's scaremongering. Boy! I ain't seen anyone try and fight back with Osgood, he thought. He's brave.

Glenroy glared at Bullet. The trio trudged on, walking through the knee-high rough grass that steadily dipped into a valley. They walked across a sloping football pitch where the wooden goalposts were warped and the crossbars bent. Finally, they reached the children's play area. A set of swings and a broken see-saw were protected by an arc of huge oak trees. Brave boys would hold contests to see who could climb the highest in the cloud-reaching branches, attempting to claim highly-prized birds' nests. If any of these nests contained eggs then the boy who had attained this trophy was given the utmost peer respect.

The threesome reached a small stone bridge where a stream hastened on its journey. Under the bridge was a popular spot for hide-and-seekers. The bold would venture into the darkness of the tunnel and hide. As they crossed the narrow stone walkway, Glenroy caught sight of somebody on the bank of the stream. 'Oh no! That's Stanton's brother, Stanton used to be Osgood's best mate; we're gonna get beat up, 'cos he'll tell him we're with Bullet. Elvin also told me that Jeremiah's only got two teeth left.'

Carlton looked towards the bank of the stream, which was edged by oddly shaped shrubbery that none of the boys could name. A lonesome figure was sitting down in a shadow of bushes, staring into the rushing water. He picked up a pebble and threw it into the stream, trying to imitate a bouncing bomb.

Carlton led the way as they approached Curvis. 'What you doing?' Carlton asked the crouched figure.

'I dunno.'

Curvis was wearing grey shorts and his jutting knees had gathered dried mud. His large narrow nose implied that one of his parents was white. His complexion was milky coffee and his hair gave him the appearance of a brown Dennis the Menace.

'Come on, Carlton,' Glenroy insisted, wondering what time it was. 'I've got to get home . . . I'm gonna be in big trouble.'

'Did you see the fight?' Carlton asked Curvis, ignoring Glenroy's pleas. Carlton was fascinated by his quietness, never joining in or following the shenanigans at school. At break-times Curvis kept himself company, walking as if in a dream and noticing nothing. 'Osgood beat up Bullet 'cos Bullet was calling him names.'

'Don't like fights.' Curvis stared into the water as if something dramatic was about to happen. Then he turned around to study the battered face of Bullet. 'Osgood don't like anyone calling him names. He's like my brother. They were best mates.' He returned his gaze to the water. 'I'd keep out of Osgood's way.'

'I ran out of school,' said Bullet. 'Osgood's gang ran after me and caught me on the field.'

'Well, he's beaten you up now, Osgood don't usually beat up kids twice – only if they say something.'

'Carlton!' Glenroy interrupted, looking fiercely at his best friend and the route home.

Glenroy had to wait five minutes until Carlton and Bullet rejoined him. The boys strolled on lazily out of the field under the warm sun until they reached the quiet orbital road that ringed most of Pinewood Oaks.

A few lonely cars were parked on the road outside the Georgian houses. Young children were playing outside, enjoying the last of the spring sunshine. Boys rode by on squeaky, heavy bikes. The more adventurous hurtled down from the hill, piloting dodgy, home-made trolleys. On the grass, teenagers were getting bruised in a brutal game of British Bulldog. Black and white plastic footballs were kicked against outhouse walls where the goals were chalked in white. Girls were juggling greying tennis balls on red walls and others sang pop songs while skipping ropes. A sulky teenager watched all the proceedings from a chestnut tree, perched on a large branch.

On one rusty-looking old bike, a small boy of about seven years old was learning how to ride. He was being assisted by an older girl who was frantically pushing the saddle, trying to keep the bike upright. 'Brenton! Pedal you idiot, pedal.'

Glenroy observed the scene and boasted, 'I learnt to ride a bike when I was five. He's useless. Look at him. I didn't need no help when I was that small.'

'You're a liar,' rebuked Carlton. Carlton pushed Glenroy playfully. 'I remember when you learnt to ride a bike. You fell off so many times you always had to go to the sick bay.'

'No, I didn't.' Glenroy felt a little embarrassed as Bullet managed a smile at the joke. Glenroy and Carlton proceeded to have a mock fight in the road while Bullet meandered a few yards behind his friends.

After walking another fifty yards or so, the juniors neared Bullet's house. Carlton, while holding Glenroy's neck in an arm-lock, mentioned to Bullet, 'Raymond Cole lives in your house, innit? He's the best footballer in Pinewood Oaks. I saw him up the top field the other day and he scored a Bobby Charlton goal. Whassisname, Lloyd Grant was the goalie, and he didn't want to touch the ball after Raymond done his shot.'

'He's not as good as Kevin Annon,' argued Glenroy, trying to squirm his neck free.

'Course he is.'

As Glenroy and Carlton disputed the matter of the best

footballer in Pinewood Oaks, Bullet ambled away to the back of his house. Before he opened the back door, he watched the quarrelling boys on the road.

Glenroy and Carlton, their wrestling antics over, jogged on, realising that tea-time was pushing on and they'd better get home quickly. They passed the blue-painted nursery building, topped off by a flat roof. On many a summer's night, boys would climb on top of the nursery and peer through the bedroom windows of the houses nearby, until an irate housefather would spot them and hail them down, threatening all kinds of physical punishments.

Screwed into the brickwork of one house was a green-painted placard, white letters spelling the word 'Holly'. Carlton ran to the front door of this house and shouted to Glenroy, 'see you later'. Remembering his strife at school, Glenroy slowed his walk and eased open the front door of the house next door. It was named 'Heather'.

Once inside his home, Glenroy wiped his feet on the large, bristled mat. Then he stepped up the three red-carpeted stairs before him and entered the hallway. He always hated the painting of a crying child that hung on a wall to the left of the entrance. The wallpaper wasn't much better – a flower-patterned light-grey, reaching right up to a high ceiling. To Glenroy's immediate right was a mahogany staircase, complete with polished banisters.

A toddler, aged about four years old, tottered in front of Glenroy in excited pursuit of a toy car. The child looked upon Glenroy and smiled. 'Everybody, Glenroy's home!' Glenroy brushed passed the infant, turning right along the hallway. 'Get out of my way,' he said casually. 'You always get in the way with your stupid cars.'

The child picked up his treasured car and stared at Glenroy as he crept along the passage.

Passing the spacious kitchen on his left, the housemother, who possessed arms big enough to stir a barrel of porridge, caught sight of Glenroy. 'And what time do you call this? Just look at your hair. Have you been fighting again?'

'No, Auntie Mary.'

The first rule a child would learn on entering any of the homes in Pinewood Oaks was to address the staff as 'Auntie' or 'Uncle'. Washing hands before any meal was compulsory and talking after bedtime was severely prohibited. Any photographs, certificates and other documents the orphan might have in their possession were taken away and filed. They were shown their place at the dinner table and cautioned about the wastage of food. Lastly, they would be told in the strictest terms *not* to infringe on the properties of Pinewood village, and other out-of-bound areas were also warned against. Following an anxious night's sleep the new child would be measured for clothes, checked for lice, have fingernails clipped, teeth and gums inspected and told of the weekly chore rota. The next afternoon the child would find himself or herself naked in the sick bay, with the resident doctor running a check from toe to scalp, asking the child's social worker about any rashes or symptoms that might be contagious.

Taking off her oven gloves, Auntie Mary inspected Glenroy from head to foot. Then she suddenly smacked his face, causing Glenroy's face to jolt ninety degrees. '*Don't* lie to me!' Glenroy squinted his eyes at the moment of impact and raised his arms automatically, backing away. The housemother raised an open right hand again, debating whether one smack was sufficient. 'Uncle Thomas said he wanted to see you as soon as you got in from school. So you'd better wash your hands and look tidy – then go to the study.'

Glenroy, soothing his face with his right palm, always thought his housemother was the nanny of the devil. He wished the bogey-man would capture her and dunk her fat head in the rushing water under the bridge, and then she might melt away, like Dracula in a film he had heard about.

He turned around and walked back along the hallway

dejectedly, then headed for the washroom, opposite the entrance of the house. The walls of the room were painted beige and the door frames and skirting had recently been glossed in brilliant white. The marble-like lino floor was bare; Glenroy always thought the flooring was made up of crushed, polished stones that someone had got from the beach. To him, this room seemed to be cooler than the rest of the house. It contained two sinks, two toilet cubicles and a cupboard where the cleaning ladies kept their items. The smell of disinfectant invaded Glenroy's nostrils. He gripped the hot-water tap as if he was strangling a dolly's neck, and clenched his teeth. 'I *hate* her,' he whispered. '*Him* and her.'

He started to wash his hands in one of the deep basins, while gazing into the mirror above the sink, wondering what punishment he would receive now. He swabbed away the hatred in his eyes. 'Don't wanna let *her* know she can hurt me.' After washing his hands, he collected a plastic comb, which had more than a few teeth missing, from a wall cabinet and proceeded to tear into his tight afro curls.

Five minutes later, he emerged from the washroom and trudged into the hallway, expecting the familiar beating. He almost stumbled on his way to the study door, his face trembling like a chocolate trifle. At the end of the hallway, he bumped into Liza, aged about seven, who had long brown pony-tails and pink ribbons in her hair. She was gripping the string hair of a tatty doll. 'You're in trouble, Glenroy.'

'Shut up, Liza!'

Liza ran up the stairs giggling, as Glenroy sweated on his fate, feeling his heartbeat accelerate within his chest. Carlton had told him to bite his finger when he was getting six of the best. That way, the pain on the backside won't be so bad. Glenroy thought he should try it. The study was at the end of the hallway, near the staircase. He knocked on the door once, giving it a light tap. Maybe this is how adults feel when they go to confession, he thought.

A voice from within the room boomed. 'Come in!'

Glenroy side-stepped his way into the study where he saw his housefather writing at a bureau in the light of a lamp. Aged about forty, he had balding ginger hair. His brown eyes were closer together than normal and his skin was pale. He had the build of a hard-working labourer who enjoyed his beer. Glenroy likened him to a ginger-haired troll he had seen in a children's fairy story. I hate you, he whispered in his mind.

The room was dominated by an expensive-looking hard-wood table with a chess board upon it. All the pieces were present in their starting positions, apart from one pawn. A red two-seater sofa was positioned under the window, looking out to the road, with cushions in lace slips neatly in place. Various pictures and paintings of boys were on the walls and window sills, most of them depicting some sporting pursuit or other. Glenroy always wondered why there were no pictures of girls.

The housefather caught Glenroy in the headlights of his stern eyes. He fingered his scraggy ginger beard and the boy guessed he was deciding on some evil punishment. His thin lips were unforgiving.

'How many times do I have to tell you *not* to misbehave in class?' the housefather growled. 'I'm sick and tired of Mr Bowles ringing me up and complaining about your behaviour. The way you're going, you'll end up in Hell. Don't they tell you in church that boys have to behave themselves or otherwise they will go to Hell? It seems like no punishment is good for you. I've a good mind to speak to Father Patrick. Do you want to end up like your mother? Crazy and no use to society?'

'No, Uncle Thomas.'

Thomas seemed to take pleasure in reminding Glenroy of his unstable mother. The boy couldn't even remember what she looked like. The only facts he had learned about his mother were from Thomas and he had been told from a very early age that the children's home would keep him safe from his dangerous mother and that he was lucky that the country provided such a fantastic service for children like him.

'Sometimes you haven't got the sense you were born with – just like your bloody mother,' Thomas continued. 'Look at you. You're fat, black as the coal we use and ugly – spitting image of your good-for-nothing mother. They should ban all mothers from having children if they're going to look like you ... I've got a good mind to give you six of the best – but I'm too busy. After you have your tea, you will go straight to bed and if I hear you talk to anybody, then you can think about your behaviour on your own. It's the only thing that works for you.'

Glenroy knew what that meant. Being locked up in the out-house every evening for two weeks, including weekends, until bedtime. With not a soul to talk to. His housefather would give him only a pencil and paper, and Glenroy would sketch images of what he thought the devil looked like – he wished he had a ginger crayon. He was glad that it wasn't February as the chill always found a way through the old windows and brickwork. When it was too cold to draw, Glenroy sat on the concrete floor in a corner. From this angle he could just see the fringes of the orchard. He would stare out of the window for hours.

He glanced at the chess board, wondering how the game was played. He noticed that one pawn was missing from the black set and scanned the table to see if he could find the missing piece. Thomas interrupted his search. 'So get your ugly, fat face out of my sight and I don't want to hear your voice this evening.'

'Yes, Uncle Thomas,' Glenroy sulked, preferring to have had six of the best rather than going to bed early. Glenroy left the room. He walked along the hallway and as he went by the kitchen, he saw his housemother stirring something in a large, grey pot. She caught sight of her charge. 'Come here!'

Glenroy walked up to her slowly. She grabbed his ear and

tweaked it into a fold, pulling his head towards her. Glenroy grimaced and nearly lost his footing. 'Dinner will be ready in ten minutes. Now sit down and behave yourself or you'll be in more trouble.'

He ambled to the end of the hallway and into the dining room. Two large dining tables were on either side, set for the evening meal. A tiled mantelpiece on the far wall had a solitary birthday card upon it, sent to one of the kids in the house by a social worker. Below this was the coal fireplace that wasn't in use. The walls were painted in a dull blue and the large sash windows had no net curtains or drapes to frame them. To the left of the entrance from the hallway there was a hatch in the wall, about the size of a chess board, through which Glenroy could see his housemother preparing the gravy. In the middle of the room was a bean bag. Glenroy walked towards it and dropped down on it, feeling sorry for himself. Why won't they let me live with my mum, he thought. Perhaps Father Patrick would.

A toy car suddenly came speeding into the room, followed by the frantic patters of an excited boy. Pushing his car around the legs of the dining chairs, the boy looked at his older peer. 'Look at this, Glenroy.' The infant pushed the battered car until it collided with the wall. Glenroy offered a contemptuous glare to the boy. 'What are you staring at, Pea Head? And stop playing with your stupid cars near the dinner table or I'll tell Auntie Mary.' Picking up his car, the youngster crawled out from under the dining table. He swept his long black hair from out of his eyes and stared at Glenroy with his round dark eyes.

'Go and play in the hallway,' Glenroy ordered, wondering why Luca always looked at him strangely.

Luca just sat down near the table, spinning the wheels of his car and started crying silently.

'Will you stop that,' Glenroy said. 'Ever since you've come here, all you do is flippin' cry. I haven't hit you.'

32

Ten minutes later, the household were eating their dinner. The smaller children, accompanied by the three staff, sat at the table near the hatch, while four teenagers, dressed in various tones of school uniform, ate on the big table in the centre of the room. From an old wireless, perched on a shelf to one side of the room, the news of the day voiced out on a low volume.

Uncle Thomas, positioned at the head of the big table, with his wife, Mary, opposite, trained his eyes on Glenroy. 'I hope you don't waste that,' he said, watching Glenroy fiddle with his food. 'You know I hate waste. You *sit* there until you finish every last morsel. You should be lucky you've got a meal to eat. Your mum always forgot to feed you, so you should be grateful for what you get.'

Glenroy forced himself to eat, getting angry at the child sitting opposite who was giggling at him.

Lisa, who was sitting beside Glenroy, was trying to hold back a lung-bursting smirk. Auntie Mary caught sight of the wide grin on Lisa's freckled features and without warning lashed her hand across the girl's face, forcing the food in her mouth to dribble over her chin. '*No* laughing at the table, or otherwise you'll be the next one who goes to bed early.'

Lisa moaned but was determined not to cry out loud. She began to eat small morsels of her sausages and mash using just her fork. She thought of horrible things happening to Mary, like getting lost in the orchard and the bogey-man kidnapping her, then eating her for breakfast with his cooking apples. The other children warily glanced at Lisa, eating their meal as if nothing dramatic had happened.

Dinner at the children's table went on with only the sound of knives and forks against plates, backdropped by the sports report on the crackling wireless of Chelsea's FA Cup run. The only conversation taking place was at the teenagers' table, where they swapped tales of teachers, canings, football and the latest pop tunes. Glenroy enjoyed his second course of apple crumble and custard, scooping his plate clean.

After dinner, Glenroy climbed the staircase, looking back at Auntie Mary watching his slow progress. On reaching the top of the stairs, he walked into the boys' dormitory, still lit by the fading, amber sun; the girls' dormitory was at the other end of the hallway. He trudged his way to the bed nearest the door. He found his pyjamas under his pillow and began to undress. Just as he was slipping on his pyjama bottoms, he saw the menacing presence of Ivor Torrey, who had entered the dorm. Long fair hair rested on the youth's shoulders. On his face he wore a heinous grin. His severe acne didn't endear him to the girls in the children's homes complex and nor did his skinny build. He fixed his eyes on Glenroy and started cackling as he watched Glenroy climb into his bed. 'Wog-a-matter? Feeling all browned off, Glenroy? Niggermind, you might feel all white in the morning, when you have your coon flakes.'

Ivor continued laughing and walked over to where Glenroy was laying. He lifted his right foot onto Glenroy's bed. 'Kiss my foot, Sambo. Go on, *kiss* it. Or I'll beat you up on the way to school.'

Frightened, Glenroy scanned the white football sock and noticed that the sole was all grey and dusty. He raised himself up and slowly bent down. He touched his lips on the dirty sock of his tormentor. Ivor smiled triumphantly and turned away to open the door and departed.

Glenroy pulled the covers over his head, dragging his pillow near his stomach and curled himself up. His body refused to sleep as he felt a bitter resentment surge through him. How can Father Patrick expect me to forgive things like that? he asked himself. When I get older, I'm gonna beat up all the people who were horrible to me and I don't care what Father Patrick might say. Glenroy pressed his palms together and slammed his eyes shut. 'Dear God, sorry for being naughty in class today. And please make mummy better so she can

34

take me away and look after me. Amen. Oh, one more thing. I know I've asked you before but can you tell the bogey-man to eat Ivor – he deserves it.'

Glenroy pulled off his covers to check that Ivor was out of sight. Satisfied, he stood on his bed and looked out of the window at the orchard, half expecting to hear the bogey-man's progress on his way to eat Ivor. Two seconds later, he was back under his bed sheets. He wondered what his mother looked like now and promised himself that when he got to be a grown-up, wherever she was, he would find her and take her away to live in a big house with seven bedrooms. And, with his mother, he would behave himself, because he didn't want her to cry if he had to go to Hell.

Glenroy refused to sleep. He was frightened of his dreams, but didn't tell anyone about his nightmares. He thought that if he did they would think him as mad as his mother. He often tried to count a million conkers but he never even got up to a hundred. Maybe all kids had these dreams, he thought, but no one talked about them. He tried to keep his eyes open but someone seemed to be pulling them closed. He often prayed to God to spare him from this torment but God never seemed to listen. Father Patrick said that God always listened to prayers, even to prayers from kids who lived in far-off countries. But maybe God doesn't listen to prayers from kids in a home. 'Dear God. I know you're really busy but this is my last prayer for the night. Please help me. I live with a horrible Auntie and a horrible Uncle. Can you make my mum better so she can take me away to live in a big house far away from here. If you do this I promise I will be good, so you can't send me to Hell. Amen.'

Soon he was asleep, but something inside him was still alert. Glenroy felt himself rising, as if he was a kite on a friendly breeze. He found himself careering on a misty, floaty journey. Images began to appear. A crazed male lion was gnawing one of his own cubs while the cub's mother was lying dead just a few feet away. The left side of her face was missing. Then a wailing teenage girl, wearing rags and a glittering tiara, laid a new born baby at the gates of that place where important people argue.

The vision changed to a naked woman behind a counter in a shop, selling her heart to a whip-lashing, ugly man who had hooves instead of feet. It blurred, then cleared to show a handcuffed, headless woman, being escorted to a castle's dungeon by elderly guards with white wigs but no faces.

The journey ended and Glenroy found himself sitting on a cloud. He was transfixed by an indistinct figure of a man. Eyes lit by a thousand November the fifths stared through Glenroy, seemingly examining his thoughts. Locks of hair, like the multicoloured ropes of a maypole, danced above his head. In his right hand he held a book, which was ten times thicker than any book Glenroy had ever seen. Gripped in his left hand, like a great king wielding his sceptre, was what looked like a gigantic tree trunk, ten times bigger than the mightiest oak in Pinewood Oaks.

He sat on a chair that glowed like a peeled tangerine when raised against the sunlight. His chameleon skin changed colours as he moved. When he spoke it was like the sound of a dinosaur walking below the ground. He opened the book and beckoned Glenroy over. Glenroy's eyes widened as he watched the book reveal a live landscape, a new world. He saw a dazzling green land with zigzagging rivers of milk. Golden sycamore trees were gently blown by the breath of the strange man sitting in the gleaming chair. Lions with green-glowing crowns, the same colour as his class-mate Jerry Peters's luminous watch, strode proudly.

The lions kept watch over their cubs and silver-coloured lambs. Happy angels, playing long trumpets, glided through the sky with wings made of cotton wool. Birds, with a multitude of eyes on their wings, like tiny flying Daleks, sang songs of praise to the man sitting on the shiny big

36

chair. Red coloured bushes, shaped like hearts, bore green and golden berries. Rich green fields, stretching for a mile, were dotted with conker trees.

Trombones blared out as if trying to speak and another page was turned. Glenroy found himself nearing a pit of sharpened, rocky teeth. He was now gripped with fear and was unable to blink. Trembling, he looked down, into the neverending depth. Petrified, desperate men tried to avoid falling by holding on to the jagged teeth on the sides of the pit. But they had no hands or feet. They were being pursued by horn-headed, five-legged dogs with long forked tongues.

Birds, with boils and burns on their faces, were flapping in the pit, finding it impossible to fly upwards. Smoke, ten times worse than in any war film, rose up out of the pit, making the birds with many eyes cough. From the mouth of the pit, a monster with ten dragon heads climbed out. From seven of these heads, seven tongues snaked out. Its body was that of a man and its legs that of a horse. Glenroy was frightened beyond belief. Between its legs was a two-headed, flame-coloured snake, and impaled on its spiked body were screaming children. Horrified, Glenroy backed away from the pit, his whole body shaking. Not even Tarzan, Superman or Doctor Who could fight this monster.

A mighty roar from the beast, like the death scream of a million Red Indians, rattled the conkers of the trees and caused the red bushes to uproot themselves. The milky rivers turned brown. The lambs and cubs struggled to maintain their footing. Towards the east the sun seemed to drop out of the sky, and in the west a violent storm gathered, shadowing the entire land. The air became very hot despite the raging wind and Glenroy thought he would surely die.

A battle began between the lions and the monster. Glenroy saw that no animal was a match for this appalling brute. Fifty lions met their death within the first minute of fighting.

The beast, crawling on all fours, moved towards the cubs and lambs.

It was at this moment that the man sitting on the throne struck his stick at the edge of the pit with earth-shattering force. Far-off mountains crumbled and the entire land began to crack, developing huge fissures. Long-haired angels carried tornado winds towards the monster, forcing it back to the mouth of the pit. It stumbled while shouting swear-words at the man sitting on the throne. It fell back into the smoking hole and while falling, got caught on the jagged teeth, tearing its body apart. A volcanic death cry shook the ground but faded as the beast fell into the core of the world.

The man, who was now standing, threw a black metal lid and covered the hole of the pit. The angels sealed it with a liquid that Glenroy couldn't identify. A sweet-smelling smoke filled the air. Raindrops that tasted of honey healed the ground. Before Glenroy's eyes, the trees grew branches that appeared to be praying.

Glenroy heard soothing music telling him to walk towards the mouth of the pit. He heard a recognisable wailing, deep within the ground, like that of a child. He attempted to remove the seal as he was being watched by angels who were shaking their heads. Suddenly, a giant scaly arm breached the lid and pulled Glenroy down into the neverending depths.

Diving into Trouble

Glenroy parted the royal-blue curtains to reveal a golden dawn. The orchard was still, yet to be aroused for the day ahead. I wonder where the bogey-man sleeps, he thought. He heard the rhythmic pecking of a raven who had taken a liking to the weather-beaten door of the outhouse that sat under the dormitory window.

As Glenroy's eyes adjusted to the morning sunlight the images of his terrible dream came back to him. He shuddered as a chill caressed his spine, causing him to blink rapidly and to shake his head. Maybe that horrible place in his nightmare was the Hell that Uncle Thomas was always talking about. He contemplated asking Father Patrick if the monster he had seen in his nightmare was the devil – but thought better of it. He willed himself to think of chocolate cakes.

Looking out of the window, the grass expanses seemed

to invite him out to play. He saw squirrels hurrying along the branches of oak trees, perhaps playing a game of tag or seeking out their breakfast. Skylarks swooped down to the ground, capturing inattentive worms between their beaks. Stupid slimy things, Glenroy thought. Why don't they just stay underground.

Closing the curtains, he looked around the dormitory and saw that everyone else was asleep. The room, apart from three double wardrobes and three chests of drawers, was bare. The tiled floor was uncovered, except for small mats beside every child's bed. Games and toys including Subbuteo table football and Monopoly were stacked on top of the wardrobes. Pictures of football teams were sellotaped to the cream-painted walls, mostly of Liverpool; and comics, like the *Beano, Whizzer* and *Chips, Tarzan* and *Spider Man* were kept in a cabinet beside the end wall. School books, pencil cases, note-pads and erasers lay on bedside tables. In Glenroy's bedside locker was a pad of paper, pencils, an armless Action Man and two greying tennis balls.

Next to Glenroy slept the eleven-year-old Ian Banks, and at the bottom of his bed was a book about the adventures of Robin Hood. Glenroy remembered that on Ian's last birthday he had asked Auntie Mary if he could have for his present the novel *Oliver Twist*. It was denied him, as Mary reasoned that boys who read *Oliver Twist* would grow rebellious and naughty. Not even the teenagers were allowed to watch the film version on television.

Glenroy listened to the hum of various breathing patterns and decided against telling Ivor Torrey that he snored loudly. Collecting his torn, itchy dressing-gown, he went downstairs. He heard Auntie Mary whistling to herself in the kitchen and hoped he wasn't too early to ask for breakfast.

The housemother had made two mugs of tea and Glenroy caught her picking the sleep out of her eyes. She glared at Glenroy, then glanced upwards to the kitchen clock that was above the cooker. Seven-fifteen. 'What are you doing up so early?' she scolded. 'Can't you have a lie-in like the rest of the kids? I can't get no bloody peace in the mornings.'

'I . . . I woke up early, Auntie. Remember, I went to bed early yesterday.'

'And the same thing will happen again even if I hear a squeal from you today!'

Mary stared blankly at the mugs of tea; one was for her husband. She considered her day ahead, thinking of the endless shrieks, moans and misbehaving that the day would surely bring. She comforted herself that at least it was Saturday and if the weather proved to be generous she could tell the younger kids to play outside and out of her way. For a moment, she reflected on her naïve young days, when she was filled with such great desire to help unfortunate children. Now she just looked forward to the end of the day, a day nearer to retirement.

Glenroy saw Mary sigh. 'Can . . . Can I have my breakfast please?' he asked, hoping he would not be sent back to bed.

'Yes, alright then. As long as you are quiet. And if you start running around and waking up the other children, I'll give you what for. Go on with you. Wait inside the dining room and I'll bring you some toast.'

'Thank you very much, Auntie.'

Glenroy walked into the dining room and sat down at the far end of the junior table. He looked at the chair where Uncle Thomas always sat, and immediately he started seeing images from his nightmare. The big throne where the giant sat, Glenroy thought, wincing as he did so. He shook his head, blinking furiously as Mary came into the room, carrying a plateful of toast. 'What's a matter with you? *Sit* at the table properly and take your elbows off. Where's your manners.'

'Sorry, Auntie Mary.'

As Mary laid the plate in front of him, he saw the toast was overdone. 'Thank you, Auntie Mary.'

Glenroy reached for the jam jar and a knife that was in the centre of the table. He covered his toast as if he was plastering a wall as Auntie Mary tutted. 'Well, Glenroy. I hope you have learnt your lesson, and today you'd better behave yourself or you'll find yourself going to bed early again. And you hate that on a Saturday, don't you?'

'Yes, Auntie Mary.' *Bleeding* witch! Glenroy said to himself. One day I'll walk to France and go to a home there. And I'll stay up as long as I want!

Squirts of jam stuck on the corners of Glenroy's mouth as he enjoyed his breakfast. When he wiped his mouth clean with a napkin, his body stiffened as he watched Uncle Thomas approaching from the hallway. 'I've just booked the swimming pool for ten o clock,' he announced cheerfully. 'So make sure you do your morning chores. You're allowed to invite one of your friends along – what about Carlton from next door? He's always well behaved; a delightful boy. Make sure you get permission from his housemother though . . . I wish you could be more like him. Maybe if you played football with him more often you could lose some of that flab and get to look like a normal boy.'

'Yes, Uncle Thomas.'

An hour later, Glenroy walked out of his back door and trotted down the steps. He skipped along the pathway to next door's back entrance and knocked loudly. He waited patiently for an answer as he tried to straighten his hand-me-down football shorts. He saw a shadow coming towards the door and heard a friendly voice. 'Is that you, Glenroy?'

'Yeah.'

The door swung open to reveal a smiling woman. Glenroy returned her good humour. She had dimples in her cheeks that kids, who did not even know her, took as a sign of kind-heartedness. Red, curly hair topped off her petite frame and her forty-one years were partly masked by her clear, unlined face. Glenroy always wanted to ask her if she could hear Uncle Thomas's voice in his study from the other side of the wall where she worked.

She ushered Glenroy inside. 'Carlton's just getting his wash. I'll tell him you're here, just wait here.' The woman smiled at Glenroy before turning around and leaving the cloakroom area. Glenroy was left to study the different kinds of children's footwear in the wooden stack of lockers. Each cabinet had a name tag on it, unlike the wire-mesh rack in which Glenroy placed his footwear at home. He noted that one kid was lucky enough to own a pair of Gola trainers. Maybe his family bought them, Glenroy guessed. He heard someone splashing about in the washroom.

Moments later, Carlton appeared, looking full of energy and zest for the day ahead. 'Wotcha, Glenroy.'

'Wotcha, Carlton. You wanna come swimming?' Glenroy asked excitedly. 'We're going at ten o clock. Uncle Thomas especially asked for you to come.'

'Nah. I'm going around the dump to see if I can get a wheel for my trolley this morning,' Carlton replied, while looking at his feet. 'And anyway, the stuff they put in the water to make it clean, itches my skin.'

'You never come swimming with me,' Glenroy complained. 'But when you ask I always go with you.'

'Well, you always ask when I'm busy,' Carlton returned, looking up. 'And I did go with you two weeks ago, that time your Auntie Mary took us when Uncle Thomas was sick.'

'Yeah, but that was the first time in a long time,' Glenroy recalled, the joy of the morning fading in his body language. He dropped the level of his voice. 'I thought you was my friend.'

'I am your friend but I'm busy this morning.'

'Why can't you go to the dump in the afternoon? I'll go with ya.'

''Cos I'm going shopping with Auntie Josephine – she's buying us some clothes.' Carlton kept glancing behind him.

'You don't have to go. I don't have to go when Auntie Mary buys my clothes. You just don't wanna go swimming 'cos you ain't my friend!'

'Aww, stop your sulking. Everyone's right at school when they say you're sulky. You're just a loser. And anyway, that's why none of your clothes fit you 'cos you're never there when Auntie Mary buys 'em.'

'I AIN'T SULKING! And I ain't a loser. And anyway, Auntie Mary says it's best for me to run around in hand-me-downs 'cos I'm saving money for her. And I got a new pair of plimsolls three weeks ago.'

Carlton couldn't help but grin. 'You're only allowed to wear 'em at school.'

'At least they'll last!'

'Auntie Josephine's buying me some Gola's. That'll make ya sulk.'

Glenroy opened the back door and stormed out of the house. 'You're the one who's a sulker!' he offered as a parting shot.

Dejected, Glenroy trudged along the road near his home. Passing the nursery, he watched the milk float crawling up the hill on its round, the bottles tinkling, which formed a musical back-up for the larks in the oak trees. Gentle breezes caressed the leaves, adding their own unique sound to the morning melody.

Glenroy looked to his left and scanned the field. He noticed it was polka-dotted with sprouting buttercups. Spring had arrived for good all of a sudden. The early morning mist which had veiled the bushes in the valley of the buttercup field was now thinning and a rich, green tapestry of tree tops filled the horizon, underneath a clear blue sky.

Glenroy watched a fox chase after a flock of birds, telling himself he'd have to go down the valley later on to see if he could locate the fox's den. He ran down the road for another fifty yards or so until he came to another pair of cottages on his right-hand side, identical to his and Carlton's homes. He paced up to the back door of the house nearest the road and again knocked loudly. The heavy door creaked open to reveal a black teenager of about fourteen years old. Dressed in football kit and a tracksuit top he looked upon Glenroy as if he was an underling. 'I s'pose you want Elvin?'

'Yeah . . . Please,' Glenroy replied, remembering his manners to an older boy. Those who didn't were sometimes thrown into the stream on the way to school.

'Elvin! That idiot Glenroy is at the back door.'

The youth departed as the wiry figure of Elvin appeared. He had an acorn-shaped face with sad, dark eyes. His short, tufty hair was crying out for hair oil and his knees looked like sand-papered doorknobs.

'You wanna come swimming?' Glenroy asked.

Elvin's face lit up, as if Glenroy was the first friend he had received for months. 'Yeah, if I'm allowed.'

'My uncle booked it for ten o clock, so make sure you get permission. Then call for me at quarter to ten.'

'Didn't you ask Carlton to come?' asked Elvin, suspicious as to why Glenroy was inviting him.

'Yeah, but he's doing something.'

For a short second, the despondent look in Elvin's eyes returned. 'Did you see the fight yesterday? Osgood beat up that new boy.'

Glenroy wiped his nose, feeling a slight pinch of hay fever. 'I was there. Didn't you see me? I was trying to tell Osgood to leave him alone. Osgood listens to me.'

'Oh yeah. Well, it didn't make much difference. He beat Bullet up anyway. I see you walking with Carlton and Bullet after the fight.'

'Yeah, we went to teach him how to fight.'

'Don't you mean that Carlton went to teach him?'

'Look, I can fight, it's just that none of you lot have seen me in action lately.' Glenroy launched himself into shadow-boxing, throwing a right and a left upper cut, weaving and dancing around.

Elvin managed to stop himself from laughing too much. He looked above Glenroy's head, hearing the sound of the milk float. 'That Bullet's in my class. He's weird. When the teacher ain't looking he takes out his stupid toy soldiers from a jamboree bag.'

Glenroy laughed. 'Serves him right he got beat up if he plays with little boys' toys.'

'Elvin!' An adult voice came from the kitchen. 'Your breakfast is ready.'

Elvin bade farewell to his mate and closed the door.

The time approached ten o'clock. Glenroy and Elvin, towels and swimming trunks under their arms, hared towards the swimming pool, taking a short cut through the orchard along a narrow, twisted, dried mud path. The orchard, fronted by unclipped hedges, grew more dense the further it went away from Glenroy's house, where the trees stopped and unnavigable blackberry bushes grew wildly, along with the tallest stinging nettles the kids had ever seen. Not even the teenagers would attempt to make a secret camp here. Generations of children thought this was the domain of the bogey-man.

As Glenroy and Elvin left the fruit trees behind them, they entered a field of long, pale grass that climbed to their waists. Grasshoppers debated openly, and other creatures that Glenroy and Elvin couldn't name, shrieked their strange shrieks. Glenroy once boasted that he'd seen a snake the size of a fireman's hose which had a mouth that opened as wide as a dustbin. Curvis told any of his peers who were patient enough to listen that if you saw a mantis eat another mantis, then that was a sign for the bogey-man to appear.

'Africa' country stretched out for half a mile or so, until it met the circular road where one enterprising housefather had set up allotments, growing his own potatoes, tomatoes and other vegetables. Fifty yards beyond the allotments, bisecting an untamed field, a chicken-wire fence marked the eastern border of the homes complex. Beyond that, rising up into the distance, sweeping through the Kent border, was farmland.

The two pals left the field through a hedge-gap on its south side. Their footsteps sounded heavier as they skipped along the tarmac approaching the building complex, overlooked by the water tower, where the swimming pool was situated. The two boys often wondered how old the swimming pool building was – full of red-slated, angled roofs, concrete walkways and a network of black pipes that were almost big enough for a football to be kicked through. Whoever built this wasn't worried about how it looked.

They could both smell the hot steam that came from the laundry and they heard the irritating din of work tools coming from the engineers' building. Council workmen loathed working in this location because of the walking distances; it was two and a half miles to the nearest bus stop. Carlton had got on friendly terms with a painter who worked at the depot and on many occasions Carlton was sent to the shops to buy a drink for the decorator, receiving ten pence for his five-mile round trip. In the summer months he spent his money on strawberry-iced jubblys and teased Glenroy with them.

Pinewood Oaks had its own team of carpenters, plumbers, engineers, glaziers, gardeners and many other workmen, mainly performing repair and maintenance tasks. In the factory beside the water tower, part-time women workers darned socks, repaired clothes, laundered bed sheets and sewed council name-tags on garments for the new arrivals. The work force were discouraged from building any sort of relationship with the children and it was strictly forbidden for any workers to take a child outside the grounds of the complex, even if it was a trip to the shops.

Elvin and Glenroy neared the red-bricked building of

the swimming pool, which was covered by a factory-like, wired-glass roof. Uncle Thomas's mud-splattered jeep was parked outside the blue doors. Glenroy and Elvin entered the building and were met by a riot of squawks, echoing around the pool's red-painted walls.

'Uncle Thomas never gives me a lift to the swimming pool,' Glenroy complained, walking towards the cubicles that were situated on the right-hand side of the pool.

Elvin, entering the booth next door to Glenroy, replied, 'That's because you're one of the oldest now, innit.'

'No, I ain't. What about Colin? He's ten and he got a lift, the little squirt.'

Elvin closed the door of his chamber and secured the small lock. 'That's because he's not in your house, stupid. Uncle Thomas promised Colin's housemother that he's gonna teach him how to swim.'

'Don't call me stupid, acorn head.'

Minutes later, the two boys joined the fray in the pool. Everyone seemed to be enjoying themselves, with the able swimmers diving and jumping into the deep end and the younger children at the shallow end, their arms wrapped in plastic blow-up supports, being schooled by Uncle Thomas, who was wearing a very tight pair of red swimming trunks. Polystyrene white floats drifted on the surface of the pool.

The older children fought for the use of a single pair of goggles. Glenroy and Elvin, both competent swimmers, were playing tag in and out of the water. Uncle Thomas kept on shouting at the children not to run.

Before the children knew it, the time had crept up close to eleven o'clock. Thomas beckoned everybody out of the water. The housefather dried himself whilst walking up and down the length of the pool, making sure everybody was in their cubicles. He grabbed another towel from a chair and paced quickly towards the booths where Elvin and Glenroy were changing. Then, coming to a halt, he banged his fist on

Elvin's door. 'Hey, Elvin. I've got your towel,' Thomas said in a friendly manner. 'You must have left it on a chair.'

Elvin opened his cubicle door and Thomas quickly walked inside. The boy was naked, dripping with water, and looked at the towel very confused. The smell of chlorine still lingered on his body. Thomas put on his best smile, stroking Elvin's wet hair. Elvin flinched and grabbed the towel. Thomas, not letting go of the towel, began to dry Elvin's back. His other hand, as if by accident, stroked Elvin's genitals. He smiled again. 'Clumsy me.'

Elvin stood motionless, frightened beyond belief, wanting to tug the towel off Thomas and wrap it around his waist and cover himself. But he couldn't. His petrified eyes were glued to the wet floor. He never thought of grown-ups doing dirty stuff. Why was Thomas being rude? The six foot plus adult had now relaxed his grip on the towel. Elvin grabbed it immediately and pressed it tight on his stomach, his hands shaking. He saw Thomas's penis bulge inside his trunks. Elvin turned around, facing the wall, still holding his towel against his abdomen, exposing his back. He became conscious of the sound of his own breathing. He felt a large hand stroke his hair, then caress his back. He closed his eyes, praying for the touching to stop. His throat became dry as his young mind told him this couldn't be happening. Suddenly, he felt Thomas's hand slide over his backside before leaving his body. Elvin then heard the door click and close again. It was a minute before he turned around to make sure that Thomas had departed.

Glenroy heard Thomas's voice as he emerged from the cubicle. He wondered what Elvin had done to warrant Thomas entering his cubicle and, apparently, discipline him. On the way home, through the orchard, Glenroy decided to ask about the incident with the towel. 'Did Uncle Thomas tell you off for messing about with your towel near the water?'

Elvin, who was walking with his eyes staring at the ground, wanted the trees to answer the question. 'Yeah he did,' he

49

stuttered, not looking up. 'But I made sure I put it in the cubicle. One of the stupid kids in your house must've took it out.'

They walked on in silence. Normally, they would play a game of tag on the way home or hide behind bushes and shrubbery as they watched others go by while they made jungle sounds. This time they pressed on in silence. 'Did he beat you?' asked Glenroy.

'No. He, er, sort of told me off about the towel,' replied Elvin, still finding it difficult to complete a sentence. 'And, he, er. Yeah, he said that I should come to swimming classes. 'Cos, er. Yeah. He said there's something wrong with my front crawl. But I don't want to go. I hate your Uncle.'

Glenroy was baffled. He kicked a twig. 'Why do you hate him? He didn't beat you. You should be lucky. If that was me he would have sent me home and give me a beating later when he got back.'

'I just don't like him,' Elvin insisted, quickening the pace of his walk into a sprint. 'I ain't coming swimming with you again.'

Glenroy chased his pal and leaped on his back playfully. 'Gotcha, acorn head,' he cried as they fell forward. The front of Elvin's T-shirt turned light-brown as it pressed against the dried mud. Elvin twisted around, trying to break free. 'GET LOST! LEAVE ME ALONE!'

Glenroy attempted a grip he had seen on Saturday afternoon wrestling. 'Say you submit, acorn head! Say you submit!'

'GET OFF! TAKE A RUN AND JUMP. GET OFF ME!'

Elvin pushed Glenroy away, tears now visible on his face, and scampered off. Glenroy, giving up on the chase and realising it wasn't a game anymore, watched motionless. Maybe I called him acorn head too much, Glenroy thought. The nightmare he had last night suddenly came to the forefront of his mind. He couldn't put his finger on it but Elvin's shouting was similar to the sound he had heard while standing at the pit of the monster. He turned around on the spot, studying the trees, and then ran as hard as he could out of the orchard.

PART TWO

Tight Circuit

2 June 1976

Curvis worked the rusty spanner around the nut of the front wheel of a bike, securing it to its axle. He hoisted the front forks and spun the metal hoop, searching for any signs of a kink; he was satisfied with his work. 'That's a lot better, innit,' he said proudly. 'It's got a little buckle on it but you can hardly see it.'

Carlton inspected the spinning disk like a jeweller squinting his eye over a gem. 'Yeah. It's going around straight,' he admitted. 'But if I fall off the thing, I'm still going to blame you.'

'Fuck you! If it weren't for me you wouldn't have no bike,' joked Curvis, wielding his spanner in mock anger. He spotted a speck of oil on the bike frame and wiped it off with a cloth.

'What d'you mean? It was me who found the thing at the

55

dump,' argued Carlton, not wanting to allow his friend to take all the credit. 'And I was the one who painted it. And I got the brakes.'

'Only after you took apart that bike that was outside the chippy last month. How would you feel if you came out of a shop and see that some bastard had taken your brakes?'

Carlton smirked, remembering the incident well. 'I'm sure whoever's bike it belonged to, their parents can probably afford a replacement; especially those posh fuckers who live in those big houses near the chippy.'

The two friends were inside the outhouse behind Carlton's home, surrounded by bits of wood and bike frames, nuts, bolts, washers, worn spanners, chipped screwdrivers and tins of small, empty oil cans. Curvis had grown to almost six foot and there seemed to be not an ounce of flesh on his taut body. His misshapen afro was left to its own devices and his slender fingers had grown unusually long. Although not as tall, Carlton now had fully developed shoulders and chest that promised perfect power. His limbs had thickened considerably and his jaw had squared into a face of determination. Crippled bike frames, punctured tyres, mangled spokes and broken trolley wheels were piled in an undignified heap in a corner of the dusty room. A snow sledge, with a frayed rope attached to it, awaited the winter months in another corner. Forgotten, headless Action Men and one-eyed dolls were kept in a cardboard box with other broken toys under the window frame.

Carlton peered through a cracked, blackened window. 'Hey! Bullet, Glenroy, come here,' he hailed.

Bullet and Glenroy were entangled in a grappling contest, trying to head-lock each other. Bullet, who had grown his hair long, now owned powerful, squat legs that enabled him to compete for the local schools sprint championships. Although just five foot eight, he had big hands with fleshy fingers, enabling him to climb the most challenging trees.

His face was oval-shaped and he now had a hint of cheek in his eyes that attracted teenage girls in Pinewood Oaks, although he was unaware of it. Glenroy now weighed over fourteen stone. His round, cherubic face had developed faint laughter lines close to his eyes and his double chin was nearing completion. Compared to the rest of his body his hands and feet were small.

Bullet and Glenroy heard Carlton's call. They untangled themselves and looked towards the window. They could just make out Carlton beckoning to them. Two spanner turns later they entered the gloom of the outhouse and watched Carlton sitting imperiously on his bike as Curvis collected his tools from the dusty, concrete floor.

'Can't you two keep your hands off each other?' mocked Carlton. 'You're like two bloody poofs!'

'Oh, shut up!' returned Glenroy. 'You're the only poof round here.'

'Least I don't play kiss-chase with boys,' Carlton sniped.

'You're just saying that 'cos you ain't got the guts to take us on in a wrestling match,' countered Bullet, punching the air in front of him like Bruce Lee.

'Take you two losers on?' Carlton laughed. 'I could beat the both of you even if I was in a straitjacket!'

Without warning, Glenroy leaped at Carlton, strangling him, while Bullet grabbed Carlton's left arm, twisting it behind his back. The bike fell to the floor. Curvis grimaced, slapping the palm of his right hand to his forehead.

'Say you submit,' Bullet urged.

'Aaaarrggg, get off, you wankers!'

Bullet tightened his hold. 'Say you submit!'

'Uuhhhggghh, aaarrrgghhh. Alright, alright. I submit.'

Bullet loosened his grip, smiling triumphantly. 'Easy . . . What was you saying before?'

'Hummpphh. You just caught me by surprise,' Carlton grinned. 'You're still losers.'

The friends laughed as Curvis shook his head, observing the damaged paintwork on the bike.

Glenroy asked, 'So you're going in the race with that? You ain't got no chance; you ain't gonna beat me.'

'Why?' Carlton snapped, feeling a terrible insult. 'All because you bullied Elvin into borrowing his bike for the race. Anyway, how the fuck did Elvin get the money for his new bike?'

'My Uncle Thomas give him most of the money,' answered Glenroy. 'Elvin agreed last week to help him teach the under-elevens to swim. They had a long talk in his study and he came out with the money. It's funny 'cos Elvin used to hate swimming with us.'

Curvis turned his face away from the conversation. Carlton looked at Curvis as if they were sharing a secret; Glenroy was unaware of this but Bullet wondered what the secret was. I hate the way they do that, he said to himself.

Carlton wheeled his bike out of the outhouse and onto the path. The children from Carlton's household, playing a game of rounders on an adjacent field, cheered their hero as he mounted the bike. 'You're looking at the winner!' he shouted to them, pumping his fist into the air.

Ten minutes later, Carlton and his friends arrived at the rendezvous point for the start of the bike race; it was outside Violet House, whose sports-loving housefather had organised the event. Some competitors were cruising around on their bikes. Others were completing last-minute checks on breaks and pedals. Most were dressed in football shorts and white vests. Carlton was wearing cut-down jeans and a white T-shirt. The housefather, a portly figure who had his long hair tied in a pony-tail, with a beard to rival a black-haired Santa Claus, was strutting about with his business face on, fingering his whistle and looking smart in a designer tracksuit.

Glenroy, wearing a non-designer tracksuit, looked for Elvin, who was seated on his brand-new racing bike, his right hand keeping balance against a lamp-post. 'Hey, Elvin. You done the brakes?' asked Glenroy, trying to sound professional. 'Have you oiled the cogs and chain? You're s'posed to do those things 'cos you're my bike engineer; Carlton's got Bullet.'

'What for?' replied Elvin, not particularly enthusiastic about Glenroy borrowing his bike. 'The bike's brand-new, innit. And 'cos it's new, don't pull the brakes too hard, otherwise you'll go head over tit.'

'Me, fall off?' laughed Glenroy confidently. 'Don't be an idiot – have I ever fallen off?'

'YES!' shouted five voices who were listening to the exchange.

Meanwhile, Curvis climbed a tree, perching himself on a branch overlooking the starting line. Hands behind his head, he studied the proceedings beneath him. He saw Bullet, championing Carlton's case to anybody who would listen.

Around twenty bikers mustered together along the starting point. The housefather formed the racers into a level line before a road bump as if he was starting an Olympic final. Glenroy muscled his way into the middle of the line-up, stealing a few inches. He was soon put in place by the eagle-eyed starter taking the opportunity to test his whistle.

Carlton's face was stiff with concentration. Mellor, slightly older than Carlton, wearing a Chelsea football club woolly hat, glanced across the line with apprehension all over his face. Others only had eyes for the road ahead. It was a relatively flat start, they would race three hundred yards or so before a sharp left in front of the community centre.

Mr Knowles walked ten yards past the start, whistle in mouth. Then he blew with enough gusto to play a trumpet. The faces of the bikers strained as they pedalled furiously to gain a good start.

Spectators yelled out their support from under the shade of trees. Curvis was joined in the tree by a clumsy Elvin. They both watched the racers disappear into the sun-hazed distance.

Curvis looked down at Bullet, who was fiercely shouting his encouragement. 'Save your shouting 'til he comes round the last bend.'

'On that bike Carlton needs all the shouting he can get,' returned Bullet. 'He said he'll buy us all jubblys if he wins.'

'If I was you I'd save my pennies for an ice-pole,' someone laughed.

'And if I was you I'd shut my mouth,' Bullet challenged.

'I've seen an elephant with a lighter frame than Carlton's bike.'

'And I've seen a Muppet with more teeth than you might have if you don't fucking shut up!'

Elvin and Curvis both heard a child's scream. They turned their heads and near the bushes that acted as the borderline of the Pinewood Oaks compound, they saw a young girl being spanked severely by her housefather. She was no older than six. As her housefather dragged her by the arm, there were no cries of protest from the spectators. Mr Knowles acted as if he heard nothing, turning his back on the girl's plight and feigning a deaf ear to her shrieks.

Curvis predicted, 'Lightwood's gonna win it.'

Elvin was surprised that Curvis spoke, for he had been feeling that Curvis hadn't even acknowledged his presence. 'He's good at cross-country and he's got stamina,' reasoned Curvis. 'The others will all rush off and burn themselves out. Around Pinewood Oaks is about three and a half miles, and the way most of them set off, they ain't gonna last.'

'Where do you reckon Glenroy and Carlton will finish?' asked Elvin.

'Carlton will never give up. He hates to lose anything. Glenroy . . .'

Curvis tailed off but Elvin guessed Curvis had no confidence in Glenroy whatsoever. 'Will be last?' Elvin completed the sentence. 'I hope he ain't too fat for my new bike. He might squash my thin tyres – they use them kind of tyres in the Tour de France.'

Meanwhile, at the front of the race, Glenroy had stolen a lead of about three bike lengths. The riders behind him were tightly packed. Everyone was beginning to sweat. They were reaching speeds of thirty miles an hour as they raced downhill. Kids stationed in the piggery that had been converted into a play area were cheering and shouting. Others lined the pavement, willing on their favourites. They saw one racer hit a kerb, fall and slide on his back across the unforgiving asphalt.

The bikers left the valley and their faces were creased even more as they began the climb that would take them by the nursery. Skateboarders frantically rolled off the road and made hurried landings on the grass as the racers pedalled towards them. The incline had taken a lot out of Glenroy. His thighs seemed to be carrying lead weights, and his calves had stiffened like setting glue. Mellor had caught up with him on the left-handed arched turn at the top end of the orchard. Carlton and Lightwood were in the middle of the pack, pacing themselves for the final push at the end of the race. They raced under the shade of a sycamore tree; Carlton knew this was the halfway mark.

Mellor, glancing at Glenroy and gaining inspiration from his obvious exhaustion, surged ahead to take the outright lead. Widening gaps began to appear between the racers. They flashed past the swimming pool and Carlton proceeded to make his calculated move. He neared the leaders. Lightwood stalked him, taking huge gulps of air and trying to control his breathing.

The cyclists swooped downhill. Past the water tower which looked down on them. The race began in earnest with everybody realising that to fall behind now would mean certain defeat. No slowing down to ride over the ramps. The children playing in the valley near the stream had spotted them, and moved accordingly. They raced over the bridge all

61

in their top gears and then steeled themselves again for the ascent that would take them past the children's play area that was surrounded by a semi-circle of oaks. Glenroy's legs simply would not respond to his brain. He thought the insides of his legs had turned to gunge. He rocked from side to side, was eventually passed by other racers and, as he dropped substantially behind the leaders, he slowed and gave up the race. 'Aaaarrrggg! My leg!' he feigned injury.

Up front, Mellor had a two-bike length lead but was being chased by Carlton. Gradually and surely, Carlton was catching him up. The leader glanced back in alarm while hastily changing his gears. They reached the brow of the hill and turned left into the finishing straight. Carlton was just half a bike length down.

The spectators, two hundred yards away at the finishing road-ramp, caught sight of the leaders. Carlton employed every muscle in his body as he forced himself past Mellor. Curvis and Elvin jumped down from the tree, shouting encouragement. Other supporters did likewise, including Bullet. 'COME ON, CARLTON. PUMP THOSE FUCKING LEGS!'

Lightwood, with a huge effort, overtook Mellor and was now closing on Carlton. Fifty yards to go. Carlton was one bike length ahead. Twenty-five yards to go. Carlton grimaced like a man suffering Japanese torture, his face caked in sweat, his calf muscles glistening in the sun, his arms taut on the handlebars. Head down. In a flash Carlton glanced at Lightwood and saw his doom. The two leaders came dangerously close together. Lightwood emitted a desperate grunt, his backside off the seat. He was inches away from the lead. Carlton had no more to give, his body yielding to exhaustion. Lightwood was ecstatic as he rolled over the ramp centimetres ahead of Carlton. His friends all performed jigs of delight and they ran after him.

Mellor came home in third place, about twenty yards behind the front two. As soon as he dismounted his bike, he collapsed on the grass underneath a tree, panting furiously. A girl went to tend to him with a bottle of water. Carlton lay on his back on the pavement, breathing hard, unable to move his limbs. Curvis and Elvin ambled towards him, proud of their friend's efforts. 'Fuck me!' exclaimed Curvis. 'When you came into the straight I thought you was gonna win.'

Carlton's spent face turned into anger. 'So did I!' Abruptly he got to his feet and kicked the front wheel of the bike. 'Fucking Lightwood! He only won 'cos he had a better bike than me. I'm gonna ask the wanker for another race tomorrow . . . Can't fucking believe I lost.'

'Don't take it out on the bike,' rebuked Curvis.

'But you done better than expected,' said Elvin, not understanding Carlton's anger. 'You pushed Lightwood as close as you could get.'

'Don't matter how close,' Carlton said with a glare. 'I still fucking lost! . . . Someone get me a fucking drink.'

Elvin ran over to a girl who was carrying a bottle of water. He returned to Carlton and gave him the water. Carlton half-emptied the one-litre bottle in one go. 'Can't believe I fucking lost!'

Mr Knowles, examining his stop watch, declared, 'Lightwood, that was a Pinewood Oaks record. Four minutes and six seconds. Well done, son. That was the best finish for years. You'll get your tenner later on.' Mr Knowles then turned to Carlton. 'Good show, Carlton, we all thought as you came around the last bend that you had it in the bag. Hard lines. Perhaps you need a better bike?'

Carlton nodded, his face still stormy. 'By the way, what happened to Glenroy?' Mr Knowles enquired.

'What? Ain't he finished yet?' Carlton replied, scanning the finishers sprawled on the grass and tarmac.

'No sign of him,' said Mr Knowles. 'He didn't fall, did he?'

'Probably,' one passer-by quipped.

Carlton, walking like he had jelly in his legs, was baffled.

'I don't think so,' he answered, a hint of concern in his expression. 'I passed him just by the bridge near the stream.'

'He probably gave up,' offered Curvis.

Elvin picked up Carlton's bike. 'I hope he hasn't mashed up my new bike.'

Bullet, walking away from Lightwood after telling him how lucky he was in his victory, suggested, 'Come on, we better go and look for him. Knowing Glenroy, he probably crashed into a tree!'

The friends set off across the sloping field. They could see the stream sparkling silver in the distance underneath an orange, setting sun. A group of young girls were playing rounders in the gathering gloom. 'Fuck Glenroy, let's watch this,' Elvin laughed.

'Elvin, the oldest girl there is about eleven,' rebuked Bullet. 'Are you some kind of perv or what?'

Elvin grinned to himself as the others shook their heads. 'Ain't it about time you fancied a girl your own age?' said Carlton, addressing Elvin.

'I don't fancy none of 'em,' snapped Elvin, his voice suddenly raised. 'I'm just messing about.'

Curvis, examining Elvin's reaction, offered a knowing smile. 'I think all of you are pervs,' he grinned. 'Bullet and Glenroy have always played kiss-chase since they've known each other. Elvin likes to watch little girls play rounders, and Carlton's got a crush on Auntie Clare who works in Acacia House.'

'All because I said she was pretty, it doesn't mean I've got a crush on her,' countered Carlton. 'Bloody hell, you lot are so immature.'

'She's only twenty-two,' Bullet remarked. 'I must admit, when I saw her in those shorts the other day, she did look a bit tasty. And Curvis, if you say that I play kiss-chase with Glenroy again, you can say hello to the acorns I'll be throwing at ya next time you're in a tree.'

'She was sunbathing the other day at the back of her house,' Elvin revealed. 'She only had a bikini on and she undone her top. I climbed a tree, trying to keep out of sight, hoping she would get up so I could get a look.'

'You perv!' Carlton cried. 'I bet you stayed in that tree for hours.'

'Two hours,' Elvin replied. 'I fucking fell on my way down. Fucking branch snapped!'

Everybody laughed, except Curvis, who simply shook his head, looking appalled.

They continued to stroll downhill across the baked grass. The street lights, set about thirty yards apart, switched themselves on, illuminating the orbital road. One of the girls playing rounders, fielding in the deep, recognised Carlton. 'Carlton, wotcha!' she hailed, raising her hand and waving at the embarrassed Carlton.

Carlton's friends chuckled as they neared the small stone bridge. Elvin mounted Carlton's bike as the others walked on. Bullet leaped onto the stone wall, the stream five foot below him. Underneath the umbrella of branches and leaves, he saw Glenroy who was throwing stones in the water. 'There he is,' pointed Bullet. 'Down there.'

The quartet looked down along the banks of the stream and saw Glenroy with his head bowed. Elvin pedalled over the grass towards Glenroy, anxiety spreading over his face. 'Where's my bike?'

Glenroy, turning around, watched Elvin approach him with a blank expression. He said nothing. Elvin spotted his bike lying on the grass near a cluster of bushes. He dismounted and went over to run a check. 'What happened to you,' Curvis chuckled. 'Someone threw a stick in your spokes?'

'My foot slipped and I fell on the grass,' Glenroy lied. 'I just missed crashing into the wall. It wasn't worth rejoining the race. But I could've won if it wasn't for the fall.'

65

'Oh yeah. Likely story,' rejected Carlton. 'You were knackered.' Curvis and Bullet were both holding back belly laughs.

'No I wasn't tired!' Glenroy stormed. 'I was saving myself for the finish! Like them professional bikers in the Tour de France.'

The others laughed heartily as Glenroy moodily threw another pebble into the stream. Elvin ambled towards his friends, satisfied that his bike was not damaged. 'Hey, Elvin,' Carlton called. 'Glenroy reckons his foot slipped off the pedal and he nearly crashed into the wall of the bridge.'

Elvin grinned, shaking his head. 'Come off it! Mellor was telling me you was knackered.'

'Well, Mellor's a fucking liar!' Glenroy raged, suddenly losing his temper. 'You always believe anything he says. If it weren't for Elvin's stupid bike I would have won ... I was pretending to be tired.'

Glenroy's friends laughed again, this time rolling on the grass. Glenroy stood up suddenly. 'I'm going home. I dunno why you lot come to look for me if all you can do is take the piss.'

'Stop sulking, you loser. Hang up, I'll go with ya.' Carlton mounted his bike and quickly caught up with him. 'What's a matter with you?' he asked. 'I know you're sulky but fuck me! Today's got to be your biggest strop yet.'

Glenroy didn't reply and walked on, head down.

'For fuck's sake. You in a strop just because of the bike race?' Carlton asked.

'NO!'

'Then what the fuck is it?'

'Why should I tell you? You just want to take the piss.'

'Oh, for fuck's sake!'

'It's Uncle Thomas.'

Carlton leaped off his bike and led it by the handlebars. 'What's Uncle Thomas done to you now?'

'The bastard reckons I stole ten pounds,' Glenroy replied,

hatred seeping into his face. 'And he's gonna speak to my social worker tomorrow. And he told Father Patrick – he wasn't gonna let me out tonight – I had to beg. Uncle Thomas says he's had enough of me and threatened to send me to Stanford House.'

'Stanford House!' Carlton exclaimed, his face giving way to shock. 'Fuckin' hell, you don't wanna go there! That's where they sent Curvis's brother two years ago, and you know what happened to him!'

Stanton, Curvis's elder brother, had been sent to Stanford House for continuous violent outbursts at his children's home in Kent. It all began when Stanton turned a teenager four years ago and was refused permission to visit Curvis. Stanford House was a youth detention centre with a bad reputation. Tales of baton-wielding staff and metal straitjackets were exchanged by gossiping kids like football cards in Pinewood Oaks. Reports that had trickled down the children's home grapevine said that Stanton had now lost his mind.

Glenroy nodded. 'Yeah, I know. But I didn't nick the ten pounds. And you know my social worker is gonna believe him – they always do. Fucking social wankers.'

Glenroy looked at Carlton, expecting his friend to condemn his housefather. 'Well, I did tell you to change that useless bitch of a social worker you got, innit,' Carlton said. 'She don't do fuck-all for you. She's a loser.'

'I wish I was in your house,' Glenroy lamented.

Carlton nodded, realising he was lucky to be under the care of Auntie Josephine.

'I ain't going to Stanford House,' Glenroy affirmed. 'I'll do anything than go to that shit-hole ... I'll even run away.'

Carlton studied Glenroy's face and realised he was very serious, as serious as he had ever seen him. He stopped to pick up a blade of grass and inserted it inside his mouth. He started chewing. 'You run away,' he mocked. '*You!* What do you know about running away? Look at that time years ago when you started off walking to France.'

'Back then I didn't know it was over the sea.'

'You turned around at the back gates ... You wouldn't survive a day on your own.'

A strange smile appeared on Glenroy's face, as if he had been waiting for this moment for a very long time. 'Who says I'm going on my own,' he said.

Carlton was visibly stunned. '*What!*' he exclaimed and then paused. 'It's Curvis, innit. You're gonna go with Curvis?' Surely Curvis would not contemplate running away with Glenroy, Carlton thought. Nah, Curvis got too much sense.

'Yep,' Glenroy replied with assurance. 'We spoke last week about it but he's been on punishment until today, so we haven't had a chance to go over it. He's still mad about his Auntie not letting him see Stanton. He still won't talk to her.'

'I thought 'cos he was allowed out today, Curvis sorted it out. He still ain't talking to her?'

'Nope. He told me today he'd rather go to Stanford House than talk to that "stuck up, aristocratic, baboon-arsed bitch" . . . I think I got that right. It could have been "fucked up, aristocratic, baboon-faced bitch". I can't remember.'

Carlton laughed, nearly dropping his bike, but he knew what this meant. Curvis had as much motivation as Glenroy for running away. Curvis once told him that if they stopped him from visiting his brother, then he would run away to make his point. And when Curvis said he'd do something, he'd always did it.

They approached the orchard, with Carlton wondering what was going through Curvis's mind. If Glenroy and Curvis were about to run away, he would be obliged to go with them. Bullet would too. They were his friends and besides, the authorities would put intolerable pressure on him, pressure that Auntie Josephine could not protect him from. What am I gonna do? he asked himself.

Carlton studied Glenroy's face again. 'You two are serious about this, innit?'

'Yep. Ain't no way I'm going to Stanford House – they beat you up three times a day and put you in straitjackets there. No fucking way!'

'Have you told Bullet about this?'

'Nope. I was gonna tell him today, but he was too busy with your bike – we wanted to tell you lot together.'

'We'll have to talk about this – all four of us,' Carlton proposed. 'You must realise that if you and Curvis leg it, they'll be asking me and Bullet a lot of questions, and they'll be watching us all the time.'

Glenroy's spirits uplifted. 'When? Tomorrow after school?'

'Nah. I've got sports for the rest of the week after school. It'll have to be Saturday. When you see Curvis and Bullet tomorrow, tell 'em.'

'So would you come?' asked Glenroy.

Carlton's expression couldn't hide his reluctance. 'I . . . I dunno. I want to know what Bullet makes of it. I know you lot's life in this place is shit. But Auntie Josephine treats me . . .' Carlton tailed off and looked up through the branches. Stars were appearing in the night sky. 'If me and Bullet didn't go it would fuck up things for me and him. FUCKING HELL.'

Glenroy cut his eyes at his friend but didn't hold this expression for long as Carlton suddenly laughed. 'Imagine it. All four of us on the run. That'll give Uncle Thomas and 'em something to think about. And it would wipe the snobby smile off Curvis's bitch of a housemother. Bullet's Uncle Rodney will probably call it desertion, fucking army-loving wanker. If I was Bullet, I'd tell him where to stick his shoe inspections and all that standing to attention bollocks. The man needs help.'

'So you coming then?' grinned Glenroy.

'I dunno. It could lead all four of us to Stanford House.

And they'll have one big fucking problem finding a straitjacket to fit you.'

'Fuck you. You're still upset 'cos you lost to Lightwood . . . Well, if you don't come with us, we'll go without you and you can stay with Auntie Josephine and kiss her arse for all I care.'

'Not my fault I'm lucky and living in her house . . . She's been good to me. I know you lot have lived through shit. But I ain't got no big reason to do a runner.'

'That's alright for you to say,' Glenroy countered, hating the fact that Carlton had a relatively peaceful home life. 'What did you say last year? That we are all brothers and we should do everything together. Well, some brother you are! I bet Bullet comes, and that will leave you on your own.'

Carlton was also thinking of that summer's day last year. He and his friends had watched a cowboy film on a rainy Sunday afternoon. All four had been mesmerised by a scene in which an Indian and a white man had slashed their palms, clasping their hands together in an act of brotherly love. It was Bullet's idea to re-enact the scene in the darkness of the damp orchard, all of them masking their pain with locked lips and tightening cheeks. Curvis had even stolen a small tube of antiseptic cream to prevent any hand becoming infected. Carlton and Bullet said they didn't need the cream, reasoning that the cowboy and Indian hadn't used it. Glenroy smothered his right palm with the lotion. They vowed to stand together and support each other, no matter what happens. As they went home that night, they sensed a kind of family belonging that had been denied them all their lives. Carlton knew that it was a bond that couldn't be broken. 'If everyone agrees,' he said finally, 'I'll go with you . . . but it has to be planned good.'

'Of course it will! You know Curvis. He's probably planning it now.' Glenroy nodded and a huge smile covered his face. They strolled off towards home as unseen gnats circled above their heads and the first hooting of an owl could be heard from a towering roadside oak tree. 'So we gonna have a meeting on Saturday to talk about all this?' Glenroy said, seeking confirmation.

'Yeah. I s'pose so.'

Before entering his home, Carlton caught sight of Auntie Josephine through a dining-room window. He felt a surge of guilt. She was preparing a table for breakfast.

Democracy

Situated at the centre of the homes complex, on the rim of a children's play area with swings and see-saws, and close to dense woodland that would shield the sun until lunch-time, was an aluminium climbing frame. It was round like a big metal football with gaping holes in it. Draped on the frame were three male teenagers. A stocky figure perched on the top, balanced perfectly. He had long, brown hair and infant sideburns, small pimples around his nose and his face seemed more red than white. He was wearing a blue, sweat-stained vest. His friends, who were slightly below him but all displaying the same aplomb upon the frame, were listening to his animated argument.

'I like that, oh yeah, I like that,' disputed Bullet. 'You expect me to convince Carlton that we should leg it! For fuck's sake, you can't expect me and Carlton to come with you all because we're best friends.' Bullet watched his friends, pleading with his brown eyes for them to understand. Shit! This is gonna fuck up my football trials later on in the month, Bullet thought. But I can't tell 'em *that*.

'Yeah, Bullet,' Curvis shook his head, displaying a calmness that irked Bullet. 'You said to me the other week how you was fighting with your Uncle and how he beat you up. What did you say at the time? That you wanted to move from your house. Especially as your social worker didn't believe you. Uncle Rodney's been picking on you for years. You seem to have forgotten how he used his cane on you.'

Bullet wiped his slowly dripping runny nose. Curvis was right, he told himself. I'll never fucking forget it. He remembered the canings only too well and felt embarrassed. Curvis resumed in a soft tone. 'Well, if you do a runner, then they'll have to take you serious, innit. They're bound to give you a transfer. Just tell your social worker that you ran away 'cos Uncle Rodney keeps beating you up . . . Look at that time he busted your mouth wide open and took you to the dentist, he told them you fell off a bike. The man's a fucking psycho. No kid should take that kind of beating.'

'Yeah,' Glenroy agreed. 'If that was me I'd hit him with a fucking coal shovel.'

'I can't remember you ever hitting Uncle Thomas back. And you never complained when that ginger-haired bastard used to lock you up in the fucking outhouse. You didn't exactly smash the windows to try and escape. So *don't* come with your bollocks about fucking coal shovels.'

'When did Uncle Rodney last hit you?' asked Curvis.

'Uncle Rodney last beat me up in April,' admitted Bullet, shamefaced. 'After me and Elvin nicked tomatoes from Uncle Sam's allotments. He hasn't touched me since.' Bullet fingered the area just above his top lip where there was a small scar. If you ran away, Uncle Rodney might think I'm not disciplined enough for the army, Bullet's internal voice said to him.

'He might not've touched you since,' countered Curvis, 'but he still gives you stupid punishments. Look at that time he wouldn't let you stay up and watch the Ali fight? For fuck's sake, you only forgot to clean your football boots!'

'Yeah,' Bullet concurred. 'He was a right bastard for that. Believe me, that night I wanted to do him something in his sleep.'

Curvis half smiled, thinking Bullet was yielding to his argument. He looked at Bullet whose face was flushed with humiliation. 'Alright, alright!' Bullet exclaimed. 'Say we all run away. Where are we going to go? I bet you ain't thought of that, have you? You haven't planned fuck all!'

'What are you fucking talking about?' Curvis raised his voice, his intelligence insulted. 'I dunno what Glenroy has told you but I know where I'm going!'

Bullet turned to Glenroy, eyeing him like a teacher watches a pupil. 'Alright, Glenroy. Where are you going to go?'

Glenroy was picking off the seven petals of a bright, colourful flower he had found while strolling near the allotments. His face, betraying his confusion, was more of an answer than his reply. 'Er, with Curvis, innit.'

'See. He don't know where the fuck he's going,' berated Bullet.

'Yes I do,' retaliated Glenroy. 'I just ain't gonna tell ya if you ain't interested. You'll probably grass on us anyway!'

It was Bullet's turn to feel insulted. His eyebrows angled sharply. 'Fuck you! I ain't no fucking grass! Have I grassed on any of you since I've known you?' he challenged, searching his friends' eyes.

Bullet's temper unnerved Glenroy and made him slip, losing his grip on the climbing frame. He stretched out an arm and grabbed on to a bar. The flower he was holding, now only with three petals, danced in the air. Curvis watched it drop softly to the ground as Glenroy composed himself. 'Yes you have!' Glenroy said. 'What about that time we were nicking wood from Acacia House the night before bonfire night?'

'That was fucking years ago,' replied Bullet. 'How old were we? About ten I think. You can't bring that up.'

'Well, you said you haven't grassed. But you have!' insisted Glenroy.

'If I remember rightly, it was your fault I got caught anyway!' snarled Bullet. 'You were supposed to be my fucking look-out. Didn't look very good, did ya? I mean, how can you miss somebody with one of those giant battery torches in his hand and his Alsatian running about like it ain't been fed!'

'I couldn't see properly. It was misty that night.'

'Misty that night! The only mist around was inside your brain!'

'Fuck you! It was a stupid idea anyway.'

'Maybe stupid but you're still a fucking lawn tongue – a *grass*.'

'You fucking carry on and see I don't make your head green by pushing it into big fucking nettles.'

'You can come and fucking try.'

Curvis watched his two friends, shaking his head. He looked around to see if Carlton was approaching, but couldn't see him. The row raged on. 'Alright, you two,' Curvis finally interrupted. 'You're like two old women.'

There was peace for a few seconds. Nosy gnats hovered above the climbing frame, taking position near Bullet's head. Something disturbed the shrubbery. Curvis was the first one to turn around, but whatever it was had gone. Glenroy decided to change the topic, fearful of Bullet's rising temper. 'You hear what happened to Kevin Annon?'

'Nah,' Curvis answered. 'What's Kevin done now?'

'You know he plays for the Crystal Palace youth team,' Glenroy answered. 'Well, he was playing a game for them when a defender called him Oliver Orphan. Kevin chased after him, head-butted him and then he took off his football boot and smacked him round the face.'

'All because someone called him Oliver Orphan?' remarked Curvis, closing his eyes for a second to rid himself of the violent image in his brain. 'That's what outside kids call us all the time. Kevin better get used to it if he wants to be a footballer.'

Bullet shook his head. 'He's a bloody nutter!' I would've done the same fucking thing, Bullet convinced himself. No bastard outsider will call *me* Oliver Orphan and get away with it.

'You can call Kevin anything,' added Glenroy. 'But if he hears someone call him Oliver Orphan he goes mental. Don't you remember last year when he nicked the carving knife off his Auntie and chased after Lightwood. That all started 'cos they were calling each other names.'

'He's a nutter,' commented Bullet. 'And lucky he hasn't gone to Stanford House. If it weren't for football he would've gone by now.'

'After last night, Mellor's on punishment,' said Curvis, deciding to swap some gossip until Bullet calmed down.

'Why? What's he done this time?' asked Glenroy.

'You know Sonia's housemother is hassling him 'cos Sonia goes out with him. Well, Mellor decided to get his own back, 'cos he didn't like the way Sonia's housemother came up his house and complained about Mellor climbing up the drainpipe to Sonia's bedroom. Apparently, Sonia wasn't there, but a small girl was. She thought she saw the bogey-man.'

Everybody laughed. The gnats backed away. Curvis continued. 'Last night, Sonia sneaked Mellor into her house. He was hiding in the stairway cupboard with a white bedsheet over him. He waited in there 'til about eleven o clock when Sonia's Auntie was switching off all the lights in the house. When she came to turn off the stairway light, Mellor came out shouting, Wooo, wooo, wooo, with the sheet over his head. Sonia told me her Auntie absolutely shit herself. Sonia reckoned that all the cows in Kent must have heard her scream. Mellor just stood, trying to say it was just a joke. But he forgot to take the sheet off. Then he done a runner. Uncle Maurice had to call out the doctor for the silly cow.'

Everyone laughed, enjoying the break from the serious matter of the day.

'He's a fucking nutter,' commented Bullet.

'What happened to him?' asked Glenroy.

'I think he's on punishment 'til he's about thirty.'

Then, from one of the paths, twisting its way from seemingly impenetrable bushes, emerged the imposing figure of Carlton. Dressed in a tight, red Adidas T-shirt and blue jogging bottoms, he walked slowly to the climbing frame.

'You're late,' yelled Glenroy.

'Shut up,' spat back Carlton, not in the mood to put up with Glenroy today. A fizzing dragonfly had followed Carlton from the bushes and he sensed its presence, waiting for the moment to pounce and destroy it. Bullet, anxious for Carlton to lend support to his argument, jumped from his lofty position down to the ground, landing awkwardly. As he composed himself, he saw Carlton set off in pursuit of the dragonfly, cursing as he went.

'Leave it alone,' said Curvis. 'What's it done to you?'

'One of them bastards stung me the other day,' reported Carlton, pointing to a blemish on his right forearm. He nevertheless gave up the chase, ambling up to the climbing frame. He leaned on it, looking at each one of his friends in turn. 'So you lot come to any decision or you've been arguing like you usually do?'

'We're serious, you know,' affirmed Glenroy. 'We ain't messing about ... Me and Curvis are definitely doing a runner.'

Carlton turned to Bullet. 'What do you say?'

Bullet wished he had never been posed the question.

To him, his friends were his family. He remembered how Carlton, Curvis and Glenroy had looked after him when he was friendless in Pinewood Oaks. Osgood, the school bully, had decided to terrorise some other kid once he knew that Bullet was a friend of Curvis. The one thing that frightened him most was the thought of losing his friends. And running away would show Uncle Rodney that he couldn't push him around, telling him what to do.

'Well, to be honest,' Bullet finally answered, 'Uncle Rodney don't beat me up so much but I can't take his stupid punishments – I'd rather take the fucking beatings. I haven't got too long to go here but I wanna move out of Uncle Rodney's house . . . We've always said that we'll do everything together.' He looked at the scar on his right palm. 'So, er, I'm gonna go.'

Glenroy looked at Bullet with a plastic smile as Curvis nodded. Bullet searched the eyes of his friends. Carlton's expression was hard to read. He half-shrugged his shoulders then eyed Glenroy fiercely. 'What have you been telling him?' He really wanted to direct the question to Curvis but knew Curvis would probably come up with a smart answer.

'What?' Glenroy answered, faking surprise at the question. 'To Bullet? Nothing! He made up his own mind, innit.'

'Fucking hell! You lot have put me in an impossible position. Ain't my fault I live in Auntie Josephine's house and she treats me alright – much better than your bitches of housemothers. But if I go with you lot, it'll be like kicking Auntie Josephine in the guts. And the authorities will think she treated me bad.'

'I want the authorities to *know* they treat us bad,' commented Glenroy.

'That's the first common-sense thing you've said all day,' commented Curvis.

'Well, I know that's true,' admitted Carlton. 'Uncle Thomas is an evil bastard who should be shot in the bollocks . . . I'm just not sure about running away.' There's got to be something else we can do, Carlton said to himself.

Curvis looked at Carlton and they both exchanged something secret in their eyes. He leaped down from the frame and picked up a small twig. He pointed it at Carlton and it had the desired effect of claiming everyone's attention. Carlton looked bemused as he gazed at the twig in Curvis's hand. Curvis then eye-drilled his friend, as if he was a hypnotist. Glenroy and Bullet swapped glances of apprehension. Curvis finally broke the silence. 'All these years I've known you,' he said to Carlton in a slow, gentle voice. 'You've had it easy. Nothing bad has ever happened to you that I know of. We don't even know why you're in this damn place – you've never told us.'

Carlton's lips moved, as if primed for retaliation, and his temper tremored inside his throat. I *hate* the way he does that. I'll never tell you. Carlton stood still, only offering Curvis a blank stare. Curvis continued. 'We all know about each other apart from you. Glenroy's mum is in some mental place. Bullet was left on the doorstep of some social services office, and my old man thought the reason people had kids was to beat them up as soon as they could walk. But you, I don't know. I don't really want to know. I s'pose you'll tell us when you're ready. But I know this. For what? Six years we've done everything together, helped each other build our own bikes and trolleys, got in trouble, lied for each other, played knock-down ginger, ran about playing British Bulldog and tim-tam-tommy, and been in punch-ups.'

Feeling more uncomfortable with Curvis's gaze than his words, Carlton watched the dragonfly, winging its way near the climbing frame. Curvis resumed. 'I don't think you fully realise what us three go through. Auntie Josephine spoils you. When was the last time you weren't allowed out?'

Glenroy and Bullet, who had never heard Curvis speak in such a confrontational tone, wondered if Carlton was going to belt him one. Carlton ambled to a logged enclosure that looked like a boxing ring with branches instead of ropes. He climbed onto the top rung, pondering what to do. Curvis thought the dragonfly was wise not to follow him. Carlton stooped down and plucked out a long blade of grass, inserting it in his mouth. Through the trees, he could make out the incline of road that led to his home and wondered what effect his running away might have on Auntie Josephine. He glanced at his mates and thought it would be intolerable if he was left on his own, and he knew that every waking moment his mind would dwell on his friends. He felt he had to go, for good or for bad. Curvis was right about most of the stuff he talked about, he told himself. But why should I tell Curvis and Bullet about why I'm in here. Glenroy'd better keep his mouth shut or I'll break his head. I should've *never* told him.

'Hey, Curvis,' Glenroy whispered. 'That was a bit strong, weren't it?'

'Yeah, but sometimes he lives in his own dream-world. Everything is not rosy in this place even though he might share biscuits and cups of teas with Saint Josephine.'

'I'm gonna see how he is,' said Bullet, pushing himself off the frame.

'No. Leave him be,' insisted Curvis. 'Let him think.'

After five more minutes, Carlton slowly loped back to his mates, wearing a defeated expression. He eyed Curvis, as if he was telling him, if anything goes wrong, it is your fault. 'Yeah, I'll go,' he said quietly. 'I mean, someone has to look after Glenroy if you do a runner, innit.'

'I don't need anybody to look after me,' returned Glenroy, his round face breaking out into a smile.

'Oh yes you do,' laughed Bullet, releasing the tension they were all feeling.

Glenroy stole behind the back of Bullet. He licked the palm of his right hand then smacked his friend on the back of his neck. Bullet spun around, only to see Glenroy scampering away towards the bushes. Bullet was quick to take up the chase. 'Come here, you nutter!'

Carlton and Curvis watched them, chuckling. 'Them two will be chasing each other when they're old men,' said Curvis.

Carlton picked up a fresh blade of grass and placed it in the corner of his mouth. Curvis wondered if Carlton was a cow in a previous life. In between chews, Carlton asked. 'So when and where do we go? Or haven't you thought about that?'

'I've been thinking about it for the past few weeks, and I don't think it's a good idea to hide in the grounds of Pinewood Oaks. We should go to the Pinewood Hills – I know the area good.'

Carlton inspected the grass he was gnawing then put it back in his mouth. Speak for yourself, he thought.

Curvis resumed. 'While you lot are playing football or something, I sometimes go up there and walk about.'

'We know. No offence but everyone apart from us lot thinks you're mental. They don't say it in front of me and Bullet . . . Can't you at least play in goal now and again? Just to shut 'em up.'

'No! Why do something you don't like? Don't give a fuck what anyone else thinks.' He smiled at his friend. 'There's a scout place up there which they use when they go camping. Hopefully, when we go up there, there'll be fuck all scouts around.'

'And what if there is?'

'Then we'll just hide out in the woods. Nobody will find us. I know the place too good.'

'Speak for yourself! I've only been up there when me and Bullet went up to the golf course near the woods. We nicked the balls from the greens and then watched from our hiding places. It was a fucking laugh.'

Curvis scratched his long nose. 'Can you think of any-where better?'

'Well, no. You're right when you say we can't hide in Pinewood Oaks. They'll comb the place thoroughly . . . Yeah, I s'pose Pinewood Hills is alright. *They* won't be expecting that. I don't know about Glenroy though. He gets lost in the bloody orchard.'

'He'll be with us, innit. He'll be alright, as long as he don't do anything stupid.'

Carlton kicked a clump of grass. '*When?*'

'Next week. We're gonna have to nick some money, blankets, food, you know, things to help us.'

'What's this about your brother that Glenroy's been telling me?' Carlton asked, showing concern.

'Stanton was moved from his detention centre in Ashford. He only spent a few months there after he was at Stanford House. And my Auntie won't tell me where they moved him to. I think he beat up about four screws in Ashford 'cos they moved him to a lower cell on ground level – he couldn't see the fields from his new cell and he freaked out. Went mad. Anyway, I told my Auntie I ain't speaking to her until she tells me where he is. *Fuck* her.'

Carlton saw the bitterness in Curvis's eyes and realised that running away was the only way Curvis could wreak some revenge. Carlton began to climb the grey frame. 'Stanton can look after himself,' he offered.

'Not if he don't see me.' Curvis looked towards the ground as a dark pessimism swept over him. 'When I saw him last month he looked like he was on the verge of cracking up. He was chatting like how he wanted to kill all the screws and police. My Auntie says he's a bad influence on me. I don't know why she says it 'cos I don't get into serious trouble.'

Carlton's eyes scanned the bushes and peering through the gaps of trees, wondered where Bullet and Glenroy were. His gaze finally returned to his friend sitting beside him. It would be fascinating to see Curvis fight one day, he thought. His attention was then drawn to the field sloping upwards from

82

the play area to where it met Lime House at the crest of the hill; Sonia and two of her younger sisters lived here with seven other children. Bare-trunked housefathers, taking advantage of the hot weather, had set up a variety of outdoor activities, including rounders and tip and run cricket. Meanwhile, an endless procession of piloted trolleys and bikes raced down the road, doing their best to evade footballs, tennis balls and inattentive small children. Carlton thought to himself that all the kids on view seemed so free and happy. But he knew, that just like him and his friends, they all had tales to tell.

'Your housemother is a real bitch. I couldn't put up with what you lot put up with. It'd do my head in,' said Carlton.

'I have to admit it,' said Curvis. 'We're all a little jealous of you having Auntie Josephine as a housemother. Especially Glenroy. It's hard for him 'cos he knows you live alright and you're just separated by a fucking wall. And on his side he's been getting all kinds of abu . . . and shit.'

Carlton knew Curvis could not bring himself to say the word. He wondered if Curvis knew his secret. Carlton avoided Curvis's gaze. 'That's one thing me and Auntie Josephine still argue about,' said Carlton. 'Growing up we heard all the screams and shit, *him* hitting the kids. And Auntie Josephine done fuck all about it. Even now I tell her to report that ginger-haired fucker . . . But she never has. Sometimes I've seen her cry about it at night. Thinking of the little kids in Glenroy's house. I feel like killing him myself.'

Awayday

Sunday, 6 June 1976. 9.30 a.m.

While the other children were sleeping in, Glenroy, who had risen with the sound of the raven pecking the outhouse door, took the opportunity to finish his weekend homework. Uncle Thomas had praised his efforts the previous day for his essay for the religious education class. His article had told the biblical story, in his own words, of how Joshua broke down the walls of Jericho. Thomas rarely commended Glenroy on his school work and it came as a surprise. That showed him, Glenroy thought at the time. I ain't a dunce and I ain't mad like my mum. What would Father Patrick have to say about it, he wondered with a satisfied grin.

After hastily finishing a questionnaire about the Industrial Revolution for his history homework, he hurriedly made his way out the back door and headed through the orchard, beyond the pale, long grass, to Curvis's cottage. Glenroy squinted as his eyes became accustomed to the already hot, bright sun. He heard crickets squawking as he ran through 'Africa country', wanting to see Curvis before he left Pinewood Oaks for the day to visit his blood uncle in south London.

As he approached the cottage, he saw a housefather tending his allotment, wearing nothing but shorts and sandals. Some of the older kids in his charge had to work on his patch of land as part of their chores. 'Go around!' the man said sternly. 'Don't you dare walk across the allotments.'

As Glenroy thought of a reply, he saw Curvis emerging from his front door, wearing a T-shirt and knee-length, cut-off jeans and carrying a small plastic bag. 'Curvis, Curvis,' Glenroy called.

Curvis looked up over the allotments and saw his friend jumping up and down on the spot, waving his arms. Curvis started slowly towards him, mindful of the housefather's eyes upon him. 'Didn't I tell you before I went in last night that I was going away for the day?' Curvis said.

'Yeah,' Glenroy replied, palming the sweat off his forehead. 'I thought I'd walk up the road with ya.'

On their way, they saw the paper boy, struggling with his burden of Sunday papers on an old, heavy bike that squeaked annoyingly, upsetting the tranquillity of the morning. Visibly straining, the paper boy cycled by Glenroy and Curvis, nearly toppling over as he went over a road ramp.

'Hey, Brenton,' laughed Glenroy. 'You've got a puncture!'

Brenton, just in his teens and dressed in hand-me-down shorts and a yellow tracksuit top, turned around in alarm to look at his back wheel. He was relieved to find it still in shape. Glenroy let out a manic giggle.

'You're wicked,' Curvis said to Glenroy as Brenton zig-zagged down the road.

'No, just having a laugh.'

The road steadily rose towards the Lodge and the fields to

the left sloped down to a valley of thorns, berries and bushes. Curvis and Glenroy often wondered what life was like for the kids playing in expansive back gardens beyond the narrow strip of grass that was fenced off to their right.

'What happened about the ten pound Uncle Thomas reckoned you nicked?' asked Curvis.

'The bastard phoned up my social worker about it, and he's coming down for a case meeting in two weeks. Uncle Thomas wants to send me away. He reckons I've been nicking all the time.'

'He's probably nicking the money himself. Never liked your Uncle. He's an evil bastard. After running away maybe you might get a chance in a different house. That'll be best.'

'There's a lot of young kids who are scared of him,' Glenroy concurred. 'Elvin used to hate Uncle Thomas. But now he's started to help him take swimming lessons! Probably 'cos he got a bike out of it.'

For a brief second, Curvis's face registered a terrible revulsion which he hoped Glenroy could not read. He wanted to change the subject. 'When you and Bullet decided to play tag for the rest of yesterday afternoon, me and Carlton thought the best place for us to go is the Pinewood Hills – we can make camp there. We might go next week – if we can get all our supplies.'

'Pinewood Hills! Fucking hell . . . What supplies?' asked Glenroy.

'What do you mean, what supplies?' scolded Curvis, mocking his friend's intelligence. 'Do you think we're gonna do a runner and take nothing with us? We've got to make sure we've got money, blankets, extra clothes and food – if we can get it.'

Five minutes later, Curvis and Glenroy reached the Lodge which overlooked the southern entrance to Pinewood Oaks. The red-brick perimeter wall had a gap big enough for one car to enter or depart. Pinewood Village high street ran along past the wall. The high street had a grocer's shop, baker, florist, newsagent, confectionist, antique dealer, an estate agent, post office and the Pinewood Inn public house; a sign outside the pub informed the public about the wonders of its beer garden. Tree-lined avenues led off the high street with semi-detached houses with smart porches and bright-coloured patios.

They saw a green bus climbing up the main road, heading east. They both looked at each other, wondering how they would feel when they were out of the complex on the run. They turned left where they made for the newsagent's. Curvis bought a CurlyWurly chocolate bar while Glenroy stood outside, remembering that only one Pinewood Oaks kid was allowed inside the shop at any time. They crossed the road and walked past the Pinewood Inn to the bus stop. A fat, middle-aged woman, wearing a flower-patterned dress and carrying a brown sausage dog, was already waiting at the stop. She looked at the two boys with such contempt that Curvis thought that kids from the home might as well have their own bus stop.

'So, what time will you be back?' asked Glenroy, keeping his voice low.

'About six, earlier if possible. I don't like going to my uncle's. All he does is drink beer and watch cricket on a Sunday.'

A double-decker green bus arrived twenty minutes later. Curvis boarded it and bade a fond farewell to his friend. The bus picked up a fair speed heading west, leaving the village of Pinewood and passing through narrow roads with large houses fronted by generous front gardens. Sitting in the upper deck, Curvis could see the landscape of the Surrey South Downs. From his vantage point, to his left, partly hidden by hills, he sighted the nearest town of Spurleigh. To his right, he saw sloping hills spotted with motionless sheep. The fields were criss-crossed by a network of hedges and rusty-coloured paths that never went in a straight line. Over the past few weeks, the heatwave had reduced the once green landscape to a lighter hue. Curvis rebuked himself for not buying a drink back in Pinewood.

Curvis thought about his alcohol-loving father. Maybe if he had had two shillings to rub together, he might not have taken out his frustrations on his family. His uncle had told him how his father was always struggling to hold down a job. Curvis remembered how he had cowered in the corner of his small bedroom, holding onto his beloved Stanton around the neck. He could still hear the terrified screams of his gravely wounded mother, who could do nothing to help – her nose broken and her left eye closed and grotesquely swollen. Blood was seeping from the back of her head and it seemed she had lost consciousness. All there was to protect him was his brave brother, Stanton. And it was Stanton who took most of the blows that were intended for him, now that his father was satisfied with the damage inflicted on his mother. Even now Curvis could smell the stench of beer from his father's breath, and the vision of his mother's face had never left him; the slowly closing eye when death finally came upon her. From that moment on, *that* memory was implanted inside his brain, like a single-page photo album.

Curvis could not remember much of his mother, although if he wanted to he could sketch a true portrait, capturing her very essence. But the words she said, the motherly things she offered him, were now elusive memories. It was a cruel Fate, he thought, that denied him of these memories. All that was left to him was that one image.

Fifteen minutes later, he reached the village of Claremont, a little bigger than Pinewood; the bus stopped outside its two-track train station. He caught a train to East Croydon, a journey lasting sixteen minutes. Jumping off the train, he boarded a bus for Stockwell, south London. Arriving in the city, Curvis noticed how everyone walked much quicker here and went past each other without acknowledging each other's presence. He wondered how the residents in the council blocks could live stacked on top of each other. He looked around, fearful of the teenagers idling in the forecourt. They all seemed to be observing his every move. Why do so many black people live around here? he asked himself.

Broken bricks lay near a large metal bin, which was holding up a busted door. Next to this was a splintered window frame surrounded by shards of glass. A burst football was resting beside a burnt-out car, and small children could be heard, running along the balconies. The question of living with his uncle in this place was not one Curvis would ever consider.

He trotted up the litter-laden steps of one of the blocks, trying to ignore the stench of stale food from the dustbins. Reaching the fourth floor he walked along the balcony, taking in the view of central Stockwell. He felt almost claustrophobic as he scanned the council blocks all around him. Looking north in the distance he could see the chimneys of Battersea Power Station and beyond that he spotted the Post Office Tower. At the third door, he tapped the letter box.

'Ah who dat?' boomed out a suspicious voice.

'It's me,' Curvis answered reluctantly. 'Curvis.'

The door opened. Curvis was greeted by a middle-aged West Indian man with a prominent stomach. His receding hair was greying and his face bore the look of constant struggle. Curvis thought Uncle Cecil had probably just as many problems as himself.

Curvis was led past a cramped kitchen which had empty, take-away chicken boxes on the floor. He saw his uncle's British Rail jacket hooked on a peg in the undecorated hallway. Reaching the lounge, where the main feature was a framed picture of Muhammad Ali, looking proud in a black jacket and bow tie, Curvis was ushered to sit down in a tatty armchair.

Cecil asked his nephew, 'So you t'ink 'bout wha' I was talking 'bout last time when you was 'ere? I did talk to your social worker an' 'im say it would be a good idea.'

No fucking way! Curvis thought. Curvis didn't want to show he was ungrateful for the offer. 'I dunno. It would mean having to change schools and everything. And I don't really like it around here – I would miss my friends.'

'Hey, bwai,' Cecil raised his voice, his face creasing with arrogance. 'Me nuh understand you. You always complain 'bout de way dem people treat you inna de home. Me nah affe invite you fe stay. I'm doing dis of my own free will, an' you treat de offer like it no big t'ing.'

Curvis observed Cecil, wondering why he was so keen now to give him a home but not so charitable in the past. His uncle had puffy cheeks below a pair of dark, severe eyes, the kind of eyes that said 'don't fuck with me'. Curvis guessed he hadn't shaved for a few days; black and white stubble appeared very dry on his square chin. He probably drinks just like my old man, he said to himself.

Curvis tried to make himself comfortable in the chair. 'Why now? It would have been alright if you wanted me to stay when I was a kid. But now? It will take time for me to get used to.'

'Listen, bwai. Me's de only family you 'ave.'

Curvis looked away, thinking to himself that Stanton *was* the only family he had. Cecil continued. 'Alright, my place is small an' I live inna council block. But it's 'ome an' it could be your 'ome. De way you describe dat place where you is, dat can never be called a 'ome . . . It's not my fault my brudder killed your mudder . . . Lord bless her and may she rest in peace . . . I just waan fe do my part.'

'It's too late,' Curvis said, almost in a whisper.

'Wha' you say? Don't be facety wid me y'know!'

Just then, a white woman, aged about thirty, came into the room. She was wearing a dressing gown, her long auburn hair masking half her face. Cecil smiled at her, thinking of a recent, pleasant memory. He hauled himself upright. 'Curvis, dis is Maureen, my woman.'

90

Curvis didn't look at her for more than a second. 'Morning, Maureen,' he greeted politely. I wonder how long she'll last with *him*, he thought.

'So you're the one Cecil has been talking about. He tells me that you are gonna live with us soon.'

Curvis cut his eyes at his uncle. Maureen continued, her voice and expression going way over what was necessary. 'He's very concerned about you, especially after what happened to your brother.'

Cecil winced as Maureen mentioned his other nephew. Curvis fixed his eyes on his uncle, refusing to blink, and in a slow, hushed voice, asked him. 'Did my social worker tell you where they moved Stanton?'

'Er, yeah. But everybody decided dat der is no point in you knowing where him der. He's a bad influence on you.'

Curvis glared at Cecil as if he had lasers in his eyes. Cecil tried to smile away the obvious tension as Maureen looked at them both, thinking her proposed role as substitute mother for Curvis was in serious doubt. Curvis released his gaze and began to speak in that deliberate way of his: every syllable clear and precise. 'You know, that's what they all tell me in the home . . . I didn't expect to hear it from your mouth . . . Maybe those meetings you had with my social worker and the others, where they give you nice little biscuits and coffees in nice little mugs, has brainwashed you . . . Stanton *is* my brother . . . It seems that no one understands that, including you . . . He has looked after me better than anybody else can or might do . . . Now it's up to me to look out for him . . . I know he needs me.'

Cecil glanced at Maureen, searching for a reassuring look. Then he looked at his nephew, thinking that his slow vocal delivery was just like his father's. This chilled his bones. Maybe it's better if he doesn't come here and live, Cecil thought to himself. This kid has got the voice of a murderer and the face of an innocent elf.

'Look after you?' Cecil finally countered. 'So beating every-body who has so much looked 'pon you is minding you? Stanton love to fight too much. Did dem tell you wha' he done to de man inna detention centre?'

'No . . . I was told he just beat him up. The man must have done something to him for Stanton to do him.'

Cecil reclined into his chair, a smug smile creeping on to his face. 'Jus' because de man call him somet'ing like mixed up skunk. Stanton beat up de man so badly, de man inna hospital inna coma. Stanton too violent, man – he mus' ah get it from his fader.'

'After the life he had, it's little wonder why Stanton grew up so violent,' countered Curvis, his face full of grief. 'I can remember when he used to stand up to my old man, trying to defend me and Mum.'

Cecil glanced at Maureen, trying to conceal his guilt. Maureen gently shook her head. Cecil got up as his girlfriend went to the kitchen. He walked lazily to the window, where the paint was cracked and peeling on the frame. 'So you waan put flowers 'pon your mudder's grave come dis July?'

'Yeah . . . It will be nine years,' Curvis replied in a near whisper. *That* image returned to his mind's eye.

'I know t'ings 'ave been rough wid you, but we nuh waan you following Stanton,' advised Cecil. 'Der is some 'ope fe you.'

Curvis scowled. 'So everyone has given up on him? I will *never* do that . . . *Never.*'

'Wha' do you waan me fe do?' asked Cecil, raising his hands, yielding to frustration. 'I cyan't help him now, can I? Me never place 'im inna jailhouse.'

Curvis's eyes betrayed the fury he was now feeling, but his voice remained calm and controlled. 'Well, I'm gonna try and help him. I'll find out where he is without you or anyone's help. I ain't gonna leave him where he is . . . To rot. Like *you* are doing.'

Cecil could not hold back his frustration any longer. 'You nah go near 'im! Y'hear me, bwai. Dat kinda t'inking will nuh do anyone any raas good!'

'And what you gonna do if I see him? Beat me up?'

The tension eased when Maureen reappeared carrying on a tray glasses filled with orange squash; she had tipped a tot of rum in Cecil's glass. Cecil snatched his drink and disappeared into the bedroom, leaving Maureen and Curvis sitting opposite each other. Maureen tried a reassuring smile. 'He's only trying to do the best for you.'

'Is he?' Was this your idea? he thought. And he went along with it just to get in your good books?

Curvis spent most of the afternoon on the balcony, sniffing the smell of roasting chicken and boiling vegetables. He sipped cold drinks and observed young kids playing tip and run cricket in the forecourt of the estate. Others idled around in groups, talking, Curvis thought, in an urgent, threatening way. Their slang words were foreign to him and Curvis thought he would never fit in there. His uncle tried to persuade him to go downstairs and join the other boys, but Curvis declined. Maureen was busy in the kitchen, while Cecil lay horizontal in the lounge, watching cricket. 'Shot 'im boss,' he would exclaim as Viv Richards stroked the ball for yet another boundary.

Curvis pondered on what his brother was doing at this particular time. He looked up to the sky and thought it was inhuman to keep prisoners inside their cells in this relentless heatwave. Then his thoughts turned to running away from home, convincing himself that now he had more reasons than one to hide away in the Pinewood Hills.

He had his own name for the area in the forest – Mummy's Garden. Every week or so he would walk up there, locating the same, isolated spot. Reaching his destination, he would sit down and talk to his mother, telling her all the things that had happened to him during the past seven days, and informing her about Stanton. He would listen attentively to the stirring leaves, the shrill language of the larks and the pockets of breezes that curled around the pines, sure in his mind that in the midst of all this natural sound, the gentle voice of his mother was beckoning him.

Curvis had no doubt that once he and his friends reached the haven of the Pinewood Hills, his mother would watch over him, guiding him at night and be their look-out during the day.

Militant

Tuesday, 8 June 1976

The clamour coming from the dining room as the children prepared themselves for dinner was unrelenting. The younger children wanted to sit wherever they liked, resulting in a tug of war with two chairs and plenty of name-calling.

Bullet shook his head in exasperation at the rumpus, forgetting what he had been like as a child. Being the eldest in the household, he tried to establish order. 'Donna! Sit at your usual seat.'

'But I don't wanna sit next to Lester,' Donna replied, her seven-year-old hands wrenching a chair off another child.

'Sit there or I'll scorch your backside,' commanded the housemother who had just entered the dining room, wearing an apron and oven gloves draped on her right shoulder. She was a slight woman, nearing her fifties, but her voice carried the weight of someone a few stones heavier.

95

Sulking, Donna released her hold on the chair and sat down at the table, beside her housemother's place; kids in the household called this the slap-chair. Donna and Lester swapped glares.

Bullet was the last to be seated at the far end of the table. He silently seethed at Uncle Rodney's refusal of his request to eat his dinner on a tray in the front room watching television. Behind him was a radiogram which was big enough for two small children to hide in. The privilege of sitting at the foot of the table, opposite Uncle Rodney, was offered to Bullet by his housefather last year when the eldest boy in the household left the home to start life in the army. Bullet felt it was tradition gone mad.

The housemother patiently served the roast beef, potatoes, cabbage, greens and carrots to the hungry horde, making sure all the younger children had the same portions. The din of children's voices and the housemother's disciplinary cries cancelled out the cluttering of knife and fork against plates.

Then, the sound of the front door opening and closing seemed to have a bewitching effect on the children. A man, near to retirement age, with an upright stance, marched along the hallway and into the dining room. The children fell silent. The housemother gained confidence with the presence of the man, who was wearing a blazer with a shirt and tie. 'Aren't you forgetting something, children?' she prompted.

In perfect unison, the children greeted the man. 'Evening, Uncle Rodney.'

Loosening his tie, Rodney stood still, inspecting his charges, the proud countenance he displayed learned after many years in the armed forces. His moustache was thick enough to tickle his nostrils and mask his top lip. His tall, lean frame was sculptured by the exercise regime he had performed faithfully every morning for as long as Bullet could remember. 'Have you been behaving yourselves, children?'

As one, the youngsters answered, 'Yes, Uncle Rodney.'

Rodney smiled and sat down at the head of the table, acknowledging his wife with a nod. They had been married for years, but the only time Bullet ever saw any signs of affection between them was when Rodney offered his arm to his wife on their annual pilgrimage to Whitehall for Remembrance Sunday.

Dinner was consumed quietly, with the children showing impeccable manners. Bullet was the first one to finish his meal. Following his request to be excused from the dinner table, he ambled along the hallway, passing the kitchen on his right and the front room on his left. At the end of the passage, facing Uncle Rodney's study, he turned right into the room where all the shoes were kept in a wire-mesh rack. An airing cupboard was opposite, its hot vents escaping through a cracked door. Next to this, and below a sash window, were two deep sinks, big enough to bathe year-old baby twins. At the far end of the room, just beyond the downstairs toilets, sunlight stole through the wire-mesh window of the back door, creating a visible beam, adding to the heat. The staff hated this room.

Bullet found the shoe polish and brushes in a bottom compartment of the rack and began buffing, knowing that Rodney would inspect his work upon completion. Why should I still be doing this? he asked himself. Twenty minutes later, Rodney strode into the room with his hands held behind his back, like royalty. He regarded Bullet for a long second. 'Brian, when you finish your duties, I want to see you in my study.'

'What about?' replied Bullet, trying to recall any wrong deed he might have done recently.

'You'll find out,' Rodney answered ominously, an arrogant grin on his face.

Five minutes later, Bullet entered Rodney's study, still trying to think of any misdemeanour. A large, framed portrait of the Queen, wearing all her regal robes, watched over the room from the end wall. On the mantelpiece were framed black and white photographs of RAF personnel, grinning in uniforms with the backdrop of Spitfire fighter planes; Rodney's Christmas gifts to Bullet three years on the trot when he was a child had been Airfix model planes.

Rodney was standing beside his desk at the other side of the room. He poured himself a shot of whisky and invited Bullet to sit in an armchair in the corner of the room. Rodney, straight-backed, strode over to the large sash windows with a view of the orbital road of Pinewood Oaks. He tutted as he saw boys and girls riding their skateboards. 'Have you thought about what you are going to do when you leave school?' Rodney asked, still looking out through the window.

'Er, kind of,' Bullet replied hesitatingly. 'I'd like to be a footballer.'

'Everyone your age wants to be a footballer, but only one in ten thousand make it . . . I've been reading your school reports, and they don't make good reading.'

Bullet craned his neck in an attempt to see who was outside the window. Rodney continued after gently shaking his glass and downing the contents. 'A young man like you needs discipline! So you can learn right from wrong and learn to be a decent citizen. I don't know why they scrapped National Service years ago. A few years in the army never did anyone any harm.'

Finally, Rodney turned around and faced his charge, his chin held high. 'Old people are being mugged in the streets! Louts are fighting each other at football matches . . . I used to go to the Arsenal when I was a kid. Watched the best players of the time like Alex James, Charlie Drake, Tommy Lawton and Dixie Dean with sixty or seventy thousand others. There was *never* any trouble. But now? Kids have *no* respect for their elders and none for the police.'

Bullet slouched in the armchair, preparing himself for a long speech; he hoped Rodney wouldn't venture into the often told details of the Battle of Britain. Rodney resumed. 'Brian, I think you should enlist in the army. They will teach you a trade and give you all the discipline you need. After you have completed four years' service or so, you will come out equipped to be a respectable young man.'

Bullet's face dropped. 'But my PE teacher reckons I should be good enough to go for football trials. All my friends say I'm good enough as well – they reckon I should go for it.'

Raising his voice but controlling it, Rodney argued, 'This is not about what your friends think. They don't live your life and you can't do something they think is right. It was your friends who told you to go and make trouble on that National Front march at the end of April . . . I mean, you are not coloured. These National Front people are not against you. It's got nothing to do with you.'

Bullet tried to mask his feelings, but his eyes betrayed him. Rodney took offence and returned the glare, his chin raised even higher. 'I don't like the influence your coloured friends have on you,' he stressed. 'I mean, I am no way a racist. But it is a fact that coloured people cannot be as well disciplined as the rest of us. It is not their fault. It's not that long ago, perhaps in my grandfather's time, that they started to be civilised. And it will take them many more years to learn how to live properly in a civilised world. Coloured kids are more likely to get into trouble than you. It is also a fact that coloured children do not do as well as the rest of us at school. They find learning difficult and their attention span is lacking. The best hope for your coloured friends is to take up athletics or boxing. I have to admit they are better than the rest of us when it comes to that.'

Bullet searched for an argument. He knew that Rodney was wrong, but didn't know how to put it across. He finally came up with, 'Carlton's brainy.'

'Yes, but he is the exception to the rule. Besides, he has

99

serious problems with his discipline; he's got a chip on his shoulder.'

Bullet fidgeted in the armchair. He wanted to shout at his housefather, but something stopped him. At this moment, he wished he had Curvis's ability to find the right words. Maybe he didn't have to find arguments, Bullet thought. Rodney might listen to action, like running away. That would wipe the smug smile off his face. *White* kids can have discipline problems as well. Bullet got up to his feet, a hint of a grin creeping over his lips. 'Is that all, Uncle Rodney?' he asked with perfect politeness.

'Yes. Go on with you.' Bullet hated this phrase.

Half an hour later, Bullet heard a knock on the back door just as he was slipping on his trainers. He was still thinking about his meeting with Uncle Rodney. He talks to me like I'm a little kid. *Go on with you!* I shoulda told him to go on and fuck himself. He opened the door to reveal a smiling Elvin, his tall, meagre frame topped off by a very dry, tangled afro. 'You coming out, Bullet?'

'Yeah, just getting ready.'

The two friends jogged out of the back door underneath a still fiery evening sun and headed to a field where they spotted teenagers playing cricket. The players had an audience of four teenage girls, someone in a tree overlooking the square-leg boundary and Mellor.

Bullet spotted Mellor, lying on the grass, eating a bag of crisps. He went over to him, taking a wide path from the onlooking girls. 'Where's Carlton, Glenroy and Curvis?' he asked urgently.

'Glenroy's at swimming – his Uncle's teaching the posh kids who live near Pinewood Oaks dis evening. And Carlton and Curvis went off somewhere – don't know where.'

'Which way did they go?'

'Didn't see,' Mellor replied. 'It's weird that Carlton missed out on a game of cricket – he's the best player in Pinewood

Oaks. Everyone was wondering why he ain't playing. Maybe Curvis is his bum chum.'

'*Fuck you*,' spat Elvin. '*Don't* say that about Curvis!'

'Alright, alright. Keep your jockstrap on. Just joking.'

'Hi, Bullet!' one of the girls hailed, waving her right hand. 'Come over 'ere.'

Bullet pretended he didn't hear. Why does she always call my fucking name in front of everybody like that? He glanced at Mellor and saw he was grinning. 'Fuck off, Mellor. Did you put her up to it?'

'No! Caroline likes ya. Don't be a fucking chicken and go over to her.'

'Bullet!' Caroline called again. 'Bullet, I know you can hear me!'

Bullet's face reddened and he turned his back to Mellor. Elvin was suppressing a smirk. Bullet wanted to run off somewhere but thought that would be too obvious and even those involved in the cricket might say he was running away from a girl. He continued to ignore Caroline and took in the cricket, glancing at Caroline out of the corner of his eyes, fearful of any approach.

He watched the bowler start his run-up and thought about the way Uncle Rodney treated him. He compared his life to the slinger of the bruised ball. It was inevitable to Bullet that the batsman would find the boundary again and, sure enough, he did, hooking the ball expertly to the road, the fielders not even moving. Then the batsman casually walked a couple of paces and prodded the pitch with the end of his bat. Bullet likened the batsman to Pinewood Oaks authority: an irresistible force that couldn't be bowled to. The stroke player won't look that good if there is no ball bowled at him, Bullet thought. And Uncle Rodney can't tell me what to do if I ain't there. He glanced at Caroline again. Just *stay* there, he willed. Fucking stay there, you crazy bitch.

Accusation

10 June 1976

The school sports hall echoed to the sound of male adolescent voices as a competitive game of basketball was underway. Ten pairs of thundering soles shook the wooden floor. Two PE teachers, both dressed in T-shirts and loose tracksuit bottoms, ran up and down the sidelines of the court, shouting out instructions to their respective teams, pointing and gesturing as if their lives depended on the result.

On the court, a black, stocky teenager had just skilfully stolen the ball from the opposing team. He bounded his way to the unguarded basket, attempting to up to score. Realising that if the black youth scored it meant sure defeat, a defender pushed the attacker forcefully in the back, propelling the youth to an unfriendly encounter with the wall. A whistle was blown. Frustrated shouts came from the team who were about to secure victory. The dazed teenager groggily got to his feet with all feeling for sportsmanship suddenly evaporating. He rushed towards his grinning fouler. 'Who the fuck are you pushing? You fucking tosspot!'

Without warning, the teenager swung his right fist and connected with the jaw of his fouler, sending him to the floor. Immediately a brawl broke out, with the two teams swapping kicks, punches and obscenities. The two teachers darted on to the court to try and stop the fracas. 'Carlton! Get to the changing rooms right now!' the taller tutor ordered, embarrassed by his pupil's violence.

'But he's been pushing me all through the fucking game! The loser deserves a good kicking.'

'Carlton! Move or you'll be looking at a suspension,' the teacher replied, while pulling the members of his own team to their side of the court.

'That fucking loser started it,' yelled Carlton, still as angry as hell.

The players in both teams stopped the pushing and jostling as Carlton reluctantly made his way to the changing rooms. Once inside, he threw himself on the wooden bench and reached for a towel from inside his sports bag. He buried his face in the towel before wiping the sweat off his temples and forehead. He felt that once more his teacher had made an example of him.

A few minutes later, Carlton could hear the game restarting and the shouts that accompanied it. He ambled over to one of the sinks by the showers and ran the cold water tap, splashing his face in order to cool not just his head but his temper. He sat back down again, beside the peg which held his school uniform. He proceeded to dress slowly and wearily, whispering swearwords. 'Fucking bastard. I'll have him outside school!' He brooded on how much he hated his PE teacher, who always picked on him. Maybe I'm an easy scapegoat 'cos I come from a home, he thought.

Carlton had achieved considerable respect for sports at his

school. He was the first-choice centre forward in the football team, and they had just won the Surrey schools cup. He was a fearsome opening bowler for the cricket team, modelling his extra long run-up on the West Indian bowler, Michael Holding, and he could run a hundred metres in eleven seconds dead. He wasn't bad at field events either, especially the long jump.

At home he had all his certificates framed, hanging in his dormitory above his bed. His medals were displayed in his housemother's study. But Carlton felt there was no pleasing Mr Fleet, his PE teacher. It suddenly dawned on him that he never really got on with any male teachers.

By the time he'd laced up his shoes, the game had finished. His team mates trudged into the changing room displaying defeated faces. Carlton thought they must've lost the game. 'Did we lose?' he asked.

'No. We won 55–48,' answered one of Carlton's team mates. 'That wanker who pushed you was sent off after he barged Hillsey. If he hadn't gone I reckon there would have been another roll.'

'I might get the loser when we're leaving here,' replied Carlton with venom in his voice.

'No you won't!' roared Mr Fleet, who had stealthily entered the changing room. 'How many times have I told you not to retaliate when you're provoked?' he shouted, hands on hips and drilling Carlton with his eyes. 'They can't beat us so they try and get you wound up. And they *did*. Didn't they?'

Carlton looked around at his team mates, trying to buy sympathy with the look of injustice on his face. By their expression it seemed they agreed with the teacher, perhaps thinking that Carlton lost his temper too much.

'If their teacher reports that you punched one of their players, starting this free-for-all, then the whole team might get banned. And I'm not going to risk that . . . So, you, Carlton, will not be playing again.'

The team drew in a synchronised breath. Carlton's face stilled with shock, his mouth open. It took him half a minute to find his tongue. 'What do you mean, I won't be playing again? That loser started it!' Carlton searched the faces of his friends, hoping for vocal support.

'But you shouldn't have retaliated,' Mr Fleet snapped, daring his team to argue the point.

'He pushed me into the fucking wall!'

'And *he* would've got disciplined if you had given me the chance! *You* have blown your top once too often.'

'Maybe if you was on *my* side more often I wouldn't need to blow my top.'

'*I'm* the referee! Get that into your thick head! I'm sick and tired of it, Carlton. You go against everything I tell you.'

'Maybe if you talked any sense I wouldn't have to.'

'I'm *not* taking talk like that. I've stood up for you in the past, and without sport you are nothing ... *Nothing!* ... This will be your last game.'

Carlton stilled his movement, lifted his head slightly and glared at Mr Fleet as if he was waiting for another *nothing* to come from Mr Fleet's lips before he hit him. 'Nothing?' His voice was calm. 'That's what you always thought, innit? That I'm nothing.'

Mr Fleet's eyes concurred.

'Carlton's our best player,' said a white teenager in almost a whisper, undressing and preparing for a shower.

Carlton glared at Mr Fleet. He looked like a relic from the rock and roll era, he thought. With those ridiculous black sideburns. I wonder if he can fight? Probably got a solid punch but I'd be too quick for him. I would fuck him up if we ever come to blows. No way he could handle me. I'll let you off this time, you bastard. But next time I'll have ya. Call me nothing again and see what happens. Carlton dropped his stare, yielding to Mr Fleet's authority. His colleagues had watched the stand-off. They were thankful when Carlton looked away.

Satisfied he had restored order and established his authority, Mr Fleet left the changing room, ordering, 'Hurry up and get dressed, I want to lock up.'

Half an hour later, Carlton was walking along a road with one of his schoolfriends. Their school was two miles west of Pinewood Oaks, populated mainly by kids who resided around Spurleigh. More often than not, Carlton would walk to and from school, saving his bus fare for sports magazines which he bought at weekends.

They reached the main street of Pinewood and ambled into a shop where they were watched with suspicious eyes.

'Hey, Hillsey, got two pence?'

'Yeah, hold up.'

They bought themselves a bar of chocolate each. Back out on the street again, both were feeling weary after the intense game. 'So you gonna watch from now on then?' asked Hillsey between bites.

'Nah. There's only two games left before we break up anyway. Fleet knew that loser was causing trouble from the start, but he didn't do anything about it. And if Fleet bans me from playing basketball, then I ain't running in the schools athletic finals either. Fleet can go and fuck himself.'

'What about cricket?' probed Hillsey, hoping that at least Carlton would play in the final of the district schools competition.

'Fuck that as well. The whole school can go and fuck themselves, I ain't doing no more sports for the school,' stressed Carlton, quickening his stride.

Hillsey didn't try to persuade his friend to change his mind. He might think differently tomorrow, he thought. He decided to change the subject. 'What do you think Miss Osbourne's gonna do about the detention you never went to?'

'Fuck Miss Osbourne. She can't take a joke. When I said, did she buy her dresses from Oxfam, I was only messing about.'

106

Hillsey laughed while unbuttoning his shirt, feeling the heat. 'Yeah. But when you said her bum needs rebuilding like how them scientists fixed up the six-million-dollar man, you might've gone too far.'

After bidding goodbye to his friend, Carlton entered the grounds of Pinewood Oaks and saw the old man sitting behind the counter in the Lodge, talking on the phone. Behind him was a vast selection of keys hanging from nails on a wooden board.

The grass on either side of the road, tormented by the harsh sun for the past week, seemed more yellow than green. The large trees, mostly oaks and chestnuts, were just beginning to show signs of forming their seed. The drive sloped gently, almost unnoticed, sweeping north. A hundred and fifty yards inside the grounds, Pinewood Oaks unfurled into a beautiful rural open estate, leafy and grassy as anything the aristocracy could boast.

Formerly farmland, the 140 acres of Pinewood Oaks had been bought by an inner London council board of guardians at the beginning of the twentieth century. Deprived of space in their own council district, the intention of the guardians was to provide a secure village environment for dispossessed children. Neighbours were not so enthusiastic about the enterprise and even less keen on the kids being brought in from the slums of London.

Carlton marched on quickly, feeling pangs of hunger; he still had a good mile to walk. After fifty yards or so, the first of the cottages, called Almond, was on his left and trees that gave way to thick bushes and clusters of ferns on his right. He heard a muffled voice. 'Carlton, why you so late?'

A coloured head protruded out from the shrubbery. Carlton recognised the face. 'Elvin, what the fuck are you doing there? You've got a green afro!'

'Last night we were playing run-outs here and I lost ten

pence.' Elvin began to swipe his hair and a shower of grass formed a green halo around his head.

'You're trying to find ten pence there!' Carlton said. 'You'll be looking for it until you're an old man.'

'I know I lost it here, so I might as well look for it. Don't want no other bastard to find it and run off to the shop and buy some gobstoppers.'

Carlton laughed. 'If you find it, you can look for all the money I've lost in the fields and bushes around here. I'll give you half of what you find.'

Elvin hacked away the shrubbery with his feet. 'Do you think I'm stupid or what? Look for your own money!'

Shaking his head, Carlton started for home once more. 'I might see you later. If you find that ten pence you can buy me a packet of crisps. But don't look too hard, will ya.'

'Alright then . . . Bullet was around here somewhere. He called for you about half an hour ago.'

'What does he want?' Carlton asked.

'Something secret. He wouldn't tell me, he reckons I've got a big mouth.'

'Well, we don't call you Jaws for nothing . . . If you see Bullet, tell him I'll see him later.'

'Yeah, alright.'

Carlton strolled on, veering off the pavement to his right, crossing a parched field that sloped down to a valley of thorns and nettles. Once he reached the valley, he took a dried mud path that bisected the undergrowth. Dust accumulated on his shoes and the hems of his trousers. He could hear younger children playing in the distance. 'Tim-tam-tommy, tim-tam-tommy, coming ready or not!' a young voice cried out. Carlton reminisced about his younger days when he had played this game, a version of hide and seek in the bushes. Carlton smiled, remembering that nobody ever found Curvis when they played tim-tam-tommy.

Carlton emerged from the scrub and out into yet another

dry field. He saw the flat roof-top of the nursery on the horizon, shimmering in the evening June sun. He ran up the hill, deviating to his left where he joined the homes complex orbital road. Children were riding down the hill on two- and three-wheeled bikes. Others rolled down on second-hand roller-skates, trying to pick up speed as they went over the newly laid road-ramps. The risk involved in hurtling over the ramps was lost on the kids.

'Carlton, look at me! I can ride a bike now!' said one kid on a bike.

'About time an' all. So I haven't wasted my time teaching you then . . . Who's on duty tonight?'

'Auntie Josephine.'

Carlton ran the rest of the way to his house and entered his home by the front door. He leaped up the three steps and only slowed down when he set foot in the hallway, mindful of the rule against running in the house. The passage was decorated in a silver-coloured wallpaper with white flecks. Two waist-high green plants stood at either end, resting on a tough-wearing, brown carpet. Carlton made his way to the kitchen where he saw Auntie Josephine wiping a table.

'Good evening, Carlton,' Josephine greeted him with a warm smile. 'Did you win your game?'

'Yeah, we won.'

'Good for you! You're turning out to be a great sportsman. You'll be in the newspapers one day.'

Carlton looked fondly at his housemother and noticed the flecks of grey in her blonde hair that had appeared during the past few months. He couldn't erase the incident with Mr Fleet out of his mind. 'Say I don't make it in sports, Auntie Josephine. Do you think I could get a decent job?'

'Of course! You're very bright . . . What brought this up?' She looked at him inquisitively.

'Er, nothing . . . I was just thinking in case I got a bad injury.' Carlton wasn't convinced by Josephine's reply to his question.

Maybe Fleet's right, he mused. *I get by in lessons but I ain't good at 'em.*

'What did I say to you about thinking negative?' Josephine stressed. 'Think *positive* . . .' She regarded him kindly and stroked his hair. 'Why don't you change? I'll heat up your dinner . . . I tell you what, though. Working in the kitchen in this weather is bloody murder!'

A few minutes later, Carlton was seated downstairs, eating his dinner of lamb chops, roast potatoes, cabbage and carrots. Opposite him sat his housemother, smoking a cigarette, making sure she blew her smoke away from the young man.

'So, Carlton, will you be late again? I'm off tomorrow, so I'll have to tell Auntie Margaret and Auntie Sophie whether to save your dinner or not.'

'No. I'll be coming home normal time tomorrow.'

'Well, I suppose you'll need your rest. You've been doing sports all this week, haven't you? Maybe tomorrow you can catch up on your homework?'

Before Carlton could think of an excuse, a small white girl, with tears smudged to her cheeks, came running into the dining room. 'Auntie, Auntie. Phillip pushed me over on purpose.'

'Where is Phillip!' asked Josephine. 'Can't you kids play quietly around the back? Tell Phillip I want him. It's nearly half past seven anyway and you all have to come in and get ready for your hot cocoa and bedtime.'

Josephine felt her patience was being tested again and wondered why her boss thought that looking after nine kids on her own was easy. She had already had to compose herself after one of the kids had dropped their dinner all over the hallway carpet. Why couldn't he give her more relief staff? Deep down she knew why. *Where are you going to find staff prepared to work for a pittance in a stressful job around these parts?*

The long-haired girl ran into the hallway and out the back door, shouting. 'Phillip, Phillip. Auntie wants you now!'

110

Josephine inhaled fiercely on her cigarette. 'No rest for the good, is there?' she said to Carlton, offering him a wry smile.

A few seconds later, a boy of about seven walked slowly into the dining room with his head bowed. Josephine knew he was guilty. Not meeting the eyes of his housemother, he defended his case. 'She started it, you always blame me.'

'Is that so, Phillip?' Josephine stared sternly at the boy. 'I'm sick and tired of you picking on Mandy every night. *You* can go to bed first.'

'But she started it!' argued Phillip, still looking down near his feet.

'Look, Phillip, *do* what you're told,' insisted Josephine, feeling at her wits' end, exhausted by the perpetual quarrelling of the younger children.

Phillip tramped out of the dining room. Josephine stubbed out her cigarette and looked at Carlton, finishing off his last potato. 'So, you haven't told me how you did in that geography test today?'

'I think I done alright. I got a bit stuck about the olden days crop rotation and all that stuff. But apart from that, I reckon I done alright.' I would've done alright if I'd done the revising, Carlton rebuked himself.

'Well, I told you to do your revising if you wanted a top mark, didn't I?' scolded Josephine, her voice raised a notch. 'But *you* wanted to play football with Brian and your other friends! You can't play football every night. You have to leave *some* time for homework.'

Carlton grudgingly nodded his head. 'Yeah, I s'pose you're right. But it's hard staying in the house doing homework when everybody else is out, especially in this weather.'

'I know that, Carlton,' replied Josephine, her tone more gentle. 'But you have to think about your future.'

What future? Carlton thought. Mr Fleet's image gatecrashed his brain. *You're nothing!* He resumed eating his dinner while

111

Josephine lit up another cigarette. Soon after, the younger children were in bed, but not until there had been more squawking, telling tales on each other and vying for attention. Later, as Carlton relaxed watching *Love Thy Neighbour* on TV, he heard a loud knock on the back door. Josephine, not happy with the calm being disrupted, commented, 'I bet that's Glenroy. Isn't this his church youth club night?'

Carlton rose from his armchair. 'Yeah, you're right. I hope he hasn't skived off, you know what Uncle Thomas is like.'

Josephine nodded offering a knowing grimace.

Carlton went along the hallway and turned right, entering the laundry room. He saw the distinctive lean frame of Curvis through a misted wire-glass window. Carlton opened the door to reveal a thoughtful-looking Curvis. 'You coming out?' he asked. 'You're not too tired, are ya?'

'Yeah. I *am* bloody tired. I also had a ruck playing basketball . . . You wanna talk about . . . things?'

'Yeah.'

Two minutes later, they were sitting down in a deserted field, Curvis wrapping a buttercup around his index finger while Carlton gnawed a blade of grass.

'So on Saturday,' Carlton began. 'We're still gonna meet up the top field by the sycamore tree?'

'Yeah, it's the best place,' Curvis reaffirmed. 'No one's gonna be there in the middle of the night. We can go through the bushes and climb over the fence which goes to an alleyway. It leads to the road outside.'

'Did you speak with Glenroy and Bullet today?'

'Yeah, everyone knows what to do.'

'Why can't we just walk out the front gate?' Carlton asked. 'No one's about that time of night.'

'Yeah, but you never know,' Curvis answered, his tone serious. 'It's too risky – someone might be up at the Lodge. And Mr Williams sometimes drives up and down in his car on patrol. If we go the top field way then no bastard will see us.'

Mr Williams was the Pinewood Oaks' troubleshooter; all unsavoury incidents were reported to him, and he was the link between the council and the staff who ran the cottages. Every Monday morning he would drive up to London to report to his seniors on matters arising or problems within Pinewood Oaks. He lived in a rent-free cottage within the grounds with his own family.

'Mr-fucking-Williams! The lazy bastard should do some fucking work in the daytime so he wouldn't have to prowl about at night. Doesn't he ever sleep?'

'Yeah, he does actually. His kids are not allowed to disturb him from one in the afternoon 'til six. If they make any noise, I heard they get a beating.'

'It's like fucking Colditz . . . We still have to cross the main road. You know what the residents around here are like – they see a black face they'll be on the phone straightaway.'

'I know, I know,' replied Curvis. 'But it's better we come out of a side road than out of the entrance of Pinewood Oaks . . . We might be stopped by that vampire Williams before we even get out of the grounds.'

'Two in the morning we meet by the sycamore tree?'

'Yeah. Any earlier someone might be up and about. The housefather in Laburnum is always up late on a Saturday night. He's a weird bastard – plays solitaire in his study. You and Glenroy have to pass Laburnum on the way to the top field. Keep close to the bushes!'

'You know it gets light about half-four in the morning?'

'Yeah, but by then we should be safe in the hills. I reckon it'll take us one and a half hours. Hour and a quarter if it weren't for Glenroy.'

'You sure you know where you'll be going in the fucking dark? You can easily get lost up there. Ramblers get lost in the fucking daytime!'

'I'm gonna nick my housemother's big torch. She keeps it

under the stairs. And Bullet is bringing his. I just hope the batteries last – they're fucking expensive.'

'I still don't feel easy about nicking the petty cash box from under Auntie Josephine's bed. It's like some kind of betrayal. Can't see why one of you lot can't nick a petty cash box.'

'We don't know where the fuck they hide it! *You* know where Auntie Josephine keeps hers. And it won't be like you're nicking from her. It's council money and they will replace it. Don't worry about it. Can't fucking last with our own money.'

'Fuck knows what I'll do if she wakes up.'

'You'll be alright. Just pretend you're wriggling through the grass and scaring girls like we used to do in Africa country.'

'Alright for you to say.'

'Don't forget to nick all the grub you can . . . I told Glenroy not to bother 'cos he's too clumsy. Besides, I think they lock the larder door in his house.'

'I think you're right. When his housemother bakes cakes, she gives most of 'em to the staff. They only get treats when the Marks and Spencer van comes with their out-of-date grub.'

Carlton yawned and Curvis took this as a cue for taking his leave. He stood up and noticed the sky had darkened. 'Carlton. You realise you can't take your bike.'

'Yeah, I thought about that. It fucking grieves me. Who knows if I'll see it again.' Carlton *had* thought about his bike and had planned to bring it along if Curvis hadn't mentioned it . . . 'I can carry it on my shoulder.'

'Carlton, we're going to the hills. You can't ride it up there.'

'Don't plan to . . . I can hide it somewhere.'

'Carlton!' Curvis knew a glare would be enough to tell Carlton that bringing his bike would be unfeasible.

Two hours later, Curvis sat up in his bed. He scanned the dormitory with his small torch and found all his junior room-mates fast asleep. Someone had forgotten to pack away a snakes and ladders board that was on the blue-carpeted floor; there'll be cussing in the morning, Curvis thought. A poster of the Liverpool football team, looking out above a child's bed, had Kevin Keegan's head missing, and a boy's best clothes were laid out neatly next to his bed, draped on a chair. Stan's social worker must be coming tomorrow, Curvis guessed.

Curvis, having trouble getting to sleep and feeling very hot, pushed the covers off his chest. Then he stood up and pushed up the sash window to its limit, hoping the night breezes would cool him down. He looked skywards and the half-crescent moon was now shining brilliantly. Curvis could sense a slight current of air, but guessed most of it was trapped by the oak trees surrounding the cottage. Looking at the star-lit canopy, he offered a whisper. 'We're gonna be on our way soon, Mum. I feel scared thinking about it. Maybe Carlton should be the leader . . . Don't wanna lead 'em into trouble . . . Maybe I should go on my own?'

The Scouring of the Allotments

Friday, 11 June 1976

Ten-thirty. The night air was heavy and idle. A lone lamp-post, its dim, yellow light flickering, stood like a sentinel outside a dull beige-brick building; it could not challenge the half moon's brightness. Halfway up a hill, a hundred yards south of Pinewood Oaks primary school, the flat-topped youth club was sheltered by oak leaves. The trees, with no breeze to make them murmur, were dumb.

The battered, graffiti-daubed blue door of the building opened. From the exit noisy teenagers soon filled the road. They were shouting, joking and cursing just like teenagers do. The din filtered through to the surrounding fields. Three adults stepped out of the youth club, with one of them locking the door behind him. He glared at the rowdy mob. 'Will you please go home quietly! Come on now, you've all had a good evening. *Don't* spoil it.' The man sighed, expecting more

116

complaints from the staff in charge of Yew cottage, fifty yards further up the road.

Glenroy, running around, pestering two girls, was the loudest of the teenagers. One of the adults, dressed in tight shorts and T-shirt, glared at Glenroy as if he wanted the teenager to disappear. 'Glenroy! Leave Sandra and Brenda alone! You've been agitating them all evening.' Glenroy looked back with a face of mystified innocence and went to join one of the knots of teenagers. After milling about for a minute or so, the adolescents dispersed in all directions, walking in threes and fours, their evening at the Blue Peter youth club abruptly over.

Bullet, Carlton and Curvis walked across a field, swapping accounts of the livelier moments at the club. Glenroy, seeing his friends set off, ran to catch up with them, thinking how dare they leave him behind; especially on this night when they had so much talking and planning to get through.

'Hey, Glenroy. Why don't you tell Sandra you fancy her?' teased Carlton.

'I don't fancy her,' replied Glenroy, his angry tone unnecessary.

'Oh yeah. Then why couldn't you leave her alone?' riled Carlton; he'd noticed Sandra himself but teasing Glenroy was a good way to disguise this, he thought. 'You wanted to play her at table tennis and then you followed her to play records. Why don't you admit it? You're in *love*.'

'No I ain't!' snapped Glenroy, dismayed to find his friends laughing. 'She probably fancies me!'

'Fancy you!' Bullet laughed. 'I didn't know she was blind.'

'I can always make her laugh,' said Glenroy proudly. 'I'm thinking of asking her out.' Glenroy thought for a moment what a date with Sandra would be like. He'd take her to Africa country and present her with the ripest pear he could find in the orchard. Then he'd kiss her – on the mouth!

117

'Glenroy, listen carefully,' chuckled Carlton. 'She laughs *at* you, not with you.'

'Who cares?' replied Glenroy. 'You watch, I'll be snogging her before you can say tim-tam-tommy.'

'She'll be screaming before you get a chance to pucker up your lips!' countered Bullet, secretly admiring Glenroy's fearlessness with girls.

'Shut your mouth, Bullet. At least I've got the bottle to talk to girls. All you can do is stare.'

'You don't talk to 'em, you just annoy 'em.'

'Sandra?' Carlton mused, pretending he hadn't really noticed her that much. 'Ain't she got that dad with locks? I think I saw him one time – right down his back his locks are. I wouldn't wanna fuck with him on a dark night.'

Why are they wasting breath talking about stupid girls? Curvis thought. We've got more important things to talk about.

'Sandra's dad has locks?' Glenroy asked in alarm. 'Her hair won't grow like that, will it?'

Bullet and Carlton laughed as Curvis shook his head. The friends were making slow progress across the field, the crescent moon their guiding light through the dark grass. The lamp-posts, spread apart fifty yards along the orbital road, pin-pricked the trees and bushes and created long ghost-like shadows. Realisation dawned on them that this might be the last time they walked home from the Blue Peter club together.

'Well, tomorrow is it,' announced Bullet, hands in pockets. 'I can't bloody believe it! The day come so quick.'

'Yeah. Don't forget the blankets, will ya,' returned Carlton. 'And whatever you do, don't forget to wake up. I know you love your sleep. Just remember, *be* at the sycamore up the top field by three o clock.'

'Three o clock? I thought it was two o clock.'

'I changed it,' said Curvis. 'That mad housefather in Laburnum house might be up at two.'

118

'Don't worry about me,' reassured Bullet. 'I ain't gonna go asleep. I'm gonna keep awake.'

'Which one's the sycamore tree?' asked Glenroy, shameful of his ignorance.

'Bloody hell! How many times do I have to tell you,' rebuked Curvis, his temper ignited by the sudden memory of his nightmare last night. 'It's the tree that's got those things that fall off that look like tiny boomerangs.'

'Oh yeah. I know it,' replied Glenroy unconvincingly.

'All of you should get as many blankets as you can,' stressed Curvis. 'We're gonna need them to sleep on. And Carlton, you sure you know where Auntie Josephine keeps the petty cash?'

'Yeah. How many times do I have to tell ya. Underneath her bed, innit. She's kept it under there for years now.' Carlton felt guilty as he spoke, but his facial expression offered no clue. I don't know if I can do it, his conscience was saying.

'Bullet, your Auntie still bakes cakes on a Saturday afternoon?' probed Curvis.

'Every Saturday without fail,' answered Bullet. 'She keeps 'em in a container in the larder.'

'Does your Auntie lock the larder door at night?'

'Nah. In our house everybody's too scared to do a larder raid.'

'And don't forget your sports bag,' added Curvis.

'I can get some biscuits,' announced Glenroy, not wanting to be left out of the planning.

'Well, get them if you can,' said Carlton. 'The biscuits would be nice but they ain't *that* important. You don't wanna get caught in your kitchen when we're about to leg it. Just make sure you get all the clothes you can carry and put them in a bag.'

'I won't get caught,' replied Glenroy, feeling insulted. 'Our larder is always locked but there's a window at the back. I think I can get through. I'll be like a cat burglar in the night.'

'More like a sea lion on a greasy tin roof,' Carlton joked. 'Forget it, Glenroy. I've seen the window at the back of your larder and even Elvin would get stuck – and he's as skinny as a twig.'

The quartet had reached the northern fringes of the allotment area that was protected with flimsy fencing. It was fronted by tall, fir-like trees that looked out of place in a landscape dominated by oaks and chestnuts. Beyond the fencing and masked by the tree tops, the allotments were dense and dark. Curvis squinted his eyes, peering into the blackness. 'What's that?' he called out. 'Did you see that? Someone's in the allotments.'

Silently the friends climbed the fencing and took cover underneath a tree. Thirty yards away, four silhouetted figures were lifting up what seemed to be netting and plucking something from the ground. Glenroy, eager to get a better view, and with his belly kissing the earth, wriggled closer to the scene of crime. 'It's Johnson and his mates,' he revealed in a whisper. 'Them guys who live in Ashburden.'

Curvis beckoned Glenroy with his right hand. 'Come on, let's go home,' he said in a low voice. 'If they wanna nick tomatoes and stuff, then let 'em.'

Carlton, crouching low and inching towards Glenroy, had an excitable look on his face. 'Nah. We shouldn't let guys from outside Pinewood Oaks come here and nick from the allotments. We'll probably get the blame for this. We don't want Mr Williams coming round to our houses in the morning asking his fucking questions.'

Bullet nodded, following Carlton on all fours. 'Let's give 'em a kicking!'

Then, inadvertently, Glenroy sneezed. One of the night raiders turned around and saw him crawling on the grass. He didn't seem threatened by Glenroy's portly figure. 'Hey, Johnson,' the thief called. 'It's that dunce in your class, Glenroy.'

120

'What are you spying on us for?' Johnson demanded, emerging out of the darkness, carrying a sports bag full of ill-gotten veg.

'Fuck you!' Glenroy challenged, confident that Carlton and Bullet were behind him. 'I live round here so why don't you fuck off and go back to your area.'

Johnson, not accustomed to Glenroy's bravado, ran towards him with serious intent, followed by his accomplices. Simultaneously Carlton and Bullet stood upright. Curvis remained by the tree, shaking his head. What is the point? he asked himself. Seeing Carlton, Johnson stopped short of Glenroy and glared at him with a promise of violent revenge on another day. 'Who are you telling to fuck off, you fat piece of shit,' Johnson cursed.

'He's telling you to fuck off,' Bullet sniped, sizing up Johnson's mates and sure that if matters came to a head, Carlton could take care of Johnson. 'What's a matter?' Bullet added. 'Are your ears full of shit?'

Johnson examined Carlton's physique and felt intimidated. He desperately didn't want to lose face in the situation. Carlton strolled arrogantly towards his foe, passing Glenroy. Bullet was prowling behind him, his fists clenched in anticipation. Carlton, in a low confident voice, delivered his ultimatum. 'If you want to take your goods home, you're gonna have to deal with us first . . . I don't like shit like you coming in here and nicking from our grounds.'

Johnson thought about it, and after another scan of Carlton's muscled frame, raised his right arm and beckoned his mates to follow him. He then emptied his bag, and tomatoes and other vegetables dropped to the ground. 'Come on,' he ordered. 'If they're gonna cry about it, let's go somewhere else.'

Johnson and his crew gave Carlton a wide berth, making sure not to make eye contact. They scaled the barrier and scampered into the nearest field, disappearing into the gloom.

Glenroy, forgetting that he might have to confront Johnson again at school, held up his left hand in an uncomplimentary gesture. 'Wankers!'

Bullet grinned triumphantly. 'They bottled it. Fucking shapers.'

Carlton looked around to find Curvis – he was sitting down, looking apathetic, still underneath the branches of a tree. 'What's a matter with you?' Carlton asked.

'Nothing,' Curvis replied. 'Just watching something that was unnecessary . . . Why didn't you leave 'em to it?'

''Cos this is our patch,' answered Bullet, spreading his arms and looking around him. 'If we let wankers like Johnson come inside here and push their weight around, then more will come and take the piss.'

'Our patch?' Curvis argued. 'Have you forgotten that we're leaving this fucking evil patch soon?'

'You're right,' Carlton agreed. 'But if we don't come back, other kids have gotta live here somehow. It's bad enough without the likes of Johnson.'

Glenroy ambled over to where Johnson had spilled the vegetables. He picked up a tomato and examined it. 'These tomatoes ain't even ripe,' he remarked. 'We should've let Johnson and them take 'em. By morning they would have had shit running down their legs.'

Carlton and Bullet laughed. Curvis, feeling ashamed about something, ambled over towards the fence, climbed it and walked off, not looking behind him. Carlton spotted him and set off after him. 'What's a matter now?' Carlton called to his friend.

Curvis waited until Carlton caught up with him before answering him. 'I had a really bad feeling last night,' Curvis admitted, his face full of guilt. 'It was like a warning . . . I dunno if we're doing the right thing.'

'What do you mean? Bit fucking late for *that*. Now the time has come we're all looking forward to it.'

122

'Maybe I should go on my own,' Curvis admitted. 'Maybe this is something that I need to do by myself, for my own reasons.'

'What do you mean?' Carlton stopped Curvis and stared at him. 'We all have our reasons. But we have to do this, to tell them what's it like in here. It's you who told me this.' Carlton heard Bullet and Glenroy scamper towards him.

'I mean . . . I don't wanna be the leader,' Curvis confided. 'Look at what just happened. I wasn't much help . . . I don't want to lead us into trouble.'

Careful with his words now that Glenroy and Bullet had caught up, Carlton put his arms around Curvis's shoulders. 'We are doing the right thing. I must admit at first I thought it was fucking mad, but when I thought about it, you know, all the shit going on, all the kids who are beaten up, it's a fucking great idea. No matter what happens, whoever's in charge of this fucking place is gonna be asked questions if we do a runner . . . Can you imagine Mr Williams going up to London trying to explain that we're missing. It'll wipe the fucking grin off his face.'

'Yeah,' Bullet concurred. 'Williams drives up and down the place and talks to us like we're his little children. *Fix your tie, young man. Button up your shirt.* Fuck that! I hate it when he talks to me. And like how can Uncle Rodney at my house be in charge of ten kids even though he don't like coloured kids.'

'I still don't think running away will solve all our problems,' replied Curvis, looking despondently at the ground. 'Especially with me planning it . . . I can't even fight for myself, and I get the shits every time you lot are involved with something. And tonight, even though I kept telling myself to help, I thought the whole thing wasn't called for.'

'Wasn't called for?' Carlton snapped. 'Fuck you. It was alright for you when Stanton was here and mashed up anybody who so much as pushed you. Me, Bullet and Glenroy had to fight for ourselves.'

'I didn't ask Stanton to fight my battles,' replied Curvis, displaying his palms as if he was yielding to defeat.

Carlton pulled Curvis's head and whispered in his ear. 'You know, one day you might have to fight for yourself, without Stanton or us lot helping out.'

'Don't you think I know that?' Curvis replied, his body draining of all confidence. 'Maybe I'll just let 'em hit me.'

'Fucking hell, Curvis!' Carlton swore, his face creasing into irritation. 'Sometimes you do speak a lot of shit. *Stand* up for yourself!'

Curvis recalled an incident that happened last year. He was beaten up by two school bullies; Curvis forgot the pain but the image of his father that gatecrashed his mind at the time was an experience he'd never forget. Two days after the assault, Carlton, Bullet and Glenroy arrived at Curvis's school seeking vengeance; Stanton would have been the first one to show up, but he wasn't there anymore – put away for his own good far from his brother. Curvis remembered the cuts and bruises his friends suffered on his behalf while he hid behind a school dustbin. He wondered why they wanted him as a friend.

From the allotments, the pals made their way across the field towards the banks of the stream that sparkled in the moonlight. Only the crickets and an unseen owl disturbed the perfect silence. Glenroy was on the look-out for a fox; he had yet to fulfil his promise years back of catching one. Bullet, feeling bored, leaped on Glenroy's back and had another wrestling fight. Carlton and Curvis observed them, smiling. They could now hear the rush of water, hurrying its way under the bridge, and Curvis, peering through the trees that surrounded his cottage, could see his dining-room window, illuminated by a strong light, one hundred yards away.

Carlton plucked a blade of grass and wrapped it around his right index finger. He studied it as if it held the secrets of the world. 'I think we're all getting nervous,' he said. 'I can't believe we're gonna do this, but we fucking are ... Auntie

Josephine is gonna hate me for this. You know, she's been good to me over the years – she's probably the only good one in this fucking place ... I was thinking of writing her a note, telling her I didn't run away 'cos of her.'

Curvis, lying belly down on the grass, watched the flow of the water. 'Yeah, you should,' he reassured. 'She's alright. The only housemother in this place who treats her kids like a parent.'

Carlton inserted the blade of grass in his mouth and regarded Curvis. He hesitated, then asked his friend. 'Is there another reason why you won't let Elvin come with us?'

Curvis took his time in answering. He glanced at Glenroy, who now held Bullet in a headlock thirty yards behind him. 'Yeah, two reasons. You know that in the past two months his sister has been visiting him on Sundays. Well, Elvin tells me that if things work out, he might go off and live with her ... If his social worker reckons it's alright. You know what they're like about that sort of thing. If they had their way, no one would leave here 'til they're fucking forty. Anyway, if he runs away with us, it might fuck up things for him. We ain't got fuck all to lose.'

'What's the other reason?' Carlton asked quietly, his face appearing as if he already knew the answer. Surely he doesn't know my secret, Carlton debated in his mind. Maybe he guessed it, Curvis is good that way.

Curvis glanced at Glenroy again. He closed his eyes for two seconds, his head bowed. 'Have you heard the rumours about Uncle Thomas?'

Carlton's face grew stormy at the mention of the name. Oh shit! He does know. 'Yeah. One or two kids talk about it.'

'So you know then?' asked Curvis, trying to gauge what Carlton knew about the housefather.

'That he touched up Elvin years ago?' Carlton said, almost stuttering ... 'Damaged him.' Maybe he don't know about me, he thought. He searched his friend's eyes for any kind of sign.

Curvis didn't answer.

'I felt really sorry for him,' said Carlton. 'I didn't know what to say. Didn't want him or ask him to show me the marks ... He said when it happened he started to bleed. What do you say?'

'Nothing,' replied Curvis. His eyes returned to the wrestling match. 'I just pray that he didn't do it to Glenroy.'

'Nah. He would've told us.'

'Would he? Something like that is not easy to tell your friends. Elvin only told me last spring. It happened *years* ago.'

Last spring? Carlton considered. Elvin told me four years ago. 'Nah. He would've told *me* ... Can you imagine living in his house with that shit going on? I would sleep with a fucking cricket bat in my bed.'

'Ssssshhhhh,' advised Curvis. 'Elvin made me promise that I'll never tell Glenroy. I didn't entirely agree with that 'cos Glenroy should have been warned.'

'Elvin made me promise too. But Glenroy would've told me if something happened. He's probably safe now 'cos I reckon that fucker's only interested in young boys.'

'We can't be too sure about that ... Can't see how Elvin can work at the swimming pool with that fucker though,' said Curvis.

'If it was me,' answered Carlton, his face creasing into vengeance. 'I'd have to *do* him. Fucking nonce. Maybe he don't try it on teenagers 'cos they would fight back.'

Curvis looked at his friend with suspicion, trying to read his face. Carlton felt like he was being put on trial. He started to sweat. 'It's fucking humid tonight, innit.' Carlton and Curvis lay in silence for the next ten minutes, knowing there was a lot more to the story.

Watching Glenroy and Bullet, Carlton commented. 'Can you imagine them wrestling and fighting in the Pinewood Hills? Fuck me, they just can't help themselves.'

126

Curvis got to his feet and decided to head home. He expected a familiar cussing from his housemother about his lateness, but he didn't care. He hadn't spoken a single word to her beyond 'thank you' and 'yes, Auntie' for almost three weeks now. He waved his friends farewell, as if he wouldn't see them for months. Bullet disentangled himself from Glenroy and said his goodbyes.

Carlton and Glenroy jogged through Africa country and through the silent orchard; Carlton was wondering if Glenroy had been touched by Uncle Thomas. He had often thought about this at various times over the past seven years. He kept glancing over at him as the anger grew within.

Emerging from the orchard, they both heard Glenroy's housefather's stern voice, cutting through the night. 'I thought I told you to come home straight from the club. What time do you call this? It's nearly *midnight*.'

Carlton watched his friend run all the way home and as Glenroy neared the back door and Uncle Thomas's rugged figure came into view, Carlton felt a cramping sensation in his stomach. With a rat's nest of feelings brewing inside his head, Carlton walked through his back door and into the hallway. The house was unusually quiet as the children were all in bed. Framed photographs of children and certificates of sporting excellence, mainly belonging to Carlton, were hanging from the walls, backdropped by pink-patterned wallpaper. Children's drawings and sketches were pinned on to a notice-board that hung near to the front door. Unlike other houseparents, Josephine had turned this house into a home for the children in her charge.

Carlton heard his housemother working in her study; he guessed she was balancing the accounts, a task she always did on a Friday night. Mr Williams would pick up the documents, which included expense forms, clothes expenditure and staff rotas, and take them into London on Monday morning.

He poked his head around the study door and, sure

enough, Josephine, wearing a pink dressing gown and with pen in hand, was surrounded by papers. A portable black and white television, situated in the corner of the room, was broadcasting a Dracula film with the sound off; the fiend himself was about to sink his fangs into the neck of a naïve virgin. Josephine peered over her reading glasses. 'Oh, hello, Carlton,' she greeted warmly. 'Didn't hear you come in.'

Carlton returned the smile. 'You wanna cup of tea, Auntie? I'm gonna make myself a snack before I go to bed.'

'You're a sweet, Carlton – I'll have mine black . . . Oh, I have changed everybody's sheets – none of the kids were comfortable sleeping in this heat – poor Suzy was drenched in sweat last night.'

'Thanks, Auntie.'

Carlton disappeared into the hallway, but before he reached the kitchen, he heard his housemother's voice again. 'Don't go straight to bed when you've eaten, I want a word with you.'

Seven minutes later, Carlton reappeared, balancing two cups of tea and a plateful of chocolate digestives. Josephine got to her feet wearily and took her tea, offering a smile as thanks. She sat back down and observed Carlton affectionately; she would not admit it to anybody but Carlton was always her favourite.

Carlton seated himself in a red armchair, next to a mahogany coffee table that was supporting a vase of varied flowers.

'I had a phone call from your mother today,' Josephine informed him, her face slightly twitching as she said the word 'mother'. 'She wants to visit you. I didn't really know what to say. So in the end, I told her that I'd have to speak to you first.'

Carlton, appearing embarrassed, declined to answer and looked at the television. Josephine knew that it was hard for him to accept that he had a mother somewhere. Meanwhile, Dr Van Helsing had entered Dracula's castle. Why didn't you

128

say no way? Carlton's inner voice spoke. She knows there is no way on earth that I'll see her.

Josephine bit her top lip before resuming, fighting the urge to speak with her heart. 'In my opinion, I think you should give her a chance and speak to her. She sounds really desperate and she's promised she's changed her ways . . . She reminded me and blamed me that you haven't spoken to her for seven years . . . God, I didn't realise it was that long.'

Still concentrating on the television – Dr Van Helsing was going down a dark, concrete stairwell, holding a torch of fire – Carlton spat '*No!* I don't want her down here.'

'But just try and get to know her again,' replied Josephine. 'Let bygones be bygones. You can't go through your life hating your mother . . . It's killing her that you won't see her.'

'NO! I never want to see her again. How many times do I have to tell you?'

'You shouldn't feel shame, Carlton. No one knows what she has done in the past. It's all confidential. Not even the staff know.'

'Well, I know,' Carlton answered in a sinister tone. '*I* know.'

'Yes, but you've got to put that behind you. She's probably changed into a better person now.'

'Put it behind me? How can I put it behind me when she hasn't a clue who my father is? And how could I put it behind me when she used to leave me at night on my own when I was a baby? *That's* the only thing I can remember about living with her. Being left on my own . . . Darkness. Fuc . . . Bitch.'

'You know, Carlton, there are some kids in this place who don't know any family. Look at your friend Bullet and the paper boy Brenton. They're all alone in this world.'

'I'll give you that, but I'll bet their mothers haven't dropped as low as the bitch who had me.'

'People can change, Carlton.'

'Why do you want me to see her? Whose side are you on?

I don't want to ever see that bitch again. Didn't I tell you before? She's a fucking loser and I don't want *nothing* to do with her. I can't believe you want me to see her.'

'Carlton, she's your mother.'

'I would *never* call her that . . . I've got a different name for her.' He held Josephine's gaze, almost challenging her to carry on.

Josephine dropped her head and stared at the desk. There was nothing more she could say. She kept looking down until she heard Carlton leaving the room, slamming the door; he hadn't finished his tea or his biscuits. With a tear in her eye, she went back to her work, thinking how impossible it would be to realise her dream of adopting Carlton without his mother's consent. *Damn* her, she thought. Damn her.

Carlton stomped up the stairs. Whose side is Auntie Josephine *really* on, he raged inside his head. Maybe she thinks I'm nothing. They *all* think I'm nothing!

PART THREE

Exodus

2 a.m., Sunday, 13 June 1976

Bullet, half-asleep, dreamed of the future. It was a distant place. He visualised a placard fixed upon the wall beside the entrance of Pinewood Oaks. The sign said, 'These are the names of the boy heroes, sons of Pinewood Oaks, who ran away from evil to freedom – Bullet, Glenroy, Carlton and Curvis'.

Rousing himself, shaking his head, Bullet fidgeted in his bed, willing the time to leap forward. He hadn't thought of it before but he had slept in this bed every night for the past seven years or so. He wondered what it would be like falling asleep under the stars, with tree trunks replacing the walls and leafy branches as a ceiling. I hope it don't fucking rain, he chuckled to himself. Running away to the Pinewood Hills could get them all in the newspapers, he pondered. Who knows, my mum might read about me and then demand to take me home.

Bullet tried to visualise what his mother looked like – perhaps she resembled the nice-looking lady in the washing-up liquid commercial on TV. Maybe my dad was a mercenary and got killed in some war abroad, Bullet fantasised. He could have fought in Vietnam, helping out the Americans. He could have been a footballer before that in the 1950s, playing alongside those famous players that Uncle Rodney keeps going on about. He could've tackled Stanley Matthews! Or had a header with Duncan Edwards! Yeah, he was a hero – perhaps he didn't know he had a son. Who knows? he asked himself. Mum might be dead as well. Yeah, she could've died from a bomb attack while nursing the soldiers in Vietnam, he convinced himself. That's how they met. She's a hero as well, Bullet concluded. Yeah, my parents are heroes.

Bullet, his mind spinning with images, recalled the day when Curvis, Carlton, Glenroy and himself made their first camp in the orchard. Old blankets for their floor and a tatty car seat, that Carlton had dragged from the dump, their throne. They had to take turns sitting on it and being king of the gang. He remembered their oath on that day. They had made it up after watching a cowboys and Indians film and bonded with their bloodied hands.

> *No less than four, mighty are we*
> *Three'll be like cutting off our knees*
> *Two'll be like the sinking of a crew*
> *And one'll be like killing us with a gun.*

It was the four friends' secret world. It was the place where they dreamed of becoming famous footballers, world-class bowlers and war heroes. They hid sweets under tufts of grass and concealed their 'war' weapons beneath ferns in case of attack from another gang. Bullet shaped a sword out of a stray piece of fencing and immediately challenged Glenroy. Bullet named himself D'Artagnan and Glenroy called himself Robin

134

Hood. Shouts of Touché! and Olé! filtered through the hazel and holly bushes. Carlton and Curvis would sit on a fallen bough in the glade, fiercely contesting a game of conkers.

Now, years later, Bullet and his friends were about to set up another hideaway in the Pinewood Hills. But this time it was for real. This was no longer playtime fantasy. Bullet could sense the same adrenalin and excitement he had felt then. Everyone would be talking about him back at the home, that would be cool too. Uncle Rodney's gonna get one big fucking shock when he wakes up in the morning!

Almost forgetting his tasks, Bullet slipped out of bed quietly. He put on his jeans and white T-shirt that were folded neatly on a chair next to his bed. Once dressed, he groped for the large sports bag under his bed. On the dressing table that he shared with a younger boy were his few toiletries. He placed his comb and brush into the bag. He felt his heart thump rapidly against his chest. He was already sweating. The silence was loud. The stillness of the sleeping dormitory was almost unnerving.

He opened his drawer and hurled vests, T-shirts, Y-fronts and socks into his bag. In the corner of the drawer was his globe money box. Meticulously, he put his savings into his carrier. He pulled open another drawer and found his two sweaters which he stored inside the sports bag. Might need 'em if we're still in the Pinewood Hills in the winter, he thought.

Bullet rolled across to the other side of his bed to open his bedside locker and collect his torch and pen-knife. He also decided to pack his frayed playing cards. Perhaps Glenroy might finally learn how to play blackjack, he smirked. After closing the locker door, he sat on his bed. He looked around at the still shadows, formed by the moonlight that stole through the curtains. He could feel all the other bodies asleep around him. He wondered if he would see his bedroom again, or indeed, his room-mates. He offered a silent goodbye to them all as his heartbeat gathered pace.

Zipping his bag up slowly, he stood up and started to creep towards the door. On reaching it, he looked out into the hallway. He scanned the corridor and thought he'd better take his chance now. Yes, now was the time – the only chance to get out of here. The staircase at the end of the passage seemed further away than normal. He left the dormitory door behind him and began to cross the corridor, thankful for the carpet that cushioned the creak of his well-worn trainers. Sweat stuck his hair against his temples and forehead as he passed Uncle Rodney's bedroom. Someone is going to come out, he convinced himself. He stole by the staff bedroom, his heart racing faster although he knew that it was unoccupied. Something beneath his right foot cracked. It was a clear sound, like a slap across the face. I'm done for, he fretted. Uncle Rodney might be awake reading one of his war books, or doing one of his stupid exercises. He inched on, his strides turning into chicken steps. Only with the staircase two yards away did Bullet relax; only the girls' dorm to pass, he told himself. As he turned the corner he knew there was no turning back.

He sneaked down the stairs, avoiding the patches in the old wooden frame where years of experience told him the creaks were. Once downstairs, he felt his way to the washroom where he found his towel and flannel hanging on a peg. He crept into the steamy airing cupboard, making sure he closed the door before switching on the light. He grabbed three blankets. 'So far so good,' he whispered to himself as he headed towards the back door.

Bullet took one last glance behind him and then unfastened the latch to the back door; he performed this task as if it was keyhole surgery. He opened the door and closed it behind him carefully. He breathed out a heavy sigh. He trod down the back door steps as if any undue pressure would crack the concrete. He allowed himself to glance upwards, sure that he was making too much noise. His heart resonated throughout his entire body and his face reddened with a hot flush. Finally he was in the clear. Freedom. This is what it feels like. He breathed in deep and darted into the murk of the field that led directly from the back of the house towards the piggery. Great adventure was ahead, he thought. As he walked, the surrounding trees muttered to each other.

As Bullet ran, he could feel anonymous eyes on him. He looked around and was sure he could detect indistinct sounds from the bushes around the field. He stepped on a twig and was startled by a cracking sound that to him was like a shot of an infantryman's rifle. He stopped, and scanned around him once more, although he could see no more than thirty feet in front of him. Something forced Bullet to run, run as hard as he could.

2.15 a.m.

Carlton, desperately trying to control his breathing, crawled along the carpet of Auntie Josephine's bedroom. Minutes before, sitting up in bed, he had convinced himself that Auntie Josephine was going to offload him to his mother. *She's* a traitor, he thought. No way on earth I'll ever go back to my bitch of a mother.

He could smell the perfume wafting from Josephine's dressing table. His palms were moist even before he entered the room, his face streaked in perspiration. He could hear his housemother gently exhaling through her nose, and every small fidget from her was like a major movement. Carlton tried to think of excuses in case she awoke – but he couldn't. His emotions changed and now he felt he was betraying her and a heavy guilt weighed on his conscience.

He made out the shape of Josephine's dressing-gown, draped over a chair. He stretched out his right arm under the bed and groped with his hand, brushing the bottom of the mattress. All he felt was the texture of the carpet. His hand ran

137

along the rug, searching with his fingers for the hard metal of the petty cash box. *Don't wake up*, he willed. *Don't wake up.*

With his thumb and index finger, he touched the square of the cash box. It felt cold. He nudged it towards him flipping the sharp corner with his fingers. *Please don't wake*, he said to himself. *Oh my God! Please don't wake.* His lungs felt like they were filling up. He couldn't breathe out. He needed to exhale but Carlton managed to control himself, forming his mouth into a small circle as if he was about to whistle. It seemed to take an eternity to prod the cash box out from underneath the bed. But finally he could see it. He started to slide backwards, towards the door, moving the box along the carpet. Josephine sneezed. Carlton slammed his eyes shut, shocked into stillness. He pressed his face into the carpet, wishing it would wash over him like the sea. He heard the rustling of sheets and chanced a look above the mattress.

Josephine had returned to sleep, exhaling and inhaling softly. Carlton regained his composure and slid backwards to the doorway once more. Once past the door frame, he turned his body around and crawled out into the hallway. He stood up, and walking on tip-toes crept back into his bedroom. Now I'm a fucking thief, he cursed himself.

He had already packed his bag with clothes and other items he required. It felt light now the burden of guilt was becoming heavier by the second. He collected his bag from just inside his room and placed the cash box carefully inside. Breathing easier, he made his way to the staircase, stepping down sideways.

On reaching the ground floor he stole along the hallway and into the kitchen; the hunger-inducing smell of baked chocolate fairy cakes still lingered in the room. Carlton wiped his face with his palm, unhooked a plastic bag from the kitchen door handle and proceeded to take the fairy cakes from a tin in the larder. He ate one in two bites.

Carlton knew where Josephine put up her chores rota —

pinned against a board above the double sinks. He unpinned the paper, full of descriptions of jobs for the children to carry out during the week. He found a biro in a drawer beside the sinks and proceeded to write a short note on the back of the paper. His message read: 'I'm not doing this because of the way you treat me.'

Carlton walked cautiously out of the kitchen and crept along the passage. He looked up to the staircase and half expected Auntie Josephine to be standing on the landing, staring with accusing eyes. No one was there. He'd better get moving, he said to himself, no need to linger. It's not like I want to get caught . . . Or perhaps I do. He walked swiftly to the back door and quickly pulled on his trainers. Before he departed, he checked behind him one last time. He opened the back door, emerged into the night and closed the door with a strong image of Auntie Josephine in his mind. Once down the steps, he offered a glance upwards, aimed at Josephine's bedroom. 'Sorry,' he whispered.

Then he ran into the black gloom of the hushed field with tears stinging the corners of his eyes.

2.45 a.m.

Carlton, Bullet and Glenroy had made it to the rendezvous point. The friends looked at each other, displaying differing stages of concern. Curvis had not yet arrived. No one wanted to ask where he could be. They waited under the branches of the sycamore tree at the top field, dimly illuminated by the moon and the lamp-post sixty yards away by the swimming pool. The hedges were still. The rhythmical hooting of an owl, somewhere in the depths of the orchard, pricked the silence. The sycamore tree itself stood like a muted, dark sentinel. Carlton felt it was watching him.

As the friends peered across the field, they all felt a

wrenching doubt inside their stomachs. Maybe Curvis got caught? Perhaps he changed his mind. Or, even worse, he might have left for the Pinewood Hills already, deciding to go on his own.

Glenroy gazed at the heavens; Curvis had informed him about the stars and he spotted Capella, in the south western sky, shining brightest. He could see shadows in the moon and for a reason he couldn't explain, he found himself cursing Uncle Thomas in his mind for telling him that a man lived in the moon. 'He's bottled it,' he spat. 'After all this. He's bottled it! All that fucking planning! *Do* this and *do* that and he don't even turn up.'

'He'll be here,' reassured Carlton. 'He'd better be fucking here. Don't wanna sneak the money box back under Auntie Josephine's bed.'

'Maybe that snobby bitch was up and caught him,' Glenroy panicked. 'They might be on the way up here. Curvis might've grassed.'

'Will you fucking calm down!' Carlton ordered. 'It's not even three yet.'

'Yeah, but he's always the first to arrive,' Glenroy countered, frantically looking here and there.

Bullet said nothing. He stood apart from the other two, peering into the distance, as if there were snipers at large. The eerie silence of the atmosphere unnerved them all. The night air was dense and they could almost feel the moisture creeping out of the earth. Gnats were still hovering above the hedges. In the moments when the teenagers paused talking, they could hear the crickets having a night-time debate in Africa country.

Bullet sat down and picked up a twig and proceeded to peel it with his pen-knife. 'Come on, Curvis,' he willed softly. Sneaking back in will be worse than sneaking out, he thought. I ain't going back tonight no matter what. Glenroy, trying to make out the clotted thicket where they planned to route their escape, looked crestfallen. 'What are we gonna do if he don't turn up?'

'Will you shut up, Glenroy!' snapped Carlton, raising his voice to conceal his own fears. '*Don't* get all panicky on me . . . Worse comes to the worse, you can eat all the fucking food. We'll tell 'em we come here for a night-time picnic.'

'Curvis is probably here already,' said Bullet. 'Probably laughing 'cos we're shitting ourselves.' Everyone looked up into the branches.

'Speak for yourself,' answered Glenroy. 'Ain't no one shitting themselves apart from you.'

Bullet heard a rustling from a hedge. Glenroy looked as if he was ready to die that second but stood firm. Slowly they made out a slim figure emerging from the bush. Curvis was jogging towards them, clutching a holdall in each hand. His friends almost tasted relief when they saw who it was.

'What kept you?' scolded Glenroy.

'Nothing,' Curvis replied calmly. 'It just took longer than I thought to pack my bags . . . It ain't quite three yet. Why the worry?'

'Glenroy was having a fit,' revealed Carlton. 'He reckoned you'd bottled it or got caught.'

'Well, he don't have to worry,' laughed Curvis. 'I'm here to hold his hand and wipe his nose.'

Bullet was honing a sharp point on his twig. 'So this is it, then? No turning back now, is there?'

'Why do you say that?' interrogated Glenroy, facing down his friend in best Sweeney style. 'Do you wanna go back?'

'Why d'you always start an argument?' asked Bullet. 'Just keep your mouth shut.'

'You gonna make me?' challenged Glenroy, his hands coming off his hips in anticipation.

Curvis, ignoring the quarrel, placed his bags on the grass and looked at Carlton. 'How much money did you get?'

Carlton opened the petty cash box with all his friends

looking on. There were two notes; one blue and one brown. Carlton counted the coins. 'Nineteen pound sixty.'

'Shit. Is that all?' moaned Curvis. 'I've only got three pound.' Curvis turned to Bullet, who was sticking his twig into the ground. 'How much have you got, Bullet?'

'Four pound and a lot of pennies.'

Bullet headlighted Glenroy with accusing eyes. 'And what have you got?'

Glenroy took his time in answering. 'Forty-two pence.'

'Forty-two pence!' Curvis bewailed. 'You were s'posed to be saving your money for the last two weeks.'

'I wanted to get that Bruce Lee magazine with the fold-out poster in it,' revealed Glenroy without a hint of shame. 'I'm gonna need something to read while we're on the run.'

'Then you should've broke into the nursery and nicked those Peter and Jane books,' chuckled Bullet.

'I don't fucking believe this guy,' growled Carlton. 'Forty-two pence! That will buy about three jamboree bags!'

'And if he's lucky, he might get a plastic soldier inside,' joked Bullet.

'Look, we've got nearly thirty pound,' said Curvis. 'That's gonna have to do.' Curvis wiped the sweat from his forehead and stooped down to pick up his bags. 'Come on, we'd better get a move on. Can't stand here arguing about forty-two pence until it gets light – and that'll be in another hour and a bit.'

'Oh shit!' Bullet lamented. 'With that idiot going on about his Bruce Lee poster, I've just realised I've left my Victor and football comics behind.' Bullet was serious.

'Ain't you getting a bit old for Victor comics?' asked Carlton.

'Yeah,' Glenroy agreed. 'They're for kids.'

'Grown-ups read 'em an' all,' replied Bullet.

'Well, at least I remembered to bring my pencils and paper,' Glenroy revealed.

'Well, thank fuck for that!' mocked Carlton. 'I will sleep well tonight.'

They set off, walking four abreast and heading towards the thick bushes at the other end of the top field. The terrain sloped gently downwards and they could now see the white football goalposts with their bowed cross bars. The backs of detached houses, fronted by long lawns and spacious greenhouses, came into view on the other side of a high, meshed fence. No lights were on inside. Rampant wild nettles created a natural barrier between Pinewood Oaks and the normal families and it would take a brave boy to retrieve the many tennis balls and footballs that were lost there. Finally they reached the football pitch. It was too dark to see any of the white lines marked on the turf. The four boys pressed on with their journey, not looking back.

They headed for the corner of the field where the houses stopped. Beyond that they followed the line of what seemed like impenetrable bushes. Curvis knew that in the winter the access would be easy, but in the present season the nettles and thorn bushes had grown to cover the path. He watched Bullet put his twig inside his bag and Carlton stoop to pick up a blade of grass and place it in the corner of his mouth. They stopped before the nettles and put down their bags. 'Fuck me!' Glenroy exclaimed. 'How we gonna get through there?'

'By swinging you by the feet and let your hair clear a path,' joked Curvis.

'Fuck you.'

'Look for a stick,' suggested Curvis. 'Otherwise, we'll have to use our feet.'

Bullet found a broken, slim branch by the perimeter fencing. He handed it to Carlton, who wasted no time in hacking away the scrub, his friends silently marvelling at his strength. They lined up in single file behind him, using their feet to clear a navigable path. They were careful to avoid any flying 'sick bay' leaves. Bullet took out his torch and beamed it forward so that Carlton could see his way into the murk. 'Doing this makes me feel like we're on a mission,' Bullet remarked.

'It's hardly fucking James Bond,' Carlton laughed. 'That old bloke who gives Bond weapons would have given me something for these fucking bushes.'

The four walked further into the darkness, which sucked them in like a rabbit hole. Soon the pathway became clearer as the vegetation thinned out. Wild cherry trees, growing no more than twelve feet high, came into view. 'These are the nobbler trees I've always talked about,' informed Curvis. 'In autumn, the nobblers are the juiciest in Pinewood Oaks.'

'Well, thank you, Dr Bellamy,' Carlton smirked. 'I really needed that information.'

'If we're still on the run by autumn we can come back here and pick 'em,' Glenroy suggested.

He received no answer. They threaded through the scrub before coming to a six-foot-high wooden fence. Glenroy glanced up at one of the trees. 'Tree. I'll be seeing you later.'

Carlton, at the head of the group, looked slightly disturbed. 'It's fucking creepy in here, innit? So dark. I bet Glenroy's thinking Dracula is following us . . . Or a zombie.'

'What the fuck would Dracula be doing in Pinewood?' joked Curvis. 'He's s'posed to live in Transylvania.'

'He might've got a boat and come over,' remarked Glenroy.

'He's not gonna get a bloody boat,' rebuked Bullet. 'He's scared of water – you divo!'

Curvis was the first one to climb over the fence. He reached the other side and then Carlton passed all the bags over to him. The others quickly followed, Glenroy being the clumsiest, losing his footing and scraping his left shin. They found themselves in an alleyway, strewn with litter, dead leaves and yellowed newspapers. Along one side was the thicket they had just crossed that faced into the backyards of a dozen semi-detached houses. A cat with green-luminous eyes watched from a back-garden shed. The friends looked back to where they came from. They were out. They were actually *outside* Pinewood Oaks boundaries.

'We're out!' gasped Bullet. 'We're all nutters – we're out!'

'Yeah!' Glenroy exclaimed. He did a disco twirl, spinning around on his feet twice, almost losing his balance.

'Will you shut your mouths!' ordered Carlton. 'You wanna wake up the whole of Pinewood?'

'Come on,' whispered Curvis, not wanting to hang around. He took the lead. They followed the alleyway until he came to a side road that led off Pinewood high street. Distant traffic was now audible from the roundabout where routes led to Ashburden, New Craddington and Pinewood three quarters of a mile away.

'When we get to the main road, watch out for any cars,' Carlton warned. '*Don't* cross the road if a car is coming.'

The quartet strode up the quiet cul-de-sac. They all admired the expensive cars parked in driveways, the pretty, elaborate porches and the trimmed hedges that fronted the detached houses. This was another world, Bullet thought to himself.

They arrived at a main road, one hundred yards east of the shops on Pinewood high street. Curvis stopped and listened. To his left, the road climbed steeply, snaking a shadow-strewn route deeper into the Kent countryside where specks of isolated lights imitated the stars. He spotted one vehicle's headlights in the distance and ushered his friends to retreat. The motorist flashed by at a fast speed. Curvis ran a last check. 'Run!' They bolted across the road and hastily made their way up another side street, heading south. This was like the one before. Homes, rows of sleeping families with clean, well-kept front gardens and cars in front of the gates.

'Keep your eyes peeled,' advised Carlton. 'Who knows what kind of posh fuckers peep out of bedroom windows.'

At a brisk walking pace, they passed a British Red Cross centre before turning left into another leafy avenue. On

145

this road they passed a stone office building filling the space of two houses. The sign read 'Air Corps Training Centre'. 'Whassisname, Robson used to go there, innit,' Bullet remarked. 'He must be some kind of pilot now.'

'Robson?' Carlton laughed. 'He couldn't make an Airfix model. He became an air cadet 'cos he didn't like being in the scouts.'

'I thought Robson joined the air cadets 'cos the magistrate in the juvenile court said he had to learn discipline,' commented Curvis. 'He didn't like the army cadets or the Boys Brigade and scouts. So he ended up there . . . I heard he hated it.'

They were starting to relax now, far enough away from Pinewood Oaks to feel safe. Shedding their anxiety, they marched to the end of the road. By now Curvis was feeling the weight of his two bags. They turned right, heading south again, the road steadily inclining and the houses becoming bigger and further apart. A field was at the end of the road, skirting the southern fringes of the village. Bullet, on seeing shadowed open land before him, suffered a pang of nerves. He wondered if Glenroy felt the same way. He momentarily shone his torch into Glenroy's face.

Reaching the end of the cul-de-sac, they were faced by a small recreation ground. The field had a football pitch in it, with a hillock on the centre point, then it slowly descended towards the far goal and the half-concealed trees beyond. Watchfully, they made their way along a well-trodden, dusty footpath that cut across the field. On their right, they could now see a children's play area, with swings, a slide and a roundabout. Curvis felt the play area was altogether a different place in the murk of the night. Spooky even. Beyond this was an enclosed bowling green, three grass tennis courts and a croquet lawn, appearing no less eerie.

'Which way are the Pinewood Hills?' asked Glenroy nervously, feeling tired now.

'Straight ahead, cross the road, and go left, then right,' replied Curvis, pointing the way.

Glenroy lifted his head and peered into the night. He saw the grey contours of the hills, spanning the horizon. Beyond the road and dwarfing the houses into insignificance were the first trees of the forest. The trunks standing imperiously straight were crowned by untold billions of moon-lit leaves: Glenroy thought he was at the threshold of a different world. He felt something in his stomach and wasn't sure if it was excitement or fear. Carlton's eyes were following the same trajectory as Glenroy's. He gulped and immediately checked if his friends had seen him do so.

They turned right into another cul-de-sac that led to woodland. The houses here were spectacular, fronted by tall gates and most had three cars in their drive-ways. This was where the rich lived, obviously. The houses were set apart from each other, the cul-de-sac cut off from the rest of the village.

The odd gargoyle, situated on top of the walls, stared menacingly into the night. Glenroy recoiled at the sight of one of them, that lolled out its tongue as if finishing a meal. It was like a servant of the devil. Glenroy only just managed to disguise his repulsion. He wondered why the rich would want something like this around their homes. Curvis put his right forefinger to his lips. 'Sssshhh. Last time I was up here dogs were barking all over the place.' Intimidated by his surroundings, Carlton imagined wolves. He peered into the forest and thought that the trees seemed . . . so old. Bullet imagined his mother might be living in a house like the ones around him. Who knows? he thought. With her good looks she might have married a millionaire.

They entered the woods. The leaves blocked out any sight of the night sky and the moonlight evaporated instantly. The air tasted different, tangible. It was heavier. Although the boys could feel no wind they could hear the tree tops rustling, as if they were commenting on their invasion. Curvis and Bullet shone their torches. Huge hollows and craters dominated the dusty ground, as if a titan had stomped lesser beings into the earth.

'How did them holes get there?' asked Carlton.

'Dunno,' replied Bullet. 'Might be bombs in the war.'

Just then, in the distance deeper into the forest, they could see two bright lights that looked like two angry, fallen stars. The two beams of light dipped and rose like a boat caught in a vexed sea.

'Shit!' bewailed Curvis. 'The scouts must be camping here. We'll have to go to the other side.'

The quartet turned around and headed back to the cul-de-sac. 'Every summer holiday,' Curvis explained, 'the scouts camp up here – cubs an' all. They've got some huts deeper into the forest but sometimes they pitch up their tents where they like. Some of them might have made camp near here. They're always driving around in jeeps and Land-Rovers.' Looking out for cars once more, Curvis led his company eastwards along the road opposite the recreation ground. On his left-hand side, Carlton was checking for any movements or lights being switched on in the few houses that they passed, afraid that someone might emerge and report him and his friends for loitering or trespassing.

They walked swiftly, realising their vulnerability near the houses. They could now make out the spire of a church that set a dark challenge to the height of the trees. Glenroy could just make out the tops of gravestones that jutted above the hedges that ringed the graveyard. There was a single lightbulb above the arched front door of the church, casting sharp-angled shadows. Glenroy's insides trembled.

'Are we gonna stop for the night in the graveyard?' Carlton chuckled. 'I'll bet I'll be the only one brave enough to walk in it.'

148

'Don't fuck about,' snapped Bullet, killing the intended joke. 'I've heard stories about that place.'

'It's not the one about if you knock seven times on a gravestone and some ghost comes out,' laughed Curvis, turning around to glance at the graveyard.

Bullet shone his torch on the spire. 'If you think it's such a joke, then why don't you go over there and knock seven times.'

No one even contemplated the challenge. Fifty yards further on, Curvis located another entrance to the woods. He turned left into a pathway that led south, finally reaching the New Craddington Road. On one side was a five-foot-high fence and behind it a secondary school, its playing fields stretching out into the night.

'Hey, Curvis,' Carlton called. 'I always thought you wanted to keep as far as possible from your school.'

'It wouldn't surprise me to see my PE teacher on one of his jogs,' Curvis replied. 'He's a right bastard. 'Cos even when it's freezing, he makes us go on cross country runs. All because he loves it.'

'Sounds like a nutter,' Bullet remarked.

'He sure fucking is – his favourite sport is running in the hills when it's snowing.'

They walked steadily uphill, dwarfed by the pines on their left. Glenroy at the back of the group was growing more weary. He dared himself a glance into the woods and imagined the trees exhaling on him with icy breaths. Get lost in there and you'd never find your way out, he thought. Scouts are braver than I thought. Thank God I never joined, coming to *this* place every school holiday.

Leaving the school grounds behind them, they eventually arrived in an unnervingly quiet avenue. Bullet switched off his torch as Glenroy sighed, his legs becoming heavy. They all heard the whoosh of traffic passing nearby. Lights from the head-lamps swished across the trees. Small, thatched cottages lined the road, with well-kept, tiny front gardens with wooden gates that came up as high as Carlton's knees. Bullet thought that perhaps old people lived in these small houses, preparing to die. At the end of the road, facing the main thoroughfare that cut through the forest, was a grocery shop which was formerly a cottage.

The main road climbed steeply to their left, its journey ending in Sussex. To their right it dropped sharply downhill, winding its way to Ashburden. The pines shielded the boys from the moonlight, bunched together and almost threatening anyone to enter. There was no horizon. For the first time the boys could smell the overbearing stickiness of the pine cones. Glenroy imagined that the trees were planted here when God was supposed to rest on the seventh day. Curvis peered beyond the road and into the forest. 'Now we'll tell the men from the boys . . . They'll never find us in there.'

Glenroy looked on in awe. 'Fuck me! It looks different at night, innit.'

Bullet switched on his torch again as Carlton zipped open his bag and took out a chocolate fairy cake. 'That's 'cos it's darker, you fool. Ain't nothing different about it – can't believe you're scared of fucking trees!'

'You sure you know the way in there?' asked Bullet, transfixed by the pines looming over the road. You sure it's safe? he wanted to ask.

'Bullet's right for once,' Glenroy agreed. 'I mean . . . Look. Once we get inside we might find all sorts of weirdos and men who escaped from prison.'

'Will you two stop shitting yourselves,' rebuked Curvis. 'We'll be alright . . . This is the last place where they'll look.'

'Come on, you poofs,' urged Carlton, not wanting anyone to question his courage.

They crossed the road quickly and after climbing fifty yards or so into the undergrowth, Curvis switched on his powerful torch. He found the path that snaked further into the murk.

150

They all kept close together, almost walking on each other's heels. Owls heralded their entrance as if they knew in advance the boys' destination. Something flapped above their heads.

Carlton looked up and only saw a black roof that hung above him at an unguessable height. He couldn't understand why he sensed the trees knew of his fear. He had felt it first back at the cul-de-sac where the rich people live; a strange feeling of helplessness in the presence of the forest's power. He couldn't explain it. Don't be stupid, he told himself. They're just harmless trees. Why should I be scared of fucking trees? The fingertips of branches tickled his hands and cheeks as he went on.

They climbed dusty escarpments where the soil seemed to crumble under each step and then descended steep hillocks. As they went further into the depths of the forest, the path petered out and they all felt their feet crunching through the scrub needles and pine cones. Their shoes and clothing soon changed colour, turning brown and green as they brushed the undergrowth.

They reached the summit of another steep mound. Curvis could make out in the near distance a small glade, surrounded by tangled bramble and bending pine trees, its upper reaches seeming to kiss the stars. 'We'll stop here for the night,' he said, hearing the sighs of relief. 'Bullet, take out the blankets, and Glenroy, I hope you've got those pillows in your laundry bags.'

'Yeah, course I have.'

Bullet proceeded to spread the blankets. Curvis stood the two torches at each end of the glade, beaming skywards, like the headlights of an upturned lorry Despite this they couldn't see much of the heavens. Instead they saw a green-leaf ceiling and gnarled boughs, aged beyond the boys' comprehension. The thick smell of parched earth engulfed them. In the eastern sky, rising over the Kent hills, was the halo of a pale sun. Glenroy looked around him as if he had heard a werewolf.

151

'I'm knackered,' he moaned. 'So many bloody hills! I'm sure I saw a fox a while ago. While I'm up here I'm gonna catch one of them fuckers.'

'You couldn't catch one if it was old and had two broken legs,' laughed Carlton. 'You're unfit. I keep on telling you to do some kinda sport. And you eat too much!'

Sitting down on the blankets, Curvis seemed to be in his element. 'Yeah, there are many hills around here. There are seven big ones called the Seven Sisters. They're made out of stones . . . Carlton, take out your food. I've got some Jamaican ginger cake and a load of French rolls that I nicked. All that walking has made me hungry.'

Glenroy produced a huge smile, nodding his head. 'Why are they called the Seven Sisters?' he asked.

Curvis handed out slices of cake as the friends sat together in a small circle. 'When I was about seven or eight, my housemother used to take us up here for picnics in the summer,' he revealed. 'You know, to run about and stuff. One day, me and Stanton were fucking about, playing tag or something. Auntie Rebecca told us off and she ordered us to sit on a bench and keep quiet. There was this old man sitting on the bench; he looked about a hundred. I asked him why the hills were called the Seven Sisters. He told me a story; I think he told us the story to keep us quiet; Stanton was pinching me.' Curvis paused, checking to see who was listening.

Carlton handed out his fairy cakes and while he observed his surroundings, Glenroy snatched the lion's share. 'Well! Tell the story then,' urged Carlton.

Curvis made himself comfortable on the blankets and a pillow, which he shared with Bullet. He resumed his tale. 'This old man told us that years ago, you know, even before someone made electricity, a little girl used to live here beside the woods . . . somewhere close to here. This girl came from a big family; she had six older sisters. But the little girl was the youngest by ten years. I s'pose she wasn't planned, if you know what I mean.'

'What do you mean?' asked Glenroy.

Glenroy was ignored as Curvis continued. 'Anyway, her sisters left home one by one as she got a little older. This upset the youngest 'cos she used to enjoy playing in the woods with her sisters all the time, going on walks and stuff. When the second youngest sister left home, marrying someone at just seventeen, the little girl got all lonely. She had no one to play with. And there was no television and stuff then. She didn't have no friends so she just kept her own company, playing in the woods, pretending that her sisters were there with her.'

'What happened next?' asked Bullet, relating to the story, but also looking for something decent to carve with his pen-knife.

'One day, she went out to play in the woods in the afternoon, like she usually did before having her tea. But she never came home for tea. Her parents got all worried and everything, and when night came, they called the police or whatever. There was a massive search for her, with members of the public, people of the village, helping out. But no one ever saw any trace of her again. It was like she vanished into thin air. They thought she got kidnapped, 'cos her family were kinda rich, but they never got no ransom note. 'Cos of the stress, the mum went mad and ended up in some mental place. One of the sisters reckoned she knew what happened to her, but said no one would believe her.'

Glenroy, immersed in the story, gazed into the daunting wood, his eyes not blinking. Curvis concluded. 'Because she used to play in the woods, up and down the stony hills, locals called the seven big ones, the Seven Sisters. The girl's dad sold the house and moved far away. No one ever saw the family again.'

Glenroy's eyes were still trained into the forest, as if he

153

was looking for a ghost. 'Shit!' he exclaimed. 'So, Curvis. You brought us to a place where there's a dead girl! Jesus creeps! You're mad. I'm fucking off home.'

'It's just an old man's story,' stressed Curvis. 'What he told to two brats . . . Me and Stanton. Just to keep us quiet. Stop shitting yourself!'

'So how did you remember all that after all this time?' probed Carlton, his face cynical. Fuckin' hell, Carlton thought. Maybe they had pervs like Uncle Thomas back in the olden days. Poor wretch, I bet some perv done her something. He looked around at the trees. I bet they know what happened to her, he thought.

Curvis shrugged his shoulders. 'I always remember stories that people told me.'

'It seems fucking real enough for me,' feared Bullet. 'Say we fall on the dead girl's body while we're fucking around up here.'

'Whassamatter with you lot?' laughed Curvis. 'It's just a story, for fuck's sake. This *is* the best place for us. Who's gonna find us here? This is just a bigger version of Pinewood Oaks.'

Carlton was chewing a blade of grass after his meal. 'Well, if I find the girl's body . . . Or it could be bones by now, I'll just tell the police where she is and hope some relatives of the girl's family are around so I can get a reward. They were rich, weren't they?'

'Shut up, Carlton,' rebuked Curvis. 'The story ain't true. It happened fucking ages ago – like when people used to wear those funny pointed hats – when everyone was a farmer.'

'How do you know?' asked Carlton. 'The old man could have been the killer. He might have killed lots of children. Maybe his ghost is still around, looking for kids.'

Carlton's friends all glared at him in silent condemnation. 'Whassamatter with you lot?' he said, trying to laugh off his embarrassment. 'Can't you take a joke?'

'That weren't a joke,' replied Bullet, stony-faced. 'You're just trying to scare us.'

'Well, how do you know the girl weren't murdered?' Carlton sniped, spitting out the blade of grass and picking up a leaf of bracken fern.

'Don't chew that,' warned Curvis. 'It's poisonous.'

Carlton threw the leaf away, annoyed that he couldn't locate any lengthy grass blades. 'For fuck's sake! Curvis, you could've taken us somewhere where I can get chews.' He looked up at the trees. Seems like they're watching me or something, he thought. They look so fucking old and ugly. 'Their fucking tall, aren't they? You don't really realise 'til you're up close.'

'The girl might have got carried away by ghosts and spirits,' suggested Glenroy. 'Or an UFO might have landed and got her.'

'You been eating any funny mushrooms lately?' Carlton teased.

'Or toadstools,' added Bullet. 'And tree bark, grass and anything else that grows under the sun. Slugs and shit, even.'

'No I haven't!' stressed Glenroy. 'You lot think I'm stupid 'cos I believe in UFOs, but I read a comic once, and all professors and egg-heads were saying that they're possible. So stick that up your arse and eat it!'

'Alright, keep your afro on,' pacified Curvis.

Fifteen minutes later, the friends lay down on the blankets, with the four of them sharing two pillows. The moonlight was fading but the sun's illumination was creeping towards the tips of the pines, creating an amber glow covering half the sky. No one spoke. All of them were immersed in their own waking dreams, wondering what fate had in store for them.

Glenroy was peering through the gaps in the canopy at the brightening sky. He wished for an UFO to suddenly appear, and little Martians to parachute into the forest with seven fingers on each hand and black bug-eyes. His thoughts then drifted to the girl in Curvis's story. He looked around him and noticed that Bullet's eyes were closed. He glanced upwards again, willing the extra-terrestrials to arrive, hovering over the forest and shadowing the sun. They won't say I'm stupid if that happened, Glenroy thought.

One hour later, when the birds had started to sing in the new day, Glenroy was lying uneasily with his eyes open. He turned to look at Carlton, who seemed to be enjoying a deep sleep. He peered into the wood around him and wondered what there was to be scared of. 'Bullet,' he whispered. 'Bullet.'

Carlton stirred. 'Hey, Glenroy. Can't you bloody sleep? Give it a rest, will ya. Let Bullet sleep.'

'I can't flippin' sleep either,' mumbled Bullet. 'We should've taken our beds with us!'

'And how would we carry the beds up here?' asked Glenroy.

'It was a joke,' stressed Bullet.

Glenroy foraged in Bullet's bag and found his torch. He switched it on and shone it directly at Bullet. Curvis sat up. 'Turn that fucking torch off! We've got to save our batteries and its nearly light now anyway. All because you lot can't sleep, doesn't mean I don't want to.'

Glenroy lay down once more, refusing to close his eyes. He didn't want to have a nightmare in the presence of his friends. They would call him stupid again.

Emancipation

7.45 a.m., Sunday, 13 June 1976

The sun threaded its rays through the tangled woodland, spreading its light to every crook and hollow, illuminating glorious greens and browns. The birds had woken early and greeted the morning. The leaves whispered in the fragile breeze and the owls stilled their tongues. All seemed quiet as the world began to awake.

Glenroy, who had not slept a wink during the early hours, rose to his feet and stretched his arms, performing an extravagant yawn. He couldn't remember feeling so relaxed. He looked at his three friends, who were still at rest on the dew-dampened blankets. Bullet stirred and looked around in blurry wonder, not believing he had spent the night under the one-eyed glare of the moon. He caught Glenroy's eyes, and for a moment the two friends smiled warmly at each other, both thinking how good they felt. The first day of their freedom had began.

Carlton was staring at the bush, seemingly mesmerised by a ladybird plodding along a broad leaf. He was thinking of Josephine and her reaction to the night's events. He wouldn't have liked to have seen her face when she entered his dorm offering a mug of coffee, as she usually did. Maybe she rang my mother about my disappearance, he thought. *Bitch!*

Curvis was still sleeping; he looked like he belonged in this place.

'What is the time?' Bullet asked, blinking the sleep out of his eyes.

Carlton reached to grab his bag and unzipped it to find his watch. 'Nearly eight o' clock.' He looked around. It's like a different place from the one we came to last night, he thought. More kinda friendly, welcoming. The trees really look pretty and the bird-sounds are kinda soothing.

'Hey, look!' Glenroy exclaimed, peering north where the hills dipped, pointing his right hand. 'There's a windmill down there.'

Bullet hauled himself up and joined Glenroy observing the windmill. 'Does it work?' Glenroy wondered. 'We should check it out tonight.'

'Nah, I don't think so,' Bullet answered. 'Probably hasn't worked for years.'

'We should have slept there,' added Glenroy. 'Least we'd have a roof over our heads.'

'Too risky,' said Carlton, shaking his head.

Glenroy looked ravenously at Carlton's bag. 'Any more biscuits? What we're gonna have for breakfast?'

Carlton offered his bag to Glenroy, who helped himself to a handful of digestives, giving some to Bullet. Carlton stared once more at the bush, his eyes unblinking. 'Auntie Josephine's gonna kill me; those biscuits were for the kids.'

'She's gonna kill ya anyway,' laughed Bullet. 'You've run away.'

158

'Yeah, and I can't bloody believe it!' replied Carlton, noticing that Curvis was stirring. 'She'll be worried sick.'

'Uncle Thomas will be going nuts,' grinned Glenroy. 'I can just imagine him shouting all over the place. He's probably gone to Elvin's house to ask him if he knows where we are. Ha Ha! Can you imagine him. *Where the hell is Glenroy!*'

'Uncle Rodney's probably going mental an' all,' chuckled Bullet. 'He's probably saying that you lot led me astray or you forced me into it. I bet he didn't do his exercises this morning. He can shove his discipline up his arse!'

Curvis's eye's squinted as they opened to the greeting of a strong sun. He sat himself up, focusing his eyes, then looked at Glenroy. 'So you still here then?'

'Yeah, thought I'd go back, eh?'

Curvis stood up and shook the blanket he had slept on. He wanted to scream a victory cheer for leading his friends successfully out of Pinewood Oaks but thought he'd better appear as if he was cool and in control. 'We'll go up to the café which ain't too far from here and get breakfast. But first, we've got to find a good place to hide our stuff. Oh, by the way, don't go near the windmill – scouts are always nosing around it.'

'What?' Glenroy exclaimed. 'There's a café up here. In the woods! This is gonna be better that I thought. What do they serve? I could kill a knickerbocker glory.'

'Glenroy, it's a café in the woods, not a fucking high street restaurant,' said Curvis. 'Be careful when we get there.'

'Yeah, the café's near to the road that goes through the hills, innit?' asked Carlton.

'That's right,' said Curvis. 'Usually old people drink tea and eat scones there. But you never know. We'll just go there, eat and fuck off.'

Bullet folded the blankets, wondering where to put them. Glenroy picked up the two pillows and placed them in the black bin bag and waited for directions.

'Put them down at the bottom of the hill, then put ferns over 'em,' prompted Curvis. 'No one goes down there – too many bushes. Oh, one more thing. Don't sleep with your heads too close to the trees and bushes. If you do you might wake up with earwigs and all sorts over your face.'

'Seems like they've got to Bullet already,' Carlton quipped.

Bullet trod carefully down the slippery slope, wondering how they had all managed to climb it in the dark. He crunched pine cones on the way as Glenroy followed him. Carlton and Curvis kicked away cake and biscuit wrappers towards the bushes. 'So what are we gonna do today?' asked Carlton. 'Play conkers? Tim-tam-tommy?'

'To tell the truth,' answered Curvis. 'I don't really know. Maybe later on, we can check out what the scouts are doing – they have some sort of adventure playground in their area – it should be a laugh. But we should keep our heads down during the day. Keep away from the road.'

'Haven't the scouts built those tree houses?' asked Glenroy. 'Hey, Bullet, you've finally got your wish – you can pretend to be Tarzan for the night.'

'How can you bring *that* up? I liked Tarzan years ago.'

Glenroy and Bullet had finished their task of masking the bags and began to climb the steep mound. 'Where're we gonna get our wash?' asked Glenroy.

'Well, just round the corner,' laughed Carlton. 'There's a mud sink around the next tree and it's got mud soap in it. Don't be long 'cos I want my turn.'

'Ha, ha, very funny,' replied Glenroy, hating to be the butt of any jokes.

'Tomorrow we'll go to the Spurleigh Way open air swimming pool,' announced Curvis. 'It's about three miles away.' Curvis pointed in a north-west direction. 'You can bathe all you like there.'

Carlton delved into his bag again and took out the petty

cash tin. He spilled all the cash onto the firm earth and hurled the box away. 'Fucking thing weighs my bag down.'

Curvis sighed, shaking his head. 'Make sure you hide the box before we go. Remember, it's evidence.'

Ten minutes later, satisfied that the camp was well concealed, Curvis started out, leading his friends down into a hollow with fiery nettles on each side. Everyone was relieved to escape the fierce sun for a while. The thicket here seemed untouched by human hand and untrodden by foot, but Curvis appeared to have a compass in his brain. Glenroy was close behind him, already sweating.

'That girl?' Glenroy asked. 'What was her name?'

'What girl?' replied Curvis.

'That girl in your story. What was her name?'

'Oh, her. The old man said it was Gemmele.'

'Weird name – wasn't it Gemma?'

'No, definitely Gemmele,' affirmed Curvis, wishing he had never told the tale.

After twenty minutes of climbing and slipping down hollows and stony barrows, they came to a dusty mud-path, twisting through the woods, and only the roots of the pines hampered its progress. Shafts of light penetrated the canopy, creating a golden kaleidoscope. Glenroy, Carlton and Bullet watched Curvis, wondering if he would veer right or left. Without hesitation, he turned left.

Now in the open, they were at the mercy of the June sun, forcing them to leave the path to seek shelter from the trees. Seven hundred paces later, the trail forked off into three directions, as if to purposefully confuse Sunday ramblers. But Curvis, total assurance written on his face, led the way, picking up the pace. As they went on, the heath, with its wispy pale grass, broadened and the pines appeared to be further apart. They saw a middle-aged man, sporting a flat cap and smoking one of those pipes shaped like a tiny saxophone. His Labrador dog bounded around him keenly. Bullet felt a tension in his throat. 'What do we do? Leg it?'

'No,' answered Carlton. 'Just walk normally.'

They passed the man, checking behind them to see if he turned around. Ten minutes later, Curvis had led them to a gravel car park that fronted a café, built on a plateau. 'Fucking hell,' gasped Glenroy. 'You can see for miles.' Four cars were parked in front of the café and young children were sitting down beside the walls, licking lollies and ice-cream cones. The building seemed old, its windows bearing the dust and grime of countless summers. Glenroy, at the prospect of ice-cream, hared into the diner, leaving his friends standing. They treated themselves to scones, crisps and ice-cream cones, sitting at a table near the front door. They were laughing and joking, forgetting the seriousness of their deed. Freedom tasted good.

After downing cans of fizzy drink, Curvis led his friends to a viewpoint, one hundred yards away from the café. Forged in a platform of concrete in the floor was a bronze-coloured compass the size of a beer barrel's base. A waist-high brick wall, arranged in a semi-circle, prevented viewers from falling over the cliff-like ravine. The view was magnificent. Under the crystalline blue sky, the four friends could see far-off isolated hamlets. Fields looked like a sliced green-iced cake and distant forests like untold servings of broccoli. Streams and small rivers glistened and there were sheep in the hills. Curvis, who had lost count of the amount of times he had wondered at this scenery, studied the compass in the floor. He pointed west. 'Me and Stanton would come up here when the Biggin Hill air show was on. We got a really good view of the Red Arrows and saw all the coloured smoke.'

'Coloured smoke?' Glenroy asked. 'They weren't on fire, were they?'

'No, you divo,' Carlton corrected. 'The smoke's for show – to make it look good.' He scanned the horizon and looked up at the vast expanse of blue sky. He felt a strange sense of freedom and realised that now he could do anything he liked. 'It kinda makes you giddy looking out from up here,' he commented.

'Yeah,' Bullet answered. 'Back at Pinewood Oaks, I was always jealous of the birds, flying anywhere where they like. Well, now we can go anywhere where *we* like.'

Curvis let his friends admire the scenery for another ten minutes, before heading south-west. Glenroy and Bullet raced each other down a steep dell. They ended up plunging head over heels into the bosom of the valley. Carlton laughed while Curvis smiled, thinking he had never seen Glenroy happier.

The quartet regrouped but Glenroy and Bullet were off playing tag, bolting around bending trees and hurdling over fallen branches. With no housefather or housemother to discipline them, there was no reason to stop; no reason to look over a shoulder. To an observer, they seemed just like a normal group of boys enjoying themselves; indeed, some passers-by smiled at their antics, thinking it was better for youngsters to enjoy the outdoors than sit in front of a television. Their bond seemed greater than friendship as they hugged, wrestled and leaped on each other, laughing merrily without a care in the world.

Auntie Josephine gazed at the clock in her kitchen. Half-past nine. Pulling tensely on her cigarette, her face was contorted with worry. The children in her charge had already left to go to church and Sunday school. She had two members of staff who both came into work at nine o clock. Both women were shocked to learn that Carlton had run away.

The news got worse. Josephine had been on the phone continuously since 7.30 a.m., talking to irate housemothers and housefathers and the dreaded duty social worker from the council; Mr Williams had to inform the social worker of the news. Still watching the clock, she heard her front door being impatiently tapped. She opened it hesitantly and was confronted with the bald-headed figure of Thomas. Josephine could smell the sweat of his armpits. He picked nervously at his ginger beard and didn't meet Josephine with his eyes; he looked beyond her into the house. 'Any news?' he asked. He sucked his teeth. 'I just can't believe it.'

'No,' Josephine replied, barely audible. 'Mr Williams searched around the grounds this morning but there is no sign of them . . . Come in, I'll put the kettle on.'

'Thank you, Josephine. I think I need it. I've been worried sick.'

Thomas entered the house, following Josephine into the kitchen. He seated himself down at a table next to the tall fridge. 'Is Brian's housefather on his way?'

'Yes. Rodney called me about an hour ago. He said he'll try and contact Brian's social worker, although it's a Sunday, and then he'll come down for the meeting. The duty social worker from the council might be coming down, but you know what they're like on Sundays.'

Thomas's temples were smeared with perspiration and his hands fidgety. He took out a tobacco tin from his shirt pocket and started to roll a cigarette. 'Why on earth would they run away?' he asked. He looked up and held Josephine's gaze. 'I haven't done anything to Glenroy for him to do anything this drastic.'

Josephine couldn't hold the gaze and turned away. 'Carlton left a message,' she admitted. 'He wrote that the reason he ran away wasn't *my* fault.'

'Yes. But he might be just saying that. I mean . . . There is no way that Glenroy would run away on his own. He's too easily influenced. He's quite a simple lad really.'

Josephine inhaled sharply, hands on her hips and her eyes smouldering. 'So you're saying that Carlton led him to it?'

'No, no. Just that Glenroy wouldn't have thought of it on his own.' He licked the length of his roll-up and glued the

164

paper down. Josephine watched him as he placed the cigarette between his lips and lit it. Another knock on the door cut into the rising tension. 'I'll answer it,' offered Thomas, not liking the way Josephine was looking at him.

Thomas opened the door. Rodney, his cheeks flushed and his lips stern, blustered into the hallway. Dressed in shirt and throat-gripping tie, his neck was as red as his face. Beside Rodney was a middle-aged woman with a tall, stooping figure. She held her head high and the lens of her glasses half-covered her long face. Her hair was pulled up with countless clips and her whole body was rigid. She glared at Thomas.

'Heard anything, Thomas?' Rodney asked, as if he was a major addressing a private.

Thomas beckoned the couple inside. 'Afraid not . . . I'm sure they'll come back today.'

Thomas switched his gaze to the woman and dipped his head ever so slightly. 'Morning, Miss Gallagher – Josephine is just making a pot of tea.'

Miss Gallagher acknowledged Thomas with a nod. She entered the house like the owner of a stately home setting foot in the gardener's hut. 'There was supposed to be a case meeting tomorrow morning for Curvis,' she offered. 'He has known about it since last week and he has been intolerable lately. Of all things, he wanted to attend! The cheek of that boy. He refused to even talk with his social worker until he knew where his brother Stanton was . . . Sometimes I wish Curvis would join him.'

Josephine led her peers into her study. After seating herself at her desk, Josephine glanced at the standing Rodney. 'Carlton's social worker will be down here in an hour . . . It's a good thing he gave me his home number. He said I'll have to make a report for his supervisor.'

'Yes, I have spoken to the supervisor this morning,' Rodney revealed, feeling a great embarrassment. 'Mr Holmes

165

expressed in strong terms that word of this must *not* get out – especially to the press.'

They had all heard this line before, and they had been warned about wagging tongues about other incidents within the children's home complex.

'These kids just don't realise the trouble they have caused,' Rodney continued. 'All this paper work we are going to have to do with the social services looking over our shoulders. In *twenty* years of childcare, not one of the children in my charge has ever done this before. Brian must have been influenced by the others to do this. He's a good, sensible boy, but picks the wrong friends. Friends that are not as intelligent as he is.'

'Now hold on a minute,' argued Josephine, controlling her temper and the dislike she felt for her colleagues. 'He's got a mind of his own and I say all four are equally to blame.'

'Now, there's no sense in arguing who is to blame for all this,' pacified Thomas. 'The fact is we have four runaways on our hands, and the council are going to be pressing us about why they did it.'

'It seems kids today think they can get away with anything,' lamented Miss Gallagher, not enjoying her tea. 'I'm sick and tired of all the memos I receive from the council telling me how to raise the children in my care. These people who send out these memos do not know what it is like to look after eight screaming kids. In the old days we would simply be allowed to use our own judgement and get on with it.'

'Yes, I agree,' said Rodney, nodding his head and doing his best to appear superior. 'If we could discipline the children the way we want to, you wouldn't get children running away and misbehaving. A little corporal punishment never did a child any harm; Brian will have a lot to answer for when he returns . . . You help these children all you can and they throw it back in your face.'

Josephine sipped her tea while thinking that Rodney's rightful place was in an army parade ground and he shouldn't be allowed within a hundred miles of a children's home. Thomas took a chocolate biscuit. 'So none of you has any idea where they might have gone?'

'They probably took the first train to London,' offered Miss Gallagher, pushing away her three-quarter-full cup of tea. 'The blighters! I blame these so-called modern television programmes myself. They should never have shown *Cathy Come Home*. It was entirely irresponsible. And I do *not* let the children in my charge watch *Oliver Twist* . . . They'll be walking the streets of London begging for a meal!'

Josephine knew that the shows Miss Gallagher cited were first shown in the late 1960s. But she decided not to contradict her.

'They will come scurrying home when they feel hungry,' said Rodney. 'They always do.'

'Carlton stole the petty cash,' admitted Josephine, thinking she could not hold this fact back any longer, although it hurt her. 'There was about twenty pounds in the box.'

'That doesn't surprise me,' sniped Miss Gallagher, refusing the offer of biscuits from Thomas. 'He appears the type.'

Josephine employed her sternest glare but said nothing. Rodney nodded his head. 'When they come back,' he announced, 'all of them deserve a harsh lesson. A spell of juvenile detention will do them no harm. This way they might realise how lucky they are to be living in Pinewood Oaks. Poor children in the inner cities don't have the facilities and grounds we have here.'

'Too right,' concurred Miss Gallagher. 'Children here are so fortunate.'

Josephine bit her top lip.

'Brian should know better than most why he is so fortunate,' Rodney continued. 'If it wasn't for social services, who knows what would have happened to him after his pathetic mother left him on the doorstep at Area 3 offices – I told him all the details, how he was left only with a bottle of milk ... Totally irresponsible! And we have to pick up the pieces!'

Thomas rose from his seat. 'I think I left my tobacco in the kitchen – I won't be a minute.'

Thomas left the room, closing the door behind him. Miss Gallagher looked at Rodney. 'That Glenroy is always acting the buffoon – so immature.'

'That's not fair, Ruth,' returned Josephine. 'They've all been stupid.'

Rodney took a curious interest in the book selection on the shelf. 'The police told me that once the boys have been missing for more than twenty-four hours, we will have to provide recent photographs of all the blighters,' he informed. 'The sergeant promised he will send two officers down from New Craddington by the afternoon. I did not want the police to get involved but Mr Holmes made it clear we have no choice. It troubles me because when the police start asking questions they are always suspicious of us. It's an affront to our dignity!'

Thomas returned to the room with a rolled-up cigarette between his fingers. Josephine was perturbed by Rodney's news about the police. Miss Gallagher inspected the decor of the room and was grudgingly impressed.

'Did Mr Williams question Elvin?' asked Miss Gallagher.

'Yes, but he claims he knows nothing,' answered Josephine.

'He's not going to snitch on his friends, is he?' suspected Rodney. 'Of course he knows something! If the police have to come down I hope they get it out of him.'

'No, I don't think so,' disagreed Thomas, the sweat returning to his temples and forehead. 'Unfairly, I've heard the kids call him big mouth and various other names, so I don't think the boys would have told him of their plans. Besides, Elvin is a good lad and if he did know of something, he would have informed me ... Since I taught him to swim he looks on me like a father.'

168

'I just want them home,' cried Josephine, her emotions overwhelming her. 'Who knows what they're getting up to? If they did take the first train to London, they could be in all sorts of danger.'

1.30 p.m.

The sun had reached its pinnacle and there was no escaping its heat. Carlton, Curvis, Bullet and Glenroy, the forest in their wake, had made their way to the summit of Cravell Hill, overlooking the New Craddington golf course and the hamlet itself, surrounded by trees and heath, six miles south of Pinewood Oaks. Twice as big as Pinewood, New Craddington boasted a police station and fire station. Carlton remembered the place well, once playing cricket for his school there on the neatest pitch he had ever seen. A few boys from Pinewood Oaks, who had saved their pocket money, took a green bus to the summer fair at New Craddington heath. They often returned with half-coconuts and goldfish swimming in polythene plastic bags.

'Fucking hell,' cried Glenroy. 'Didn't realise we are so high up – those stacks of hay look like lumps of brown sugar!'

The boys sat down in the shelter of the forest, forty yards away from the corkscrewing Cravell Hill road, weary of their exertions in the morning. They peered into the valley.

'If it snows a lot then those bastards who live down there get cut off,' said Curvis.

'Why? Is that the only way in?' asked Carlton, pointing to the hill. 'Never been to the other side of the place.'

'Yep,' answered Curvis, smile on his face. 'It's alright going downhill but trying to go up is almost impossible. Stanton used to nick things from abandoned cars down there.'

'You two come all this way in the snow?' asked Bullet.

'Yep, Wellington boots was a fucking good invention.'

169

Bullet noticed something coming up the hill. 'The Old Bill!' he shouted, pointing a frightened finger.

They rapidly retreated into the forest, with Glenroy the last to make it. From undercover they watched the police car skirting the bend.

'You think they saw us?' panted Bullet.

'Nah, they would've stopped if they had,' returned Carlton. 'They probably don't even know we done a runner yet.'

'Who fucking knows?' said Curvis. 'I bet Bullet's Uncle Rodney has called them already . . . Come on, let's go back to base.'

As they went back to their camp, the sighting of the police car had fired their adrenalin and they all sensed the danger of adventure. They likened themselves to war prisoners, escaping from somewhere like Colditz with the whole German army in pursuit. Even Carlton had ceased worrying about Auntie Josephine's reaction and had started to think of more daring pursuits. Bullet, pacing ahead with stick in hand, confident of the route, sang.

> *'Four of us mighty are we*
> *Three'll be like cutting off our knees*
> *Two'll be like the sinking of a crew.'*

His friends joined him in song for the last line.

> *'And one'll be like killing us with a gun!'*

10.30 p.m.

Bullet shone his torch forward as he and his friends stealthily made their way through the scouting complex in the woods. The sun had faded half an hour ago and the owls were just waking up. In single file, the four boys threaded themselves through the trees and bushes. A still blackness surrounded them. Unseen, coming from the tree trunks, they could hear the mating songs of the cicadas, a repetitive, rasping sound. Glenroy, in the middle of the quartet, queried, 'Where do these bum chums camp out? We've been walking for ages.'

'We're in the scouting grounds already,' answered Curvis. 'Sometimes they sleep in huts and sometimes tents. Look out for any camp-fires; they love to have one of those stupid sing-songs before they fuck off to bed.'

'I bet they don't sing any rude rugby songs,' chuckled Bullet.

'Snobby fucking losers,' cursed Carlton. 'They probably go through *The Sound of Music* songbook.'

They approached a small, still lake, undisturbed by any breath of wind. Its oval length was about the size of a football pitch. With the eye of a single torch, they could just make out the shapes of one-man canoes, bobbing gently on the water, attached to ropes that were tied to small, wooden moorings, speared into the firm ground. On the other side of the lake was a tiny estate of pre-fabricated huts, no higher than seven feet tall, that were moon-shadowed by giant pines. The boys noticed an array of dim, yellow lights, shining like giant fire-flies from the buildings. Carlton looked up at the trees, thinking they were the only witnesses who knew he and his friends were here. 'Let's cut the ropes,' he prompted. 'Bullet, got your pen-knife?'

'Yeah, it's in my pocket.'

Crawling on his hands and knees, Carlton reached the nearest boat. Bullet passed on his pen-knife. Curvis remained in the cover of trees acting as look-out. Glenroy looked dreamily at the water. This is like being in a film, he thought. We can do what we want. Maybe we can build a raft and come back here.

Carlton began to saw the rope. Thirty seconds later, Carlton and Bullet cackled as they observed the boat floating off towards the middle of the lake. Glenroy crept to another boat and Carlton threw the pen-knife to him. He wasted no time in sending the boat out to join its sister in the murky lake. Curvis peered nervously from his position as his three friends laughed at their own mischief.

Carlton freed another boat, but got his feet wet as he slipped on the soft mud that ringed the lake. 'Shit!'

'Let's go for a skinny dip,' suggested Glenroy. Before anyone had a chance to answer, Glenroy had already taken off his T-shirt and started to pull off his trainers.

'You perv!' mocked Bullet. 'I ain't taking off my clothes for you!'

'You're just saying that 'cos you ain't grown no pubes yet,' returned Glenroy.

'Fuck you, you queer bastard.'

'Fuck you, you army nutter!'

Carlton watched Glenroy take off his socks and pull off his jeans. 'I ain't one for taking up Glenroy's ideas,' he said. 'But this is a fucking good one; I've been sweating all day!'

'Well, I ain't taking off my pants so that perv can have a look,' said Bullet, not admitting that the water looked sorely tempting to him also. He began to undress.

'You know, sometimes I wonder if Bullet's got a willy,' laughed Glenroy.

Everybody chuckled. Curvis walked down to the edge of the lake, breaking his concentration on the huts. 'Fuck it. I'm going for a swim!'

Soon they were all neck-high in the lake, enjoying the cool water. The lake bed was soft and muddy and it was a relief to them all for their feet to be free of trainers and socks. They could smell the reeds that were clustered together around the rim of the lake and they had an excellent view of the three-quarter moon, dark spots and craters spotting its yellow, white surface. From lake level, the pines looked magnificent

172

in their size and stature, as if they were giant landlords watching over their property. For half an hour the boys swam, played water tag and marvelled at their environment, blissfully washing away the day.

Regretting that they hadn't brought any towels with them, the boys donned their clothes over wet bodies. Curvis, who was dressing at his previous look-out point, about twenty yards away from the others, was the last one to pull on his trainers. A shadow of a figure emerged from the bushes behind him.

'Oi, what the fuck are you lot doing here?' bellowed an adult voice.

Curvis turned around in panic, one trainer shoe not yet tied. He was stilled into shock, his mouth wide open.

The man, late teens or early twenties, wearing a venture scout outfit, lunged at him. 'Come here, you little runt!' The man grabbed Curvis and viced him around the neck, pulling him to the ground. 'Lawrence, Frank! I've found trespassers! Come quick.'

Glenroy, Bullet and Carlton reacted quickly, scampering to Curvis's aid, preparing their fists. They attacked the man with hands and feet. Running footsteps could be heard in the distance. Birds flew out of trees. Something four-legged ran into a hole in the ground. Carlton put together a combination of punches. Bullet held the man down. Glenroy was kicking the man's legs. Curvis was dazed. The footsteps were getting closer. 'Lawrence, Frank! Fuck off you bastards . . . I'm over here!'

'Where?'

Bullet pulled Curvis away. Glenroy offered one more kick before wondering which way to go. Carlton kept on punching. 'Shut up!' he yelled.

'There's fucking more of them,' panicked Bullet. 'Curvis, which fucking way?'

Curvis didn't reply, he was still in shock. Bullet slapped him around the face. 'Which fucking *way*!'

Curvis pointed an unsteady finger. 'Glenroy, stay close,' Bullet told Glenroy. 'Carlton, *come on!*'

'Don't you fucking hit one of my friends again!' said Carlton, caught up in a violent hysteria. The man couldn't shout anymore. The sound of crunching pine cones was all around.

'Carlton, fucking leave him,' beseeched Bullet. 'Leave him!'

Carlton finally left his bruised and battered victim and joined his friends. Curvis, regaining composure, switched on his internal compass and led the way, scampering around bushes, under branches and up and down slippery hollows. They heard voices behind them.

'Matthew's hurt! He's hurt bad. Get the first aider!'

'Fuckin' hell! Look at the state of him.'

'Don't move him. He's concussed. What madman did this, for Christ's sake?'

'Lawrence, go back and call the police. I won't sleep easily 'til the bastards that did this are caught. Fucking hell, look at the state of his face!'

The four runaways weaved their way through the forest, panting. They hastily climbed a fence that led them out of the scouting grounds. 'Bullet, shine your fucking torch,' ordered Carlton. 'I nearly ruptured myself on that bloody fence.'

'What if the venture scouts see it?'

'Just shine your fucking torch!' raged Carlton, adrenalin still surging through his veins.

'Calm down,' advised Curvis. 'They ain't following us.'

'Yeah, but you have to be safe,' replied Bullet.

'You alright, Curvis?' asked Glenroy. 'That guy looked like he wanted to strangle you to death.'

'Yeah, I'm alright,' answered Curvis, glad for the concern. 'Neck's a bit sore though.'

'Fucking loser. We should have choked him,' said Carlton. 'See how he'd like it.'

174

'I thought you weren't gonna stop punching him,' said Bullet.

'I didn't want to.' Carlton's eyes still promised violence. 'I'll do *anything* to protect you lot.'

They made their way to the other side of the forest, a trek of an hour. In the distance they could hear police sirens. 'The whole of the fucking Surrey police force gonna be looking for us now,' warned Curvis. 'But they still won't find us,' he added with a smirk. His friends didn't share the same confidence.

When they had made their base camp, Bullet laid out the blankets. They started a card game, aided by torch-light and suppered on crisps and chocolate bars. Glenroy, not all that adept at playing Black Jack, peered into the blackness that surrounded him. 'This place is weird,' he commented. 'It's like at night we're somewhere else – not in the same place like during the day.'

'Of course it's the same place,' replied Bullet, reluctant to admit that he felt Glenroy was half right.

'Glenroy's right for once,' said Carlton, watching the surprised looks from his mates. 'It's like . . . The place is alive.' He looked up at the trees. 'It's like the whole place is alive during the day and this something is . . . nice. But at night . . . it ain't nice. What do you say, Curvis?'

'Well, it is alive. Everything around us is alive. The trees, bushes, everything. I've been up here hundreds of times, and I have to admit that at night, I've noticed the whole thing kinda changes.'

Glenroy thought of the girl in Curvis's story. Maybe it's her doing, he thought. 'That girl, if she's still alive she'll be an old woman now, innit. She might be a witch! Who knows, she might be still walking around in the woods today, or tonight?'

'Glenroy, forget about her,' replied Curvis. 'She's dead.'

'Well, if nobody found her, Glenroy might be right,' offered Carlton, wanting to humour his friend.

'Come off it!' disagreed Bullet. 'If that's true, she would have been walking around here for about a hundred years. What's she gonna live on?'

'She might nick some chickens and stuff off the farms around here,' replied Carlton. 'When you think about it, it wouldn't matter how long ago it was if she was a witch. She might be still alive. Witches live for ages – up to a thousand years.'

'Who knows?' concurred Glenroy. 'She might've made her camp where no one could ever find it . . . Remember when we were kids. We always made a camp where we thought no other kids would find it.'

'Yeah, but you would always tell someone where it was,' scolded Curvis, not happy the way the conversation was developing.

'She might just come out at night-time, getting something to eat,' Glenroy continued. 'If we stay up, we might see her.'

'You're a nutter,' dismissed Bullet, shaking his head.

Carlton glanced at the trees. *They* probably saw the girl all those years ago. *They* knew her fate. Only his friends and the trees had seen his assault on the venture scout. He couldn't understand why he kept on kicking and punching when he didn't need to. Maybe it was because, up in this place he knew he'd get away with it. His friends wouldn't grass on him, nor would the trees. He didn't have to answer to Auntie Josephine no more. Didn't have to answer to Mr Williams either. They think I'm nothing anyway, he thought. My mother thought I was nothing, that's why she didn't want me. But up here with my friends I am something. I'm their protector. I can keep them from harm. *No one*'s gonna fuck with them while we're up here.

Curvis looked up to the stars, wallowing in his freedom. He tolerated the imaginings of his friends now they were in the hills; the same thing always happened to him. He spared a thought for his brother Stanton. At least while he remained

176

in the Pinewood Hills, it was him making the decisions, not social workers, housemothers or housefathers with never a thought of consulting the child. It was good to be free, he thought.

Half an hour later, they took to their sleeping positions. Even Glenroy was confident enough to close his eyes, although he dared not allow himself to fall asleep. He thought of the little girl in Curvis's story, wondering what she looked like and what games she played in the woods. Glenroy asked himself how she could not be intimidated in the darkness of the forest? He wished he could have met her. Maybe they could have been great friends, larking about in the woods and playing hide and seek. As he pondered on Gemmele, he realised that, like her, he was at the mercy of the forest. He tightened his eyelids and tried to imagine he was back in his dorm.

Bold Like Nimrod

6.45 a.m., Monday, 14 June 1976

Curvis had woken early and set off purposefully into the woods, as if he had an appointment to keep. Glenroy, who had only slept for two hours, watched him, wondering if he should ask where he was going. Curvis went on, glancing upwards to see if he could catch any sight of the crooning larks. He spotted a nest, with tiny, eager beaks protruding over the edge, awaiting their first meal of the day. Curvis thought of Glenroy and smiled to himself.

Two minutes later, he came to a tall pine, its needles growing in clumps of fours and fives, almost concealing the trunk and branches. Curvis stooped and lifted a branch so that he could sit down facing the trunk. Inscribed in the bark were two letters that Curvis had carved out six years ago; *C* for Curvis and *S* for Stanton. Below it was the figure *4* and underneath that the word *Ever*. He looked up to the heavens then closed his eyes. In his inner vision, he saw painful, bloodshot-brown eyes, set in a heart-shaped face with a long, aquiline nose. Chaotic, horse-chestnut-coloured hair framed the picture.

'Morning, Mum,' Curvis whispered. 'I dunno if you agree with what I've done. I just had to get away . . . Nearer to you. Maybe I should have come on my own.' He placed his hand on the tree gently, caressing it, feeling its rough texture. 'But they would never let me go on my own and they would've never forgave me if I didn't tell 'em I was doing a runner . . . I know you want me to find Stanton and see how he is. And I will. Those bastards won't keep me from him. I feel frightened without him. You know, 'cos he ain't there. That's why I come here, Mum. Be near to you. As long as I'm up here I know you're looking over me. If the others go, I might stay. I can't live in that place no more. Not without Stanton. It'll do my head in.' Curvis took his hand off the tree and wiped tears away from his cheeks. 'I'll talk to ya tomorrow, Mum. Gotta go, the others will be wondering where I am. Somehow I've gotta teach 'em to respect this place – *your* place.'

Five minutes later, Curvis returned to the camp to find Glenroy moaning about his hunger. Bullet was folding the blankets while Carlton seemed to be searching for something. No one wanted to admit it, but they all felt more comfortable now the sun had risen.

'Anybody seen my watch?' Carlton asked.

'I've got it,' answered Curvis, delving into his back pocket. 'It was under your pillow and I took it 'cos you looked like you was gonna roll over it . . . Did you have a bad dream?'

'Yeah, yeah. I did,' Carlton lied, not wanting to reveal the stabs of guilt that kept him from sleeping. 'Give the watch here!'

Curvis lobbed the watch over to Carlton who caught it with his right hand. He strapped it to his wrist. 'Bullet, do you have to fucking snore all night? It's like sleeping next to a combine harvester.'

'Who rattled your fucking cage,' returned Bullet. 'Besides, I can't help it, I breathe through my mouth when I'm sleeping.'

'What's that song about a combine harvester that's number one?' asked Curvis, noticing his friends were particularly grouchy this morning. Maybe they're shrugging off the effects of the night, he guessed.

'It's them trampish people who talk weird,' answered Glenroy. 'I think they're called the Weezils. When they talk, they go oooaarh, oooaarh.'

'They don't sound like that,' laughed Bullet, standing up, preparing himself for a rendition of the song. 'Well, oive got a brand new combine harvester, you've got an old donkey,' he sang, sounding more Scottish than West Country. Everyone collapsed in giggles.

Glenroy wanted more excitement. 'We going back to the scouts' place tonight?'

'Oh yeah, and have the whole fucking scout movement after us?' sneered Bullet. 'They'll take to the fucking skies and drop smoke bombs to make us come out from hiding . . . You're a nutter.'

Carlton and Curvis chuckled. Glenroy wasn't deterred. 'It was a laugh, though,' he said, grinning from ear to ear. 'Hey, Carlton, you give that bloke one hell of a beating. Reminded me of the time you beat up that rock and roll guy last year. Remember that; you tore the ring outta his ear.'

Carlton didn't want to be reminded of that incident. 'Auntie Josephine is probably getting the kids ready for school and nursery,' he remarked. 'Making their toast and cereals. Phillip is probably having a fight with Donna.' Carlton didn't want to admit it to his friends but the severe beating he had inflicted on the scout had felt good. It was empowering, he thought. I bet *that* scout don't think I'm nothing. *I* saved Curvis. Bullet could've never handled that guy on his own. When I'm like *that* no one can fuck with me.

'Kids in your house are lucky,' said Curvis. 'In my house the teenagers have to make the young ones their breakfast. My housemother says it teaches us responsibility. I said to her, she's a lazy witch. When I was talking, I'd call her Ruth. She *hated* it. The bitch even complained to my social worker.'

'Carlton's sure lucky he's in Auntie Josephine's house,' Glenroy commented. 'Even my Uncle Thomas used to treat him good.' Carlton visibly winced at the mention of the name. 'When we were little,' Glenroy continued. 'After swimming he used to buy sweets and stuff for Carlton up the shops.'

'That's 'cos I used to behave myself,' answered Carlton, very uncomfortable. 'It didn't mean I *liked* the fucker.'

'He used to buy Elvin sweets an' all,' added Bullet. 'He's never bought me anything! He don't even say hello to me.'

Carlton went quiet as he watched his friends. That's how he does it, he told himself. He used to give me sweets and the odd sixpence. Fucking bastard! I can't believe I ever liked him when I was a kid! I wonder if Thomas will come up here looking for us. If he does, I won't run from him. No fucking way! Only the trees will see what I'll do to him.

'You're luckier than most,' said Glenroy. 'And Uncle Rodney don't believe in kids eating sweets. He reminds me of that kid-snatching man in *Chitty Chitty Bang Bang.*'

'Uncle Rodney doesn't even believe in kids smiling,' offered Curvis. 'If he had his own way he'd have us marching up and down in Pinewood Oaks in army uniform, singing the fucking National Anthem.'

'He probably bursts into tears when he watches *The Dambusters*,' remarked Glenroy. 'Fucking loser. He probably fucks an Action Man instead of his wife – that's why he ain't got no kids.'

And I wonder if he fucks with kids too, Carlton thought secretly.

Glenroy was laughing as he approached Bullet, wanting his turn with the pen-knife to etch his name in the tree. Bullet gave him the blade. 'He ain't that bad,' Bullet said, displaying his palms. 'It's just that sometimes he thinks he's still in the Royal Air Force. When I first come to Pinewood Oaks, he would line us up and inspect our fingernails and behind our ears. If they were dirty, he would send us to have a bath, giving us a mighty tough scrubbing brush. But he don't do that now.'

'I think he's heard too many bombs in the war,' laughed Curvis. 'Maybe some nerve gas is still inside his brain and he thinks that all kids are Germans.'

'Nerve gas wasn't used in the Second World War,' affirmed Bullet. 'Besides, how could he hear bombs when he's dropping 'em from a plane?'

Curvis delved into his holdall and pulled out a clean, but crumpled white T-shirt. He took off the top he was wearing and donned the fresh one. 'I hope you lot got your swimming things,' he asked. 'I did tell ya all before we left.'

'Yeah,' answered Bullet.

Curvis and Bullet then looked at Glenroy, who avoided eye contact. 'On the night we done a runner,' he stuttered. 'I was all nervous and that, and I forgot my trunks.'

'I knew you would forget something,' berated Curvis. 'I'm surprised you remembered the pillows!'

'Anybody got a spare pair of shorts?' Bullet asked.

'Yeah, I have,' answered Carlton, snapping out of his silence. 'He can use my football shorts.'

Bullet pushed his pen-knife into his back pocket and trundled down the small hill. 'Stop sulking, you baby. Carlton's got a spare pair of shorts.'

Curvis watched Bullet and Glenroy with concern. He turned to Carlton. 'Take it easy on him. You know what he's like.'

'Yeah, but sometimes he does stupid things,' Carlton said,

182

impatience creeping over his face. 'Last night he started to wander about, telling me he heard some voices. He reckoned that the scouts followed us up here. Then he was going on about that girl in your story, telling me that at night she becomes a witch. I wish you'd never told the fucking tale. It's given him the creeps.'

'He's more shit scared of the dark than I realised,' admitted Curvis, stealing a glance at Glenroy. 'Maybe we should move to clearer ground.'

'Then we'll get caught – someone's bound to see us.'

'Not if we find a good spot.'

'There ain't no good spot. If we're in the open we'll be in danger. No! We'll stay here. It's only Glenroy who's scared of the dark!'

'If you say so,' yielded Curvis, slightly shocked at the angry tone of Carlton's voice.

Ten minutes later, Carlton and Curvis were smiling as they watched Glenroy and Bullet have another bout of wrestling. 'That story about the girl,' Carlton wondered. 'Is it true?'

'It's true alright,' said Curvis. 'I was up here one day and asked a woman why the stony hills are called the Seven Sisters, she practically told me the same story as the old man. She said it happened a *long* time ago.'

'Well, fuck me!' exclaimed Carlton. 'So we really could find a dead body up here.'

'Who knows?' replied Curvis, shrugging his shoulders.

'Who knows! Is that all you can say? Maybe Glenroy's right when he says there's a witch here at night.' Carlton chuckled, making it easier for Curvis to think his last comment was made in jest. But in a corner of his mind the ghost of a witch roaming the forest at night tugged his imagination.

'Don't be ridiculous.'

'Yeah, I s'pose you're right . . . Come to think of it, when we were younger, Glenroy hated the orchard. He really believed the story of the invisible bogey-man.'

Curvis said nothing in response. He, too, believed in the tale of the bogey-man when he was a kid but felt he would lose face if he admitted it. He remembered how the bogey-man was supposed to be eight feet tall, dripping with a gooey, green slime that was only displayed when he was eating a victim. He had a disfigured face that looked like mushy, stale cheese and a massive, snorting nose with nostrils that an Action Man could make camp in. The bogey-man only ventured out at night, prowling the part of the orchard where even teenagers didn't tread, looking for children who did not go home on time. If by chance the bogey-man came across kids, it would consume them through his nostrils, making a horrific grinding sound like an industrial Hoover sucking up a boulder too big for its hose. 'I think living where we do, our imaginations run a bit wild,' Curvis finally said. 'And up here it can run riot . . . Right now I wanna go swimming, I feel so sticky.'

Carlton thought about what Curvis had said. Perhaps it was just his imagination running away with him. Beating up that man last night wasn't imagination though. It was real – I could smell the tobacco on his breath. I saw his scared eyes. I know I'm protecting my friends but I didn't have to go *that* far. Maybe there is something else about this forest. Some kinda force that makes you go over the top. He didn't want to think what it was. 'So, how do we get to Spurleigh Way from here?' asked Carlton.

'It's about three miles,' answered Curvis. 'We head north west, go over the hills.' He pointed the way. 'And Spurleigh Way is on the other side of Pig Folly's Shaw.'

'Pig Folly's what? What the fuck is a shaw?'

'A small wood.' Curvis shook his head, not understanding why everyone didn't know the meaning of such words. He ferreted in his bag and drew out a weather-beaten compass. 'This will come in handy now.'

'How much is it to get in at Spurleigh Way pool?' Carlton asked, fearful of the answer.

184

'Last time I went it was forty pence for kids,' replied Curvis, watching Bullet and Glenroy who were still wrestling.

'Forty pence!' cried Carlton. 'That's a pound sixty for all of us. Ain't there no wall we can climb over?'

'Er, yeah, but we're in enough trouble already. It'll be worth paying the price. I dunno about you but I feel like I've got ladybirds crawling about in my pants and I'm itching all over. And I ain't going back to the scout lake!' Curvis raised a hand to Bullet and Glenroy. 'Hey, you two! We're going in a minute. Come and help us tidy up.'

Ten minutes later, the friends set off, carrying their swimwear and towels within their holdalls. They paced themselves sensibly, emerging out of the forest twenty minutes later in a valley. Curvis led them through copses, across two streams and over a long hill until they gazed down on the hamlet of Spurleigh. Bullet imagined a military mission with an expert team going beyond enemy lines on the journey, and while he wasn't dreaming, wished he had a football to kick on the way.

Circled by a ring road, the small town had straight avenues and detached houses with tidy front gardens, backdropped by a golf course. All the kids they saw seemed to have chopper bikes and there was even a toy shop in the high street, next door to a bank.

'Come on,' said Curvis. 'Not far to go now.' He pointed to a highway. 'The pool's at the end of that road.'

Although it was a school day, the open-air pool was packed with young bathers and toddlers, running about on the grassed banks around the swimming area, shrieking with glee. Adults were sunning themselves on long towels, and pool attendants, dressed in brightly coloured sleeveless shirts and white shorts with whistles hanging around their necks, preened themselves in the sun.

At the pool, the friends swam away their troubles, playing tag in and out of the water. They were all accomplished swimmers and dived straight into the water. Glenroy, with his fleshy torso, seemed to float on the water with minimal effort. Bullet was a busy swimmer, all arms and legs, making large splashes. By contrast, Curvis, owner of the physique of a long-distance runner, hardly disturbed the pool, performing long, elegant strokes. They remained at Spurleigh for the rest of the morning and early afternoon when Carlton suggested they'd better move on before schools were out in case any pupil on their way home recognised him.

Turning back to base by 4.30 p.m., Glenroy took out of his bag his pad of paper and pencils and started to sketch. He sat cross-legged, supporting the paper on his lap. Carlton set off to the café to collect some water, carrying three empty Coca-Cola bottles. Curvis was busy picking leaves off shrubs; he wanted to improve his friends' bedding as well as adding to the camouflage of the camp. Bullet collected all the rubbish and in a spot twenty yards away from the camp had cleared an area the size of a discus free of leaves and twigs. He had matches in his pocket, but decided, for a reason he didn't know, to try and start a fire with two sturdy twigs, gouging out a small hole in one of them.

'Bullet, what you doing?' Curvis asked, looking over to him.

'Trying to start a fire, innit. Get rid of the rubbish – it's really built up.'

Curvis dropped the leaves in his arms and rushed over to Bullet. 'Are you fucking mad? We'll all fucking burn! The heatwave has left everything really dry. If something catches alight it'll burn half the forest before we can say tim-tam-tommy.'

'Sorry,' Bullet offered. 'I was just trying to see if I could do it. Like say the batteries run out and I didn't bring my matches, we'd have to learn how to build a fire.' No need to talk to me like I'm a fucking idiot, Bullet thought. Only trying to help. Why does he do all the ordering around?

186

'Look, if you want something to do,' said Curvis, wagging his right index finger. 'Give me a hand picking those dock leaves; they're better to sleep on than the hard earth.'

Glenroy seemed to be immune to the exchange taking place. He simply concentrated on the figure he was sketching, rubber in his left hand and pencil in his right.

An hour later, Carlton returned, his bottles now filled with water. 'Next time we need water, I think I'd better go somewhere else and get it; the woman at the counter looked at me weird. She didn't charge me for the water though.'

'Yeah, you're right,' agreed Curvis. 'Must be somewhere we can get water 'round here.'

Carlton saw dock leaves covering the ground. 'Fuck me! You've been busy. I'll look forward to sleeping tonight.'

'It's alright, innit?' said Bullet. 'Me and Curvis did it. Glenroy just sat down and started to draw – lazy sod.'

Glenroy looked up, finally acknowledging Carlton's presence. 'Wotcha, Carlton. Give us one of them bottles.'

Carlton had a silly grin on his face. 'Not until you show me what you've done.' Carlton, Bullet and Curvis had never seen any of Glenroy's artistry before.

'Yeah! Let's have a look,' urged Bullet.

'No!' Glenroy refused. 'You can keep your fucking water.'

'Oh, stop being childish, Glenroy,' said Curvis disapprovingly. 'We won't laugh.'

Glenroy turned his pad upside down as Carlton approached. 'I want Bullet to promise – I know what he's like.'

'Promise, Bullet,' ordered Carlton, placing the bottles on the ground.

'Alright, alright,' Bullet replied, thinking the whole thing was immature. '*I promise.*'

Glenroy turned over his pad. His friends ran to get a look. Their eyes widened and their mouths opened.

'That's . . . that's . . .' Carlton stuttered. 'It's really good. Fucking hell. It's *really* good.'

Bullet nodded and Curvis looked at Glenroy in astonishment. 'So much detail,' Bullet remarked. 'Why didn't you tell us you were good at art? And who is it?'

Glenroy smiled his widest ever smile. 'It's Gemmele. I don't show my drawings to anybody, not even Uncle Thomas. He would say they're rubbish.'

'When we get back,' said Carlton, 'you should show the fucker. He can't think of you as mental if you show him what you can do. He'll get the shock of his life.'

'Too right,' added Curvis. 'You could go to college or something drawing like that.'

Glenroy's drawing caught the despair of a young girl. The eyes were intense, her innocent expression was framed by long hair that parted in the middle and reached down to her hips. She seemed to be scared of something. She was wearing a simple dress and was barefoot. In the background were trees that even included the contours of their bark.

Carlton couldn't remove his eyes from the sketch, and to him, the girl of Curvis's story was now made real. Maybe Glenroy has seen her, he thought. Even if he saw her in a dream it would make her real. People don't dream about drawings. He must have seen the face. He *must*'ve. How did he know she's got freckles? Or how her nose is shaped. And those eyes! Something weird is going on here.

9.30 p.m.

Miss Gallagher peered through her kitchen window and watched a policeman and a woman constable pull up in a light-blue panda car outside her cottage. They got out of the car and watched the dusk begin to settle in; the sun disappearing over the forking branches of the oak trees, creating a light green, reddish glow. The male officer knocked

188

at the letter-box impatiently. Miss Gallagher's frame came into vision through the misted glass.

'Good evening,' she greeted, smiling pleasantly. 'I was expecting you at nine o' clock . . . But you're here now. Can I get one of the children to make you a cup of tea or perhaps a cool drink? My, when will the heatwave end?'

'No, thank you,' replied the policeman. 'We've already had cold drinks at the last house.'

Miss Gallagher led the officers into the recently hoovered and dusted sitting room; usually the children would watch television here but Miss Gallagher had emptied the room two hours ago, then ordered one of her teenage charges to make it spick and span. The officers looked around them and thought the room had a clinical feel. Just the basics were here, including a large black and white television and a brown, buttoned three-piece suite. There were no pictures hanging from the straw-coloured wallpaper and no plants. The policeman pulled out a small notebook from his breast pocket and waited for Miss Gallagher to take her seat elegantly in an armchair before he spoke.

'Are you Miss Gallagher?' he asked.

'Yes, that's right. I am the officer in charge of this house,' Miss Gallagher replied automatically.

'Now, it is Curvis who resides here,' began the policeman. 'We are just calling to seek some background information about the boys who have run away. I want to make that clear because where we called previously, the gentleman seemed to think we were on a witch-hunt . . . Is there anything you can tell us to aid our search?'

'Curvis was treated very well here,' Miss Gallagher answered defiantly, looking down her nose. 'The staff treated him just like a son and I'm sure the reason he ran away was because of the influence of his friends.'

The policewoman scribbled down notes. Miss Gallagher stole a cautious glance at her. Reading his own notes, the policeman continued. 'Can you tell me the reason why Curvis was not told of his brother's whereabouts? The social worker was a bit vague on this issue.'

Miss Gallagher folded her arms abruptly. 'After a case meeting, seven weeks ago, it was decided that Stanton would have a bad effect on his brother. The decision was *not* entirely mine. All my staff concurred with the notion and it *was* approved by the social worker *and* his supervisor. You see, officer, life has been hard enough for Curvis, and we thought he could do without seeing his violent brother in a detention centre. You couldn't know of the psychological harm it would have done to the boy, who's still only fifteen.'

Leaning forward, the female officer rested her writing hand. 'Don't you think that this decision was a contributory factor in Curvis's decision to run away?'

'*No*, I do not!' Miss Gallagher inhaled sharply, trying to restrain her anger. 'Curvis knew that the decision was made for his benefit and I'm sure he understood it.'

'Did Curvis say he understood the decision?' probed the woman constable.

'Yes. I put it to him and he was calm about it. He didn't make a scene.' Miss Gallagher scratched her nose and put her hand to her mouth, as if stifling a cough. The female officer watched the housemother keenly, trying to decipher her body language. 'We have made enquiries and have learned that Curvis and his brother were extremely close, and hated to be separated,' she said bluntly, her voice tinged with frustration.

'The decision was taken to *protect* Curvis,' insisted Miss Gallagher, talking at the carpet with hands clasped together.

'But hasn't the boy a right to know where his brother is?' asked the policewoman, her personal feelings overriding her task.

'With respect! We know a lot more about teenagers than *you* do!'

190

'We are straying from our point,' said the male officer. 'Our job is to bring the boys back safe,' he said, glaring at his colleague.

'As I said before,' Miss Gallagher butted in, 'the decision was made for Curvis's well-being. You see, Stanton is nothing like Curvis. Stanton is very violent and always got into terrible fights. He was a hooligan. But Curvis is quiet and reserved and very polite, nothing like his brother. You wouldn't believe they are related.'

'Yes, I'm sure that's true, Miss Gallagher,' the policeman said, reading his notes. 'Now let's get back on touch . . . We have checked with the local bus depots and no one can remember seeing four boys board a bus in the Pinewoods area on the night or morning that they ran away. We thought we had a lead after hearing there was some trouble at the scout complex in the Pinewood Hills, but apparently the trouble-makers were all grown men in their twenties. Sometimes, after young men drink too much in the Pinewood Inn, they wander off into the hills, causing all sorts of mayhem.'

Miss Gallagher tutted.

'We are assuming that the boys must have gone on foot wherever they were heading,' the policeman resumed. 'And in most cases, runaways head for London. Yesterday we spoke to Curvis's uncle and he says he hasn't seen Curvis; he appears to be very concerned. Do you know if Curvis has any friends in the Lambeth area?'

'Not that I know of,' answered Miss Gallagher, raising her head and looking down her nose again. 'He only has friends in Pinewood Oaks, none at school. His teachers say he's a loner.'

'Yes, we heard,' said the woman officer.

'Is there anybody else who he knows outside the grounds of Pinewood Oaks?' asked the policeman. 'Any girlfriends?'

'Good gracious, no. He's very shy with girls. After school he comes straight home. He's not interested in sports, not like that uncouth Carlton boy. He doesn't even watch television that often. The only programmes he watches are those nature documentaries.'

The female officer scribbled down notes with Miss Gallagher looking on suspiciously. The housemother turned to glare at the policeman. 'So *what* other ways do you have for pursuing your enquiries? Have you actually searched for them yet?'

'We have informed most of the police stations in the Surrey, Kent border area and have also alerted the Met stations in London, presenting full descriptions of the boys. I can assure you we are doing everything we can.'

Miss Gallagher narrowed her eyes.

'We are due to check the local railway stations in the morning,' the policeman announced. 'Perhaps someone who issued tickets on that morning, or the night before, will remember four teenagers fitting our descriptions – they did have money to travel.' The policeman inspected his watch. 'If there is anything you can't think of now you can help us with, but maybe might remember tomorrow, please feel free to call us at the station. We are taking this matter very seriously indeed.'

'I should think so,' replied Miss Gallagher.

The officers stood up and made their way out of the room, not waiting for the housemother to escort them out. Miss Gallagher cursed something under her breath as she followed the police officers. They got to the front door and the policeman turned around, preparing his farewell. 'Miss Gallagher, I *do* know that the kids in this place are not easy to care for with the backgrounds most of them come from. So with that in mind, unless they commit a serious crime, as soon as we find them, we will hand them over to social services and they can take their own disciplinary measures.'

'That's good to hear, constable,' Miss Gallagher nodded. 'They may well decide to send them to a more secure unit – they have all bitten the hand that feeds them.'

'Goodbye, Miss Gallagher,' the policewoman said coolly, her eyes contemptuous. 'We will be in touch as soon as we hear something.' She closed the door behind her.

Once they reached their car, the policewoman leaned on the bonnet and turned to her colleague. 'What do you think?'

'I don't know,' the policeman replied, looking at the cottage. 'It seems everybody we have talked to tonight is hiding something. We know Curvis's motive, but surely there must be something more. Something is not quite right.'

The policewoman nodded and fished in her pockets for her car keys. 'That Mr Thomas Pearson, he was very nervous.'

'Yes, I noticed that. He certainly was smoking heavily and spoke through his fingers many times in response to our questions. He was also a bit *over*-nice.'

'Yes, he was. He would have cooked us an early Christmas dinner if we'd asked him!'

They both chuckled, taking in their surroundings and drawn by the twilight beauty of the orchard. 'But there is something very strange about him,' added the policewoman. 'I can't quite put my finger on it.'

'They're all a bit strange and eccentric,' said the policeman. 'That Rodney character who lined up the kids in his house to give us a formal greeting. He's another one, but I suppose to care for the kids in this place, you have to be a bit mad.'

'But it's that Mr Pearson,' the policewoman said, shaking her head, her face in deep thought. 'Glenroy's the boy in that house, isn't he? The way Pearson kissed that little boy on the forehead before he went to bed . . . it was unsettling. Not what Pearson did but the way the boy reacted. He flinched.'

'That's normal. No boy likes to be kissed goodnight. He probably felt embarrassed because we were there to see it.'

'Yes, I suppose you're right.' She climbed into the car and turned on the ignition. The policeman joined her in the passenger seat. 'Who knows what really happens in these places,' he said. 'The social workers wouldn't let us read the files of the boys, they all had a meeting without asking for our attendance, and they are petrified about the press hearing of this matter. It's like investigating the Masons.'

'I just feel sorry for the boys,' the policewoman said, hitting first gear and feeling the roll of a road-ramp. 'It's obvious from what we heard today that once they're caught, they'll be separated and placed God knows where . . . I wonder where they are now.'

Heat of the Night

The temperature had only dropped a few degrees lower than it had been in the afternoon sun. The bushes and tree leaves were moistened by the humidity, producing a thick scent that hung in the air; the four runaways could taste it on their lips. They moved stealthily through the tangled wood; even Glenroy was sure of his footing now.

The boys had made their way from their base to the eastern side of the forest, crossing from Surrey into Kent, beyond the Pinewood Hills and near to a bush-lined road with cats' eyes peering brightly from the asphalt. Curvis, shining his torch in front of him, led the way. Carlton was in the rear. 'Can't be much further to the big house?'

'I can't see it yet,' answered Curvis, thinking this adventure was not as great as he thought half an hour ago. 'It must be soon though.'

Glenroy was immediately behind Curvis. 'What are we gonna do when we get to the house?'

'Have a look round, innit,' replied Bullet, dreaming of a military raid on a sleeping enemy. 'The house is massive.'

Late in the afternoon, after spying on the scouts, Carlton offered to take his friends 'for a long walk and see what they come across'. Curvis made sure he used his compass so they could return safely. They had stumbled on the mansion while on their trek. None of the teenagers had ever seen a house quite like it. It was a ranch-type building which seemed to stretch out the length of a playground. Carlton was fascinated by the French shutters and the huge windows, and they all wondered who lived in such a house, deciding to revisit it at night. Bullet reckoned a footballer lived there.

'Glenroy, Bullet! Help me clear away the stingers,' ordered Curvis, standing in front of nettles with a green-meshed fence about seven foot in height on the other side. 'Fucking hell!' Curvis exclaimed. 'I didn't see the fence 'til I was right here. Look, the house is over there.' He pointed his finger. Bullet and Curvis east-wested their torches.

Fronting the mansion was a manicured garden with narrow pathways criss-crossing it. Garden chairs were placed around white tables with yellow and white striped umbrellas sprouting out of them. A pond was rimmed with a rockery, its stones knee-high. A large greenhouse, reflecting the moon and stars, was beside a wooden hut. A paved path curled its way from the back of the garden to the wooden-panelled back door of the house. No lights were on in the dwelling, its walls covered with hardwood, varnished panels.

'Some film star must live here,' said Glenroy, kicking away the nettles. 'The pond is about as big as the swimming pool at Pinewood Oaks.'

'Who's coming over then?' challenged Carlton. 'To have a look round.'

Glenroy began to climb the fence. 'Last one over is a tosspot!'

Seconds later, all four were on the other side of the green fence, adrenalin surging through them. They stood before an immaculate, colourful flowerbed. Glenroy simply walked across it. Curvis shook his head as he and the others stepped around it. They headed for the greenhouse, thinking of food. 'Glenroy,' Carlton whispered. *'Don't* wander off.'

Carlton opened the transparent greenhouse door carefully, as if there might be a bomb attached to the handle. They crept in. Potted, varied plants hung from twined baskets, the colours forming a kaleidoscope. Strange-looking buds were forming in trays on shelves and bags of peat and earth were resting on the floor. A garden manual was open on a small wooden table. Curvis noticed something. 'Hey, look, tomatoes.'

The other three joined Curvis, and without hesitation, Glenroy plucked a tomato and tasted it. Carlton's eyes were trained on the windows of the house. 'Not bad,' Glenroy remarked. 'They're better than the ones that grow in Pinewood Oaks – try one.'

They sat down on the dusty floor and tested the ripeness of the fruit. After eating his tomato in three bites, Bullet slipped out of the greenhouse and stood outside, eyeing the hut. Curiosity getting the better of him, he lifted the latch. He pushed the door ajar and, to his dismay, watched a garden fork fall helplessly to the ground. It hit the concrete floor with a thud. 'Shit!'

'Bullet! What the fuck are you doing?' boomed Carlton.

'I just pushed the door and the bleedin' thing fell down, innit.'

Curvis scanned the windows of the mansion. Glenroy started to bite into another tomato. Carlton glared at Bullet. Bullet hastily returned to the greenhouse. A light was switched on in a bedroom. The sound of startled feet descending stairs was just about audible. Curvis saw the light. 'I don't think whoever's coming is gonna give us cups of tea and custard creams. *Move!*

Something four-legged, or maybe eight-legged was approaching rapidly from the side of the house. 'Dogs! Leg it!' screamed Curvis.

Glenroy spat out his tomato and bolted out of the greenhouse, heading for the fence. Bullet and Carlton sprinted with him. Curvis, momentarily in shock, was left behind for a crucial three seconds before he started moving. Glenroy performed an almighty leap on the fence. Bullet and Carlton soon realised that Curvis might not make it. Carlton grabbed his arm. 'Come on!' The Dobermans displayed their teeth, getting closer. The barking disturbed the quiet of the night, birds fluttered in the trees. A human shadow appeared by the back door of the mansion. The dogs neared their prey. Bullet, having no time to jump on the fence and get high enough, picked up a plant pot. Carlton collected a smiling gnome with a fishing rod in his hand that was beside the pond. Curvis was rooted in fear. Canine jaws were slavering. Bullet threw the pot, missing a Doberman's head, but the creature became more cautious. Glenroy was up and over the fence, his body leaving a dent in the mesh. Carlton scored a hit with the happy gnome, striking a dog in its side. The two animals halted their advance and resorted to barking. The shadow by the door moved. Curvis, regaining his composure, sprinted to the fence. 'Give us your hand!' yelled Glenroy. 'I'll pull you over.'

Bullet and Carlton soon joined Curvis clambering over the fence. Bullet's T-shirt got caught on a stray piece of mesh. The dog sped towards Bullet.

'Pull him! Just pull him!' screamed Curvis, who was now on the other side of the fence.

'Swing your fucking legs!' yelled Glenroy.

Bullet, not heeding the advice of his friends, scrambled over the barrier, ripping his T-shirt. *This is private property,* a man bellowed. '*Get off my land or I'll be forced to call the police!*'

'Shut up and suck your dogs!' Glenroy returned. He picked up a stone and threw it at the greenhouse. A loud smash distracted the barking dogs and they went to investigate. Another bedroom light was switched on.

'What you do that for?' rebuked Curvis. 'The place is gonna be crawling with the Old Bill and we've still got to cross the road to get back to our camp!'

'Fucking snob!' Glenroy replied. 'I should've put the stone through one of the windows.'

'Do something like that again and I'll put a stone in your head,' rebuked Bullet, his anger more directed at the dogs. That was too fucking close, he sighed to himself. What would they do if I got caught? They wouldn't come back for me. Fuck doing something like this again.

Ignoring Bullet, Carlton picked up another stone and threw it, aiming at the man. Curvis didn't wait to see if the missile hit its target. For half a second Bullet glared at Carlton, primed to rebuke him but thought better of it. He turned and ran. Glenroy stood motionless, staring ahead.

'Come on, Glenroy. We'd better get on our bikes,' said Carlton. 'Fucking rich wanker.'

The intruders quickly weaved their way through the coppice, confident enough to set off in a trot, sure of their way. Curvis took the lead, shining his torch in front of him. 'This reminds me of the time Uncle Rodney told us about the war in Burma and the Malaysian jungle,' panted Bullet, wanting to divert any possible thoughts that his friends might have on his fears back at the mansion. I've *never* been so frightened, he admitted to himself.

'Here he goes again,' sighed Carlton. 'Telling us one of Uncle Rodney's war stories.'

Glenroy and Curvis nodded, feeling themselves veterans of these tales by now. Bullet was irrepressible. 'There were about a thousand Allies in the jungle surrounded by about ten thousand Japs,' Bullet began, his voice mimicking the tones of Lord Olivier who narrated *The World at War*.

'More like ten thousand Allies being chased by a thousand Japs,' chuckled Carlton. 'Those Japs were fucking mad!'

'Them tomatoes were alright,' mentioned Glenroy.

'Yeah, but we're lucky we're not a fucking dog's supper,' said Curvis.

'Don't you wanna hear the story?' moaned Bullet.

'I know the story,' said Carlton. 'Tarzan come to the rescue with his chimp and killed five thousand Japs on his own. Two thousand got killed in quicksand and the others shot themselves 'cos they couldn't take missing *The Water Margin* programme.'

'What the fuck is the Water Margin?' asked Curvis.

'That stupid programme about karate, where men jump in trees and fight on top of houses and a second later, they're fighting in mountains.'

'So you don't wanna hear how a lot of the Allied soldiers got awarded their Victoria Crosses?' snapped Bullet, his face yielding to frustration.

'Oh, go on then, if it's gonna kill ya.'

They slowed down to a march, feeling secure that no enemy was behind them. An owl watched their progress as an unseen beak hammered against a tree-trunk. 'You're right, Carlton, when you said there was quicksand,' resumed Bullet. 'But also there was those vampire leeches, bigger than Glenroy's feet.'

'Bigger than Glenroy's feet!' laughed Carlton. 'They must've looked hideous.'

'Fuck you,' riposted Glenroy. 'I ain't got big feet.'

Bullet continued. 'The Allies were running out of food and stuff and the Japs were closing in.'

'Did they remember to pack their toilet paper?' laughed Carlton. ''Cos we didn't. I scratched up my arse this morning with those dock leaves. It's fucking rough. I'm gonna look for something softer in the morning.'

'Oh, if you're not gonna listen, then fuck off,' complained Bullet.

'And Bullet,' Curvis reprimanded, 'stop doing your shitting near the camp! I nearly walked in your crap this morning.'

'Fuck me!' said Carlton. '*That* was a brush with death.'

As they neared the Pinewood Hills road, they lay flat on the ground, immersing themselves in long grass. The odd car went by and when Curvis deemed it was safe, they continued their trek back to their base, the mounds and hillocks becoming more difficult to negotiate as they grew weary. They settled for the night on the now dirty and grass-stained blankets, below which were scores of leaves. They feasted on Carlton's cakes and biscuits.

Curvis knew the food wouldn't last longer than two days and thought of seeking out allotments near the farms for a food source. He wondered why he had allowed their excursion to the mansion at night. We're starting to do stupid things, he thought. Carlton's getting more audacious by the hour. What would've happened if he had hit that guy in the head? He thinks he can do anything and get away with it. Glenroy ain't much better. It was a hell of a risk. Why didn't I say no? He admitted to himself that even he revelled in the adrenalin rush. He looked around at his surroundings and concluded that the forest was daring them to walk with danger. 'Yeah,' he whispered. 'You're daring us.'

Bullet sat up, peeling a stick with his pen-knife, honing a point. He was still thinking of his narrow escape from the dogs. He looked around into the forest as if there were wild hounds at large. Perhaps they'll attack us while we're sleeping. We're not in no fucking house to keep 'em out. *Anything* could happen in this forest, especially at night.

Carlton looked up to the stars, noticing how some shone brilliantly while others were barely visible. He watched the trees' fingertips move gently above his head before switching his gaze to Glenroy. I wonder what kinda dreams he has, he thought. He must've dreamed of Gemmele. He goes on stupid but he's *something*. He can draw. That makes him something. I could never do anything like that. How did he learn to draw so good? Fucking *how*!

Glenroy surveyed the darkness around him, then looked at Curvis. 'That girl, did she play in the woods when it was dark?'

Curvis sat up and grabbed his torch, beaming it into the hollow. 'I dunno. Can't see how she could've been scared of the dark when she lived all her life near the forest.'

'She might have run away just like us,' Glenroy suggested. 'Maybe her mum and dad used to hit her all the time. Just like what happened to me when I was younger. I wonder if real parents hit their children like the housemothers and housefathers do. Maybe they get hit three times a week instead of every day.'

Curvis thought about Glenroy's last question and quickly realised that neither he nor any of his friends had any idea of normal family life. None of them had close friends outside Pinewood Oaks and normal family life was as far away as the stars. He thought of his mother and what life would have been like if his father hadn't killed her.

Carlton interrupted his thoughts. 'Will you two ever shut up about this girl? Glenroy, you've gone on about Curvis's story *every* night since we come here. It's getting on my nerves! Anyway, I don't give a fuck what happened to her.'

'Would you say that if one of us went missing?' probed Curvis.

'Course not!'

Bullet pushed his stick into the earth. 'Maybe she was eaten by mad, nutter hounds. You ever seen that film? *The Hound of The Baskervilles*. The dog is about as big as a horse.'

'I saw it once,' revealed Carlton. 'They were mad to go after it.'

'It's just a film,' said Curvis. 'You lot really let your imaginations run mad.'

'The story of that little girl weren't a film,' affirmed Carlton. 'You told me it was definitely true.'

'Yeah,' said Bullet. 'When all this is over, I'm gonna check if she's still officially missing.'

'What will happen if we go missing?' asked Glenroy. 'Will they have a big search for us?'

'Glenroy, we are missing,' pointed out Curvis.

'No, no. Say six months from now,' said Glenroy, his face serious. He looked at his friends one by one. 'Will they just give up? Say we were murdered up here, no one would fucking know. We'll be lying dead somewhere, just like that little girl. And 'cos she didn't get a Christian burial, she's now a ghost in the daytime and a witch at night . . . No one gave her the last rites. Father Patrick told me that if someone don't get the last rites, their soul has trouble getting to heaven. That's why Gemmele's probably haunting this forest.'

For a moment they all looked at each other.

'For fuck's sake!' snapped Carlton, slamming his right fist into the ground. 'Stop bringing her up. Just fucking shut up! Father Patrick talks out of his arse!' He started to sweat and wished he had the courage to tell Curvis that this place frightened him and they should leave for open ground. He was beginning to feel claustrophobic here. He thought it was ridiculous. Claustrophobic in a fucking forest! To him, the perspiration of his forehead began to smell like chlorine. The chlorine of the swimming pool back in Pinewood Oaks . . . In *that* cubicle . . . Uncle Thomas. His insides shook and he desperately tried to rid himself of the image.

'They'll soon realise that we're up here,' said Curvis. 'Especially after last night and what happened with the scouts. The Old Bill might have already looked for us in the daytime. Let 'em search until we're ready to go back. Who knows, our names might be in the local papers.'

'Uncle Thomas is gonna kill me,' said Glenroy. 'He's gonna fucking kill me.'

'Only if the witch don't get you first,' laughed Bullet.

'No he's not!' Carlton spat. 'He's *not* going to touch anyone!'

Curvis studied Carlton and thought his last statement was a promise of violence. Maybe I should take 'em to clearer ground. Bullet was looking down at the earth. He still wanted to scold Carlton for throwing the stone at the man outside the mansion. Why didn't Curvis tell him off about it? he wondered. You can't just pick fights with anybody. Even here in the forest, there have to be some rules.

An hour and a half later, Curvis, Bullet and Glenroy were asleep. Carlton was drifting in the surreal chasm between slumber and insomnia. His mind recalled an incident in the past.

He was five years old, lying in his bed. Awake. Two hours before his mother had kissed him goodnight, the lipstick still remained on his forehead. The fragrance she was wearing was unknown to him but it was nice. He liked the way she tucked him in and ruffled his hair, her hands so soft. But now she was gone. Left the house for a place he didn't know, leaving him alone. In the dark. All he had for company was a dummy. His mother had tried to wean him off it but he cried the house down in protest. He sucked on the dummy feverishly and he would keep on sucking until she returned. A few more hours he would have to wait. In the dark. Not daring to get up and turn on a light or to peer out the window for his mother's return. The room was cold. Blackness surrounded him and he felt bound to his bed. He refused to answer a call of nature, preferring to wet his bed. She'll have to see to me as soon as she gets in, he thought. She'll have to wash me. She knows I never wet my bed if she's here. But she ain't. She's gone.

Dancing in the Dark

10.15 a.m., 15 June 1976

Carlton sat up, uncomfortable from his distracted sleep; a multitude of emotions preyed on his mind: guilt, fear, anger. He plucked a blade of grass out of the ground, placed it in his mouth and sucked on it. The morning skylark's song soothed his troubles, and he could smell the dew mingle with the strong scent of the pines. His eyes squinted as he looked up at the bright June sky. He was in his rightful place, he thought to himself, beside his friends. They wouldn't leave him. He smiled as he watched his mates, resting peacefully. 'Four of us mighty are we,' he whispered.

He was glad that he had found a moment for himself for it gave him time to think. Glenroy wasn't whining, Bullet was not reciting tales from the Allied campaign in Burma, and he was not having to absorb Curvis's bitterness towards the people in charge of Pinewood Oaks. The feelings of his friends were infectious and invaded his own memories – picking out moments in the past. He hadn't dislodged the memory of his mother slapping him for wetting the bed. His mother's harsh voice still rang inside his head. *'There's a toilet in this place, fucking use it!'*

He rubbed his eyes and delved into his bag, unzipping a small compartment in his holdall and counted the cash that was remaining: seven pounds sixty. Guilt struck him again. Auntie Josephine grew large in his mind and he recalled all her kindly words of advice and encouragement. These were quickly superimposed with images of his own mother and memories of the last time he saw her – in the spring of 1974. He was already at Pinewood Oaks. That morning he had refused to see his mother and ran away to the orchard where he and his friends had made their hideout, not returning home until past midnight. His mother was distraught and Josephine had to comfort her the best way she could, telling her gently that the last green bus always departed outside Pinewood Oaks at 11.10 p.m. Josephine walked her to the bus stop, unaware that Carlton was observing from the bush. 'You fucking bitch,' Carlton had whispered.

About thirty yards away, its roots hidden by shrubbery, Carlton approached the tallest of the trees. Once he reached the base of the trunk he looked up at its looming height. 'And good morning to you,' he whispered. He was going to climb it, he told himself, gripping the branches firmly. 'Now, don't snap on me.' He skilfully ascended the tree. From its branches as he climbed higher he could see the vast area of woodland and sprawling plains beyond. The windmill stood lazily a mile away. He had an excellent view of the seven barrow hills, looping south-west, their stones sunwashed. In his mind, he saw Glenroy's sketched creation, Gemmele. Her face was so pretty and carefree. She was running and laughing, careering up and down the hills with her hair trailing in the breeze. She must have run up and down there loads of time, he thought.

'Hey, monkey,' Glenroy called. 'What you doing up there?'

'Just looking,' Carlton replied, marvelling at the glorious view, spitting out the grass from his mouth.

'What are we having for breakfast? I'm starving,' complained Glenroy, holding the drooping flesh of his stomach.

'Eat the fucking grass!' joked Carlton, descending the tree.

'Give us some money,' asked Glenroy. 'I wanna go up to that café place and buy some sandwiches.'

'Will you stop moaning! You're always thinking of your fucking stomach!'

The exchange woke Bullet. Bleary-eyed, he hauled himself up and trudged towards the tree that Carlton had appeared from. 'My bloody back,' he bewailed. 'I can't take sleeping on the ground no more – the leaves don't make much difference.'

'Then go home,' baited Glenroy.

'Why don't you go home?' returned Bullet, not in the mood for humour so early in the day. 'You're the one who's fucking scared of the dark.'

'Scared of what dark,' argued Glenroy, putting on a brave face. 'You see me crying about it?'

'Who got up in the middle of the night and shouted *What the fuck was that!* when some squirrel was running about,' mocked Bullet.

'It could've been one of them scouts creeping up on us,' riposted Glenroy.

'Oh yeah! At three o'clock in the morning?' Bullet teased. 'You thought it was the bogey-man, innit.'

'Fuck you!' Glenroy dismissed.

'Will you two fucking shut up!' reprimanded Carlton. 'You're like two girls.'

'Well, tell him,' sniped Glenroy, pointing an angry finger at Bullet. 'I wish he'd stayed at home!'

'You fucking asked me, you idiot!' volleyed Bullet.

'I wish I bloody never, now,' replied Glenroy, his face sulky.

'Shut up!' yelled Carlton, glaring at his two friends and

almost daring them to continue arguing. He felt that he couldn't tolerate their altercations any longer.

Curvis stirred, opened his eyes and watched Glenroy trundle down the mound. 'What's wrong with them two now?' he asked.

'They're arguing again,' answered Carlton. 'And getting on my fucking nerves.'

Glenroy, entertaining himself by throwing pebbles at a tree, turned to Curvis. 'Curvis, tell Carlton to give me some money so I can get something to eat.'

'How much money we got left?' asked Curvis.

'Seven pound sixty,' Carlton replied. 'I counted it this morning . . . We ain't gonna last too long with that.'

Curvis stood up and shook the blanket he had slept on. Dock leaves and tiny twigs danced in the warm air. Curvis coughed and proceeded to fold the blanket, his face in deep thought. 'Hey, Bullet,' he called. 'What time does your school have the dinner break?'

Bullet was leaning on a tree, twirling a green leaf around his thumb. 'Twelve-thirty. Why?'

'One of us should go down Elvin's school and find him,' suggested Curvis.

'See Elvin?' wondered Carlton. 'He'll tell everybody that he saw one of us.'

Glenroy, on hearing the proposal, strode purposefully up the hill. 'I'll go,' he offered.

'No!' replied Curvis. He turned to Carlton. 'Carlton, you go. No one in the school knows you.'

'There's only a few boys who know me there,' argued Glenroy.

'Nah. What happens if one of those boys sees you?' reasoned Curvis. 'It's best for Carlton to go 'cos he knows the back way around Pinewood Oaks to get to the school.'

'For fuck's sake! You don't trust me to do anything,' complained Glenroy, his arms waving about in frustration.

Curvis ignored Glenroy's pleas. His face was businesslike. 'Carlton, if you get to see Elvin, try and get him to give us some food and stuff. He can meet us later on tonight to give us the grub.'

'And what if I don't see him?' asked Carlton.

'Then you'll have to go back after school and see if you can catch him then.'

Carlton collected a pound note from inside his bag. He looked at Glenroy with caution. 'Buy four of those hot pasties, and don't take the scenic route, and *don't* stay there for too long.' He passed the cash to Glenroy.

Glenroy banked the note in his back pocket and ran down the hillock, stumbling over pine roots.

Curvis and Bullet began to tidy the area of the camp as Carlton looked on, turning something over in his mind. 'How much longer are we gonna be on the run?' he asked, his tone soft but serious. 'It's nice around here but we can't stay here for ever.'

Bullet halted his morning chores and looked at Curvis. 'He's right. Even deserters from the army get caught after a while.'

Curvis slightly bowed his head, seemingly accepting defeat on the argument. Maybe he should remain on his own, he thought. Not yet, not yet, his will told him. Not yet. He smiled. 'I dunno. I s'pose we'll go back when everybody is sick and tired of shitting in the bushes – I should've thought about taking crap paper on the night we left.'

'Which way shall I go?' asked Carlton. 'To the other side of the golf course and cut through Badgers Dyke? Then take the hawthorn path next to Hogspill Wood?'

'Yeah,' Curvis nodded. 'When you come out of Hogspill Wood, follow the road to the Pinewood library and cross at the lights. Go down to the bottom of Grove Avenue, turn left, and you're there.'

'Tell Elvin to keep his trap shut,' offered Bullet.

Curvis nodded and set off to his adopted tree where he spoke with his dead mother. Carlton and Bullet paused until Curvis was out of earshot. 'What do you reckon?' asked Bullet. 'We've made our point. We've got to go back sometime.'

'Yeah, I know,' replied Carlton. 'But are you gonna tell Curvis we should go back? You know what he's like. He'll probably want to stay up here on his own. Best to wait for him to get sick and tired of it. But I have to admit, it's a great feeling to be up here, knowing those fuckers don't have a clue where we are. It'll be a shame to go back. We can hold on for a few more days, especially if Elvin can help us out.'

Half an hour later, Glenroy returned, holding four hot pasties in white wrappers. The boys sat down to eat their breakfast. Glenroy was the first one to finish his meal.

'Should've got two each. I'm still hungry.' He threw his wrapper behind him. 'So what are we gonna do while Carlton's seeing Jaws?'

'Watch those rich people play golf and see if we can nick their balls,' suggested Bullet.

'Yeah, might as well,' agreed Glenroy, searching for a response from Curvis. 'Or we can go to Spurleigh again.' Curvis's eyes were fixed deep into the wood.

'Yeah,' Bullet agreed. 'Last time it was a laugh. Coming, Curvis?'

Curvis didn't turn around to respond to Bullet and offered his reply to the forest. 'Nah. I'll stay round here for the day. Don't feel like going nowhere.'

The others looked at each other. 'Something wrong?' asked Bullet.

'Nah, just feeling really tired.'

Carlton checked his watch and began to ready himself for his long trek, combing his hair with an afro pick. 'Turn left at Grove Avenue?'

'Yeah . . . be careful,' Curvis replied, finally turning around.

210

'I'll be back around half-two,' Carlton said. 'So don't leave me on my own for too long.'

'Tell Elvin to get us some apples and oranges and some of those shortbread biscuits that his Auntie makes,' ordered Glenroy.

'Sure you don't want roast lamb with mint sauce?' laughed Carlton, making a start. Before he left, he gave Bullet some cash.

'Sure you don't wanna come?' Bullet asked Curvis again.

'No!' Curvis answered, his frustration shocking his friends.

'Alright, keep your hair on,' said Bullet. 'Let's get ready, Glenroy. We'll leave the king of the sulks on his own.'

Two hours later, Carlton was walking through Ashburden playing field, approaching Elvin's school. Around him were dog-walkers, elderly citizens relaxing on wooden benches, stretched-out sun-bathers, and a overweight man wearing a tracksuit with a towel around his neck, walking swiftly but strangely, his arms pumping like pistons. Carlton wiped the sweat off his brow and thought the man was a nut-case.

He rested on the grass and checked his watch. 12.15 p.m. 'Only fifteen minutes to go,' he muttered to himself. He plucked a blade of grass and pushed it in his mouth. He felt he could do with a cooling drink or ice-lolly after his five-mile trek. 'A jubbly will go down nice.' He lay flat on his back, in view of the school buildings a hundred yards away. He thought of the day he first arrived in Pinewood Oaks. He asked the strange man, who was holding his hand on the journey to the children's home, where his mother was. He told him she was on holiday. That night he refused to sleep with the dormitory light switched off, waking up the whole household with his screams. Auntie Josephine had had to take him in her room where she had a lamp. This routine carried on for six weeks, with Carlton pining for his mother, not knowing if she would ever come back to claim him.

211

The bizarre-walking man had completed a lap of the playing field when Carlton stood up. Teenage shrieks and shouts were coming from the school and pupils were streaming out of the buildings. Most of them remained in the school grounds out of the sun's glare. Only a few ventured out to the playing field. Carlton saw a boy of his age and went to approach him. 'Do you know Elvin? Skinny coloured boy? He rides a bike to school.'

'Yeah,' the boy answered, chomping a ham sandwich from his lunch box. 'I think I saw him in the playground.'

'Can you take me to him?'

'Yeah, c'mon then.'

Elvin was dressed in black trousers and a white shirt that was unbuttoned to his navel, hoping to attract some girl's attention. 'Elvin!' Carlton called. 'Elvin!'

Elvin turned around and saw the dishevelled appearance of Carlton – dried mud stains on his face and his hands. Elvin's eyes clicked into animation and his mouth gaped. 'Fucking shitting hell! Where did you come from?'

Schoolboys and schoolgirls looked on curiously. Carlton looked around him. 'Come here!' he ordered.

Elvin stepped away from the girl. 'Keep your fucking voice down!' Carlton instructed. They walked towards the playing field. 'Where've you been? Pinewood Oaks has been crawling with police, me and Mellor had to go up the station to answer some questions, there's a fucking curfew going on, somebody said you were all dead, we all thought you went up to London, there are people in suits walking about, everyone's going nuts, arguing with housemothers and housefathers. Where've you been? London?' Elvin stopped for breath.

'Will you fucking slow down!'

Elvin exhaled strongly and looked at Carlton with a fond- ness that was borne out of years of friendship.

'What did you say to the police?' Carlton asked.

'Nothing,' Elvin replied proudly. 'I didn't know where you

212

was anyway. They took me and Mellor to the police station. They even questioned Sonia, asking her if you lot had any girlfriends in Pinewood and nearby.'

'So what did Sonia say?'

'Nothing – she was so cool about it. But Mellor lost his temper with the police. I heard him shouting and all that and they were shouting at him. When we got back to Pinewood Oaks, he smashed Mr Williams' window.'

'He must be on some serious punishment?'

'Yeah, but he's going nuts. He shinned down his drain-pipe to see Sonia last night and he wants her to run away with him.'

'Fucking hell. I didn't realise all this shit would've happened to you lot.'

'Yeah, like I said there's a curfew. Everyone has to be in by eight o'clock. Friends from outside have to be out of the grounds by seven. The staff are watching us like hawks, and at night we hear cars driving up and down the road.'

'Have you seen Auntie Josephine?' Carlton asked softly, fixing Elvin with a serious stare.

'No ... I heard that she went with the police up to London. But Sonia saw her and reckons she's been crying all the time.'

Carlton did not allow his feelings to show on his face. He composed himself. 'Now, Elvin, listen to me ... We're running out of money and we need food ... So what do you reckon? You reckon you can get us some nosh and meet us tonight?'

'I'll try, but it'll have to be before eight.'

'Shit!' exclaimed Carlton. 'It's still light then. We'll have to risk it.'

'So will we. Uncle Thomas followed me up the shops yesterday, like he wanted to say something to me. He looks like he's got the shits.'

'Well, don't say nothing yet, until I come back. Then we'll

tell everybody, including the social, what a fucking pervert he is. I hope he gets the fucking sack.'

'Do you think they'll listen to us?'

'Probably not me on my own. They'll never believe *me*. That's why you have to back me up and tell 'em what that bastard done to you – I'm depending on you, Elvin. Hopefully, others will say something as well.'

'So who you gonna tell first?' asked Elvin. 'I thought you would *never* tell anyone.'

Carlton took his time answering, feeling a sickly sensation in his stomach. 'Auntie Josephine. I know she'll believe me. I've been thinking about it while I've been on the run.' And I've been thinking about what that bastard done to me in that swimming cubicle, he thought to himself. Disgusting fucking animal. *Three* times. Three fucking times. Carlton had the look of vengeance in his eyes. 'I want that fucking pervert to pay.'

There was silence as Elvin studied the face of his friend. His heart was beating fast as he thought of the consequences of Carlton's plans. Then there was Carlton's savage temper to consider. He knew the rage within Carlton was about to explode, it was there in his eyes. There's no way Carlton would allow Uncle Thomas to get away with it. Elvin wondered how it would all end.

Carlton broke the silence. 'Meet us by the fence near the junior school shed just before eight o'clock, with all the food you can get. Be careful nicking the stuff.'

'Yeah, I will. What you get depends what's in the larder though.'

'Right now, we ain't too fucking picky.'

'Alright then, I won't let you down . . . Where you hiding out?'

'You don't need to know.'

Carlton placed his hand on Elvin's left shoulder and half smiled. 'Elvin, you're a good mate. You get on everybody's fucking nerves sometimes, but you're a good mate.' Elvin returned the smile with more to spare as he watched Carlton about-turn and jog away; the crazy walker was on his third lap.

Carlton returned to the camp three hours later and found Bullet meticulously carving something in a tree. He had a sheet of paper in his hand and glanced at it now and again. Glenroy was sitting down sketching, seemingly not even aware of Carlton's presence. Curvis was nowhere to be seen. 'Where's Curvis?' Carlton asked.

Not taking his eyes off the job in hand, Bullet replied, 'Gone to get some water. We've run out already . . . Did you see Elvin?'

'Yeah. We're gonna meet him later on today. He's gonna bring us some food.'

Glenroy looked up. 'Yeah, what time?'

'Before eight.'

'I hope he brings some cakes.'

Carlton sat down, tired from all his walking during the day, not really looking forward to setting off again later on. 'So what have you two been up to today?'

'Went swimming,' Bullet answered. 'Couldn't get Curvis to come with us. Then we watched some blokes playing golf.' Bullet and Glenroy both smiled mischievously. Bullet dropped his pen-knife on the ground and took out three golf balls from his pockets. 'And we got these,' Bullet continued. 'You should've seen their faces when they walked to the green. I had to put my hand over Glenroy's mouth 'cos he wanted to burst out laughing. They just didn't know what happened to their balls.'

Glenroy roared with laughter and Carlton joined in, wishing he had been there with them. 'What's that you're doing?' Carlton asked Bullet, regaining his composure.

'Oh, I bet Glenroy that I could do his drawing on the tree.' Bullet stepped two paces back. 'Not bad, eh.'

'Let me see that,' said Carlton, getting up and snatching the sheet of paper out of Bullet's hand.

Carlton visibly flinched at the image. 'I've got to give it to him,' said Bullet. 'It's brilliant.'

'Yeah, yeah, it is,' Carlton admitted.

Glenroy smiled. Carlton looked at the drawing and something troubled him deeply. From the neck down, it was more or less the same sketch that Glenroy had drawn previously, but Gemmele's face was replaced by a head with horns of such repulsion that Carlton recoiled again while analysing the deft detail. 'Where the fuck you get the idea to do this?'

'In a dream I had last night,' revealed Glenroy. 'She changes like that when the night comes.'

Carlton looked at the tree. Bullet had carved out the outline of the head and had already grooved the horns. He was now starting on the eyes. *'Jesus,'* exclaimed Carlton. 'Ain't you got nothing better to do than devil stuff?'

Glenroy and Bullet simply laughed.

7.55 p.m.

Carlton led his three mates swiftly across the playing field. The sun was setting, its beams kissing the tree tops and only aspiring footballers and teenage sweethearts were in the park. The freshening wind was still absent, and in parts of the playing field, where the grass struggled to grow, the earth was visibly cracked. No soccer players attempted any sliding tackles.

They soon reached the wooden fence that encircled the northern acres of Pinewood Oaks. The junior school loomed silently beyond it. They grouped near a tree to catch breath and they all felt like they were breaking back into prison.

'Keep your eyes peeled,' Carlton instructed. 'Who knows who we might see tonight. Be prepared to leg it.'

'Carlton,' Glenroy called, 'you should've told Elvin to meet us here in the rec.'

'Too risky – they're all being watched and the bastards

would know there was something up if they went out of the grounds.'

Carlton was the first to leap onto the fence, hauling himself up with his strong arms. He scanned the vacant playground. 'Clear,' he whispered. 'But no sign of Elvin.'

'I knew he'd let us down,' griped Glenroy. 'He probably told someone.'

Carlton leaped down to the asphalt and looked right, where beyond the chalkings of a hopscotch grid was a flat-roofed shed made of steel and iron, about twelve foot high and supported by wooden pillars five inches thick. 'Where the fuck is he?' muttered Carlton to himself.

'What's the time?' asked an anxious Bullet, clambering over the fence.

'About a minute to eight,' answered Carlton, scanning the sides of the building.

Curvis and Glenroy climbed the fence and dropped to the ground. 'He might have got caught nicking the food,' offered Carlton. 'We'll give him no more than ten minutes then we'd better leg it.'

'Sssshhh,' ordered Curvis. 'I can hear something.'

Retreating into a corner of the shed, they crouched low in readiness to sprint to the fence. Heartbeats up-tempoed. At first they saw a silhouette appear by the corner of the building, its shadow lengthened three-fold by the dropping sun. The runaways inched forward to the fence, still on their haunches. A wiry figure emerged, walking into the playground looking this way and that, carrying plastic bags. It was Elvin. They saw another figure walking behind Elvin. 'I hope that's him?' said Glenroy, pigeon-stepping out of the shed. 'Who the fuck is that with him?'

'It's fucking Sonia!' revealed Carlton. 'What the fuck is she doing here?'

The friends met in the middle of the playground. Curvis ushered everybody back inside the shed. Carlton glared at

Sonia. She was wearing a T-shirt and a two-tone skirt that met her calves. Her hair was plaited in corn-row style. She was holding two plastic bags. 'We weren't too sure if Elvin could get out, so we decided that we would both try and get here for eight.'

'What have you got then?' Glenroy asked, looking at the bags.

'Anything we could lay our hands on,' replied Sonia. 'Even Brenda nicked some food for you earlier.'

'You told Brenda?' charged Curvis. 'For fuck's sake! Who else knows?'

'Just Mellor, Brenda, Sonia and me,' answered Elvin.

Bullet watched Sonia suspiciously as Glenroy examined the contents of the plastic bags. 'Bourbons!' he exclaimed.

'I thought Mellor was on punishment,' Carlton remarked.

'He is, but he sneaked out to see me about seven o clock,' replied Sonia.

Elvin and Carlton wandered off to talk amongst themselves as Glenroy, still delving into one of the bags, plucked out an apple. With his first bite he almost halved the fruit. Sonia switched her gaze to Curvis and was met by cynical eyes. 'So you lot alright then?'

'Yeah, we're coping,' Curvis answered. 'Had a couple of scares though.'

'I dunno what Elvin's told Carlton, but all the police and staff have been on our backs. We can hardly go any-where now.'

'Yeah, we heard,' Curvis nodded. 'Thanks anyway. You've made a friend for life with Glenroy.'

Sonia laughed. Bullet seemed strangely subdued. *What's she doing here? When all this is over I'm gonna have a serious word with Elvin and tell him not to tell our secrets to fucking girls.*

'I s'pose you know that Brenda is going mad with worry for you lot . . . Especially Carlton.'

Curvis glanced in Carlton's direction. He didn't have a clue that Brenda was sweet on his friend. He was sure Carlton had no idea either. 'That's news to me,' he replied. 'We don't wanna be worrying about that.' Curvis felt a strange sense of jealousy. He never thought that one day his friends might start dating. He didn't want to think about it. 'Well, Carlton's never told me that he fancies Brenda,' he said coldly. 'He don't fancy anyone. None of us need girlfriends.'

'Yeah,' concurred Bullet. 'Don't need 'em.'

A whine of a car's engine could be heard coming down the hill, approaching the school. Carlton and Elvin were the first to move. Glenroy swiped the bags before he darted off. Sonia ran to the shed, Elvin joined her. They were breathing hard. Curvis almost ran up the fence vertically and somersaulted over. Glenroy threw the bags over. Panic got him over the barrier rather than the art of climbing. Heartbeats accelerated.

A policeman stepped out of a sky-blue panda and ambled into the school grounds. He looked this way and that. The runaways watched him through a hole in the fence. Elvin and Sonia stooped low in the shed, sure they would be caught. The heavy steps on the concrete were becoming louder. The policeman halted, scanning the length of the playground. Elvin closed his eyes. 'If he sees us, then kiss me,' Sonia whispered. 'He'll just think that we're together, going out.' Elvin grinned a ridiculous grin. The officer started to walk again. But to Sonia's relief, he turned back to his car.

'That's a fucking shame,' panted Elvin as Sonia laughed. 'But Mellor would've killed me!'

As Elvin uttered his last word, Carlton, Curvis, Bullet and Glenroy were already running across the playing field, satisfied that their friends were safe.

3.00 a.m.

The night breeze picked up, tossing the leaves of the pines to and fro. Carlton couldn't sleep. He hated it when Curvis ordered the torches to be switched off. Strangely, the snoring from his friends comforted him. But it's unnerving when you hear sounds and can't see where they are coming from. Carlton couldn't take any more and groped for a torch. He found one near Bullet's head and switched it on. Inexplicably, the beam found the tree Bullet had gouged with Glenroy's sketched image. Carlton shuddered and felt something cold in his veins. He didn't want to look but felt compelled to. He looked up at the height of the tree and then returned his gaze to the image. He felt it was alive, telling him to do something. His hands shook and he could feel his T-shirt sticking to his chest. It *was* telling him to do something. He switched off the torch, lay back down and willed the dawn to come. Suddenly, a scream pierced the night. It was Glenroy, his eyes were wide open and his face was covered in sweat. He sat up, his back as straight as a board, his head still but his lips quivering.

'Whassamatter?' Curvis asked urgently, reaching for his torch and switching it on.

'I ... I had a nightmare,' stuttered Glenroy. 'A ... A bad one.'

'Fucking hell!' exclaimed Bullet. 'You shit the life out of me!' We can't go on like this, he thought. We gotta go back now. Glenroy's cracking up.

Carlton was in shock. He tried desperately to stop his shaking. He stood up. 'We ... we should leave one of the torches on ... For Glenroy. Curvis, we'll have to find clearer ground. The forest is really making Glenroy scared.' Glenroy didn't deny this.

'OK,' Curvis agreed. 'Glenroy, you sure you'll be alright? It's only an hour or so 'til daylight. Carlton, give him something to eat.'

Glenroy nodded, grateful that no one had laughed at his plight.

Five minutes later they were eating the food that Elvin and Sonia had given to them. It was a silent meal, with all of them recognising their need for each other. Yet Bullet felt that Curvis, Carlton and himself were unable to deal with Glenroy. They probably heard that scream back at Pinewood Oaks, he thought. He was obviously frightened to death about something. He studied Glenroy, who seemed happy enough munching his bourbons. He needs help, Bullet considered. Help that we can't give him. Carlton was staring at the image gouged in the tree by Bullet. I wish I could scream out like that, he thought. But I can't. I just can't. They don't think I'm scared of anything. I'm supposed to be the strongest. They'll think I'm *nothing* if I scream.

A Perfect Rage

8.10 a.m., Wednesday, 16 June 1976

Sonia smiled into her mirror, happy with her hair, which she
had just formed into a neat, bunched pony-tail. Mellor likes
it that way, she thought. She checked her watch and realised
she'd better make a move.

At the base of the stairs, Sonia's housemother loomed,
waiting with hands on her hips, glaring and examining Sonia's
blouse. Too good-looking for her own good, Auntie Cilla
thought. 'You have been late enough times this term and if
I find out you know about those boys, then you can forget
about that skirt you wanted to buy Saturday.'

'But I'm getting it out of my allowance. It ain't your
money.'

'You show me some respect and prove you're worth the
council lavishing money on you . . . I'm not having you larking
about with that Mellor boy; it gives the house a bad name.'

'He's my boyfriend!' insisted Sonia, fearless in returning her housemother's stare.

'He *was* your boyfriend ... And what's more, due to your recent behaviour, you can forget about that hair oil and shampoo that you wanted. Besides, none of the staff knows where you can get the stuff. You'll have to carry on using the Vaseline.'

'But this girl at school told me I need *proper* oil for my hair. The ends keep breaking and it's too dry.'

'*Don't* argue with me. Vaseline is good enough for the other black children and the council shouldn't have to pay for luxuries like ethnic hair oil ... Now, go on with you.'

Sonia passed her housemother and presented her with a look of contempt. She picked up her school bag near the front door. 'Go on with you!' the housemother ordered.

The smell of recent cut grass caused Sonia to sneeze as she went outside and felt the heat of the sun. She walked up the incline towards the community centre and spotted Brenda, leaning against a lamp-post. Sonia quickened her pace. Brenda was attired in the same uniform as her friend, though her large frame suggested she was too old to wear it. 'Did you see 'em,' Brenda asked eagerly.

'Yeah, all four,' Sonia answered. They began to walk. 'They've got the bags of food, but we got a scare when a policeman came down in a car. He got out but Carlton and them were gone over the fence. Me and Elvin had to hide in the shed. We were shitting ourselves.'

'Did you get a chance to talk with Carlton?' Brenda probed.

'Nah, he was chatting with Elvin. They were a bit secretive an' all. They all looked a bit rough; marks and stains over their faces, so I reckon they must be hiding in the hills. Carlton was looking a bit wild. Something in his eyes was scary. Elvin wouldn't tell me what they were talking about.'

'I hope he's alright . . . Everyone else reckons they went up to London,' remarked Brenda.

'No way. If they went to London they wouldn't come back here asking for grub – it's too far.'

'Your housemother still asking questions?' asked Brenda.

'Yeah, all the time. Especially as I got in fifteen minutes late last night. It's getting on my fucking nerves. Even my social worker is coming down tomorrow, all 'cos my housemother reckons I'll be more truthful to him, and also 'cos she reckons I need lecturing about how to behave to be a proper lady. She and him can go and fuck themselves.'

'So, did you see Mellor last night?' asked Brenda.

'Yeah, he sneaked out about seven. He's really going mad. All that questioning is getting to him and he wants to run away and join Carlton and them . . . He wants me to go with him. He wanted me to find out where they are . . . I've never seen him cry before. He kept on saying I'm all he's got.'

Brenda looked at her friend and placed a supportive hand on her shoulder. 'You two won't be in this fucking place for ever.'

Sonia began to weep. 'I . . . I just know they're gonna move him. I just know.'

'If I know Mellor at all, he'll find a way to keep in touch. He always does.'

'I . . . I let him do it last night. He seemed so sad. Crying. It hurt. But in a funny way I felt like I was mothering him a bit. It was a weird feeling. Afterwards he was saying sorry. I don't even care if I get pregnant, 'cos if I do, they'll have to move me to somewhere. If they move him I don't wanna stay here. So I have to find a way out of this fucking prison.'

'Who knows?' Brenda said, looking behind her at the cottages. 'In ten years' time you might be married to Mellor, and I'll be married to Carlton. We'll visit each other, feeding our kids.'

Sonia broke out into a wide smile and laughed.

224

9 a.m.

Following their breakfast of apples, oranges, Madeira cake and bourbon biscuits, Curvis had led his friends to a brook near the west side of the forest. Curvis didn't know its source but it ran down off the hills from the south. It was safe to wash here as the clay banks, steeply rising above their heads, shielded them from view on one side and the pines on the other. Stripping to their Y-fronts they swabbed away a day's sweat and grime and took the opportunity to fill their bottles. The water was cold and tasted much better than the stuff they drank from the café's tap.

By mid-afternoon, they had trekked to a field near Spurleigh, where they played two-a-side football, using one of Glenroy's tennis balls. Curvis and Glenroy were little more than spectators as they watched their friends tackle ferociously for possession. When they felt too hot to continue, they threw golf balls to each other. Carlton thought up a gauntlet run where one of them, twenty yards way, had to sprint in front of the others, trying to evade golf and tennis balls; Bullet proved himself to be a marksman, not missing once with any of his throws. 'If you don't run straight then you have to stand still and we get free throws,' Carlton ruled. Curvis suggested that perhaps they should target no higher than the shoulders. Glenroy received the most hits but he took it in good humour.

They spent the early evening lying on their backs, tired from their exertions; at Glenroy's request, they played 'I spy with my little eye'. The game died when Curvis spied something beginning with 'H' that flew in the sky. Following half an hour of frantic guessing, Curvis finally revealed it was a hobby bird. The others gave up.

By 9.45 p.m., they were hungry but had eaten all the food

they had brought with them. Carlton had a plan. While explaining this, he led them to a street where they sat down on a low wall outside a row of shops. They watched the traffic go by. The sun was dipping behind the hills that overlooked the town, and the forest to the east was now cloaked in grey; the seven sisters appeared like a pale ribbon in the distance. Carlton dug into his jeans pocket and produced a five-pound note. 'So you all know what to do,' he asked quietly. He searched all eyes and received nods of understanding. 'Just act normal,' he added. 'Like you're waiting for me to get the fish and chips.'

Carlton led the way into the take-away, making sure his five-pound note was visible in his hand. Behind the counter was a man of about twenty-five who had never served more than two black people in his life. He watched the boys curiously and spotted the cash in Carlton's hand. He was turning over chips in a heated, transparent container, ready to place them on yesterday's newspapers that covered a table.

Carlton produced his most innocent smile and looked the shop assistant in the eye. Glenroy paced back and forth behind him as Curvis stood by the door, pretending to watch the traffic. Bullet stood beside Carlton, noticing the man's tattoo on his right forearm. Carlton studied the price list on the wall, giving the impression his custom was hard won. He placed his five-pound note on the counter, keeping his fingers pressed upon it. 'Can I have steak and kidney pie and chips four times, please.' He asked in his best Surrey English.

'Wrapped up or open?'

'Wrapped.'

Bullet edged nearer to the exit. Glenroy was already outside and Curvis, still standing by the entrance, was humming something, appearing perfectly calm. Carlton still had his fingers on the note as the shop assistant presented the take-away meal, wrapped up in newspapers and placed inside a large brown paper bag. Carlton snatched the food, swiped

226

the five-pound note and put it into his pocket, then bolted through the exit. Curvis and Bullet had already flown. Carlton soon passed Glenroy, who was looking behind and laughing. 'We done it!' he exclaimed. 'We fucking done it.'

'You thieving, fucking niggers!' the assistant yelled, angry with not just the shoplifters but himself.

The boys hurriedly crossed the road, leaped over a fence, and ran uphill across a field. Without looking back, they jogged on for another five minutes until they were out of sight of the town. They stopped to catch their breath and to wipe away the sweat, sitting down near the edge of a wood. Daylight had died and darkness was spreading rapidly over the sky. Looking down at the town, it seemed so far away now. Carlton served their supper.

'Hey, Carlton, did you get the man to put salt and vinegar on it,' laughed Bullet. His three friends laughed with him, but were too leg weary and hungry to respond. They finished their meal in five minutes.

It was near to midnight when they reached their base. Exhausted, they laid the blankets down. By now, they had their own sleeping positions, which they all respected. Carlton sat himself against a pine, chewing a blade of grass, seemingly in deep thought. He didn't want to come back to *this* place. He had wanted to say something when Curvis had suggested during the daytime that they should spend one more night here and then he'd scout for another camp in the morning. I'm not sure if I can take another night, he thought. How can I tell the rest without losing face? I wanna go back and tell Auntie Josephine about Thomas. I want to confront *him*. Don't wanna wait.

Bullet took out his pen-knife and searched for a suitable stick or twig to carve. Glenroy was playing with his tennis ball, juggling it from hand to hand, quietly singing a hymn to himself. '*Onward Christian soldiers . . .*' Curvis was looking up to the stars, not believing their caper back at Spurleigh.

We're getting more and more daring, he thought. We'd have never done a thing like nicking the food if we were still in Pinewood Oaks.

Glenroy lost control of his ball and it bobbled down to the hollow. Curvis, who had his torch switched on, tried to locate the ball with the torch's beam. Glenroy went off in search.

'Look for the fucking thing in the morning,' remarked Carlton. 'You'll be searching all fucking night.'

'Nah, I wanna find it now,' replied Glenroy, bending shrubs and kicking away at the roots of the bushes.

'Are you fucking stupid or something?' Carlton mocked. 'Leave the fucking ball 'til morning!'

'Curvis, lend me the torch,' Glenroy asked defiantly.

'Don't give him it,' laughed Carlton. 'Let him look for the ball in the dark.'

'Shut up, Carlton. You're just in a mood 'cos you didn't bring a ball yourself . . . Stop picking on me.'

'Well, if you weren't so stupid, I wouldn't pick on you.'

'Shut your mouth!' returned Glenroy.

'Come and make me, you idiot!' challenged Carlton.

'I don't make shit!'

'For fuck's sake, can't we ever get some peace?' pleaded Curvis.

Carlton watched Glenroy climbing the hillock, his face mean. 'Who are you calling shit? You fucking div.'

'Come on you two,' Bullet pleaded, not liking the look on Carlton's face.

'You can talk,' Carlton addressed Bullet. 'You're always arguing with that idiot . . . He's as fucking mental as his mother!'

Glenroy stopped in his tracks, his mouth agape and his eyes staring at Carlton in disbelief. Carlton's gaze dropped to the ground, knowing that he had gone too far. Curvis, shining his torch at the quarrelling couple, stood up and went to move towards them. Bullet was stilled in shock.

228

'LEAST MY MOTHER AIN'T NO WHORE,' yelled Glenroy.

The regret washing over Carlton turned into a boiling fury. His eyes narrowed and his face wrenched with violence. He took in a huge breath, as if he was summoning every bad experience he had ever had. His mother's image flashed in his brain. Before Curvis could separate them, Carlton launched himself on Glenroy, wading into him with a flurry of blows, employing all his limbs. He punched Glenroy's face. Curvis dropped the torch and leaped on Carlton's back, trying to restrain him. Bullet joined the *mêlée*, attempting to parry Carlton's blows. Glenroy dropped to the ground. The torch rolled down the mound and rested in the hollow, its beam exposing the tennis ball. But Carlton's fury would not be quelled. Bullet was struck by a wayward elbow. Curvis was strangling Carlton. 'Stop it! Stop it!' he implored.

'You fucking big-mouth bastard!' raged Carlton, now kicking his helpless victim. 'Why don't you fuck off and play with your girl ghost! You mental div! She can fucking put up with ya. No one else will!'

Glenroy tried to roll himself into a ball, adopting the foetus position.

'Leave him, Carlton! Leave him!'

Bullet bear-hugged Carlton, trying to drag him away. Curvis viced his neck. Carlton still lashed out with his feet, gripped by frenzy, his eyes unblinking. 'Uncle Thomas is *right*. You're as mad as your stupid mother!'

Bullet and Curvis summoned all their strength and finally managed to wrestle Carlton to the ground, their sweat mingling with each other's and their bodies covered in dusty green. Breathing was heavy and heartbeats raced.

'Calm down,' Curvis panted. 'Calm down. He doesn't realise what he's saying.'

Carlton glared at the writhing Glenroy, doubled up in pain. Glenroy returned the stare and something frightened him, as if he was looking into the pit of Hell. The nightmare he had suffered last night manifested itself into a long second in his mind. He was now shaking violently. Something told him to run. Run as hard as he could. He scampered off, running aimlessly into the woods, his sense of self-worth shattered, his nightmare becoming a reality inside his head.

As Curvis and Bullet were wondering where they had found the strength to restrain Carlton, they realised that Glenroy was gone. Curvis peered through the blackness; Carlton was still in his grip. 'Oh, Jesus Christ!' He looked accusingly at Carlton. 'You alright now?'

Carlton was close to tears and feeling ashamed of himself. His eyes dropped to the ground. All rage had left him. 'Yeah,' he answered.

Curvis released Carlton and let out an audible sigh. His arm muscles ached and Bullet wiped the sweat from off his face, blowing hard. Carlton stood up, tears welling in his eyes. He sheepishly trooped off and sat against a tree. His square chin was kissing his collar bone. Curvis found his torch. Bullet looked for his. They glanced at each other, realising everything had gone horribly wrong. Curvis tried to clear his head and think rationally. 'We'll have to find Glenroy,' he told Bullet, who was switching on his torch. 'Carlton, you'll be alright? We're gonna find Glenroy.'

Carlton nodded slightly, too remorseful to lift his head. 'Tell him I'm sorry.'

Curvis and Bullet carefully stepped their way down the mound, cracking pine cones under their feet. They shone their torches this way and that. 'Glenroy! Glenroy!'

Glenroy, who had sustained cuts and bruises to his face, and a dizziness that denied him co-ordination, plunged deep into the part of forest that even Curvis hadn't navigated. Not able to see beyond the sweat dripping off his eyebrows, he collided into trees, tripped over shrubs and felt the leaves lashing his face. He came to a complete halt and tried to listen for something. Something that was normal, something that he could recognise. He only heard a terrible cry of a beast. The beast in his nightmares inside his head.

His breathing accelerated. He lifted his head in order to catch more air. His head felt heavy and his body was trembling. He tried to focus his eyes and all he saw was a blackness. A blackness that was encroaching, a blackness that was in pursuit of him. 'Help me, Jesus,' he cried weakly. 'Lord help me.'

Tears were running down his puffy cheeks. His mouth was agape. He could smell his own blood and fear charged inside his stomach. The sound of the beast vibrated in his ears and he could sense a presence. He covered his ears with his palms, only to hear an echoing voice in the distance. 'Glenroy . . . Glenroy.'

To Glenroy, it sounded like a young girl's voice. 'Glenroy . . . Glenroy.'

The voice seemed to be getting closer. 'Glenroy . . . Glenroy.'

Glenroy's eyeballs darted around like a ball-bearing in a glass tumbler. His heart seemed to want to escape his chest. The sweat encasing his body turned icy cold. He ran as hard as he could muster. He launched himself forward into the forest, not looking behind, and not caring if his face smashed into a tree-trunk or his legs were speared by thorns. Finally, exhausted, he sat down, pushing his knees tight to his chest. He rubbed his eyes and attempted to focus.

'Glenroy . . . Glenroy.' It was Gemmele, running around in a radiant white night-dress. She had nothing on her blackened feet. Her eyes were red and her teeth were long and sharp. Her ears were dripping something, like wet glue, and her neck was crudely stitched in the shape of black crosses. The boils on her face were seeping blood and she had no hair, only horns. She was gesturing to him, smiling. He slammed his eyes shut and muttered the first prayer that came into his head. He shivered, not daring himself to move. He didn't move a muscle, but sweat poured off him. Then he opened his eyes slowly. Gemmele was gone. He noticed his legs and feet were bleeding, but didn't realise that blood was also soaking his forehead, mixed in with sweat, falling onto his eyelashes and impairing his vision. He felt his stomach rising through his chest and pausing just below his throat. He stood up and started to walk, dabbing his face. He had partly regained his balance and began to jog, desperately wanting to get out of the forest.

With fear giving him a reservoir of energy, he ran for twenty-five minutes, only pausing when his lungs felt about to burst. He leaped over bushes, slid down hillocks and passed through vegetation. He came to a road. A road he knew. Not thinking of his friends, he ran downhill, heading back to Pinewood Oaks.

'Glenroy! Glenroy!' called Bullet, shining his torch here and there. 'There's no fucking sign of him!'

'I haven't seen him either,' responded Curvis. 'Let's double back and check the other side of the camp.'

'Alright! But I'm getting fucking lost myself,' shouted Bullet.

'Stay where you are and shine your torch upwards. I'll meet you in a sec.'

Bullet stood motionless and shone his torch upwards, showering light on the black fingers of the canopy. 'What are we gonna do?' he muttered to himself. He heard the rustling of bushes and saw the anxious figure of Curvis. 'What are we gonna do?' Bullet asked, his body stationary but his eyes full of panic.

'I dunno,' replied Curvis. 'I just don't know.' Inside his head, Curvis knew that if Glenroy was not to return to the camp soon, they would all have to go back and report Glenroy missing, no matter what the consequences for themselves. 'Fucking Carlton and his temper!' Curvis bemoaned. 'If he'd

232

told us a long time before about his mother then none of this would've happened.'

'I've never seen Carlton like that before,' remarked Bullet. 'It's like something took over him . . . He beat Glenroy up bad. It's *this* fucking place. Carlton would have never done it in Pinewood Oaks. This place freaked him out. And it's made Glenroy go *mad*. Did you see his face? What do we fucking do? You should have never taken us here! I'm *leaving* in the morning!'

'Will you fucking calm down! I can't change it now, can I? We've just got to find him.'

'He could be anywhere by now. Say he gets lost? What we gonna say? I *can't* believe you talked me into this. From now on, *I'm* gonna start giving orders and you better fucking listen!'

Curvis was shocked at Bullet's anger and thought he'd better yield to him. He didn't want Bullet to lose his temper as well. 'Alright, alright. But we still got to find him – let's check back at the camp, he might've gone back.'

Bullet nodded, almost snorting as he tried to get a grip on his emotions.

They returned to their adopted part of the forest in twenty minutes. On their trek through the coppice, they hardly talked to each other, and they exchanged knowing glances, only too aware of their fate back at Pinewood Oaks. They saw a brooding Carlton, still sitting against a tree, peering unblinking into the dark. Tears covered his face.

'Has Glenroy been back?' asked Curvis.

Carlton shook his head, and then covered his face with his palms.

'What did you have to go mad for?' rebuked Curvis, immune to the distraught figure of Carlton. 'You know what he's like! Saying stupid things.'

Carlton buried his head into his arms. 'It wasn't stupid,' he mumbled. 'IT'S FUCKING TRUE! MY MUM IS A

233

FUCKING SLUT!' Hiding the truth is impossible now, he thought. They'll all think I'm nothing now.

Bullet and Curvis stared at each other, wondering what to say next. Bullet dropped his head, finding the scene too unbearable. It was the first time any of them had seen Carlton weep. Carlton moved his arms from his face and Curvis noticed the chewed remains of a blade of grass dangling from his mouth. 'Glenroy's probably gone back,' he said softly. 'And at first light, I'll be going back. Apart from saying sorry to Glenroy, there's something I've gotta do.' There was a deep menace in these last words, like a threat. *Glenroy would like me to fuck up Uncle Thomas,* Carlton thought. *Fuck telling Auntie Josephine, she won't believe me anyway. I'm gonna go straight for him. It should have been Thomas who got beaten up, not Glenroy. No one is gonna get in my way. Not even Curvis and Bullet . . . I'm gonna fuck him up real bad.*

'What do you mean there's something you've gotta do?' Curvis asked, worry imprinted on his features.

'You'll find out . . .' Carlton's eyes betrayed him.

Bullet searched for his pen-knife, found it, and restarted the sculpturing of his stick. 'You never know, Glenroy might come back in the night . . . If he don't, we'll leave at first light.'

Carlton closed his eyes and nodded. Curvis was crestfallen. He stood motionless for half a minute as if something inside him had died. 'You two go back,' he said. 'I'm gonna stay up here for a day or so yet.'

'Don't be so fucking stubborn!' reprimanded Bullet. 'You're coming back even if I have to drag you by your fucking feet!'

'This was my idea in the first place,' replied a dispirited Curvis. 'I shouldn't have dragged you lot into it.'

'I dunno if I can face him,' said Carlton, feeling sorry for himself.

234

'WE'RE ALL FUCKING GOING BACK TOGETHER,' ordered Bullet, his anger surprising even himself.

'He's right,' agreed Carlton. 'We should all go back together.'

Curvis turned on Carlton, his fury obvious. 'If you hadn't beat up Glenroy, then everything would've been alright!'

'It wouldn't've mattered whether he hit him or not,' reasoned Bullet. 'We would have had to go back sooner or later.'

'There's no way I'm letting Glenroy take all the shit,' Carlton stressed, his voice stammering with emotion. 'We have to assume he went back.' He eye-drilled Curvis. 'And you're coming!'

Curvis nodded, his torch-light exposing his watery eyes.

'Alright,' Bullet said. 'We'll have one more look for him and if we don't find him, we'll leave first thing in the morning.'

Curvis bowed his head, accepting defeat. He turned around and restarted his search, tears running freely down his taut cheeks. Bullet and Carlton watched him until he was out of sight. 'He's right, you know,' Carlton acknowledged. 'It might have been better if he had run away on his own.'

Bullet and Carlton set off together, not at all confident of finding Glenroy. Bullet led the way and Carlton was glad he was by his side. They did not veer too far away from the camp, thinking they could easily become lost themselves. They were thorough in their search, looking behind trees, pulling apart bushes and looking into hollows. Every now and then they could see the flicker of Curvis's torch bisecting the woodland; it was a comfort to them. They searched for almost an hour with hope evaporating as every minute went by.

Returning to the camp, Bullet turned to Carlton. 'I know we have to go back, but I tell you what, I've had the best days of my life up here, even though it got fucked up in the end.'

Carlton nodded.

'Where the fuck is Curvis?' Bullet asked. 'I haven't seen his torch shining for five minutes.'

'He won't get lost,' said Carlton. 'This place *is* his home. It's where he and Stanton had good times. He really misses his brother. I didn't know how much 'til we came up here.' Bullet sat down and looked at Carlton, his gaze demanding honesty. 'What's that something you've gotta do?'

Carlton took his time answering. 'Beat up Uncle Thomas,' he said calmly. His stare was impassive, as if he knew this was his fate from long ago. 'I don't want none of you getting involved . . . This is between me and him.'

Achilles Possession of Carlton

7.45 a.m., Friday, 18 June 1976

The clouds had thickened and the air was moist, waiting for a breeze that never came. The green of the leaves and grass in the Pinewood Hills was of a duller hue, and the morning dew took its time evaporating, covering the ground in a light, silvery film. The humid conditions enhanced the balmy smell of the pines. Curvis had risen from a disturbed sleep two hours ago in a vain search for Glenroy or any signs of his tracks. He found nothing. As he reached the summit of the mound he watched Carlton and Bullet, eating chocolate biscuits, sitting on the spread-out blankets, muttering amongst themselves.

'No sign of him,' reported Curvis. 'Not even a footprint; the ground's too hard. I hope he's gone back 'cos if he hasn't, I dunno where the fuck he is.'

Carlton moistened his dry lips with his tongue. 'He must of gone back,' he said. 'Stop worrying – when we go back,

237

we'll see him then.' He stole glances at the image Bullet had carved in the tree. He felt he wanted to do more to Thomas than just beat him up.

'For how long would we see him?' asked Curvis, his face full of dismay. 'They'll probably move us.'

Bullet glanced at the forlorn figure of Curvis and wanted to change the subject. 'Should we bring back the blankets?' he asked.

'I don't really give a shit,' answered Curvis, his mind somewhere else.

Bullet decided to leave the blankets where they were. 'I'll carry Glenroy's stuff and his drawings.'

'*I'll* take 'em,' Carlton insisted. Carlton stared ahead of him blankly, readying himself for his confrontation with Thomas. 'I've been thinking all night what Auntie Josephine is gonna do when she sees me,' he reflected. 'I don't wanna see her with a whole lot of fucking social workers and all those bastards from the council around me . . . And Mr fucking Williams. I wanna see her on my own . . . To do my explaining.'

'I definitely want to see my social worker when I see Uncle Rodney,' affirmed Bullet. 'He's gonna do his fucking nut.'

'I don't give a shit about what they say or do to me,' said Curvis. 'I just wanna get it over and done with . . . I just hope they don't move none of us.'

'So,' said Bullet, searching his friends' eyes. 'Everyone ready?'

'Yeah,' answered Carlton. 'Might as well go now. If we're lucky we might get a hot lunch,' he laughed, hiding his own apprehension.

Curvis scanned the area that had been his home for the last few days. He shook his head at the sight of sweet wrappers, orange peel and empty crisp packets that littered the ground. He stooped to check the contents of his bag and squeezed in the remainder of his soiled clothing and zipped it up.

238

Bullet gazed skywards and wondered when the storm would break. Carlton folded a pair of grass-stained jeans and placed them carefully inside his holdall. Taking in the tranquillity of the forest for the last time, Curvis spoke in a defeated tone. 'Come on. Let's go and face the music.' They picked up their bulging bags and started for home, all of them wondering about their individual fate.

Forty minutes later, they emerged into the Pinewood Hills Road, where they saw the bemused faces of four people waiting patiently for a green bus. They turned left and ambled down the hill. Carlton walked close to the kerb and felt a sail of wind as a truck raced by. He glanced up at the darkening heavens and felt his heartbeat resonate from his chest to his throat. They passed the William Blake comprehensive school, where the pupils were congregating in a playground. They all knew that 99 per cent of the pupils would go home to a family and a normal life. They were going home now.

At the bottom of the hill they turned right. The Pinewood Oaks water tower came into view. They walked in silence, exchanging fearful glances. Pedestrians were going about their normal business and the buses were full of children journeying to school and adults commuting to work. As they reached the beginning of the perimeter wall that encircled Pinewood Oaks, the boys slowed their pace. Bullet took the lead and Curvis followed closely behind. Carlton nervously looked about. 'Say someone sees us by the Lodge?' he asked.

'Just ignore them and carry on walking,' replied Bullet.

Bullet looked behind and glanced at Carlton. He sensed something uneasy. Something violent. 'You alright, Carlton?'

Carlton nodded slightly, his attention distant.

The entrance to Pinewood Oaks came upon them quicker than they would have liked. They all looked warily at the Lodge. They saw an old man talking on the phone behind a counter. The man looked up. He quickly replaced the phone and started re-dialling.

'It's Taylor,' Bullet remarked. 'He's bound to ring up everybody and tell them he saw us.'

'You think Taylor would have retired from working in the Lodge by now,' chuckled Bullet, trying to lighten his own tension.

They walked cautiously on, all of them glancing behind to check if anybody was following. Walking abreast on the pavement, Carlton began to sweat. His mouth was becoming dry, his thoughts focused on Thomas. He stared directly ahead and, sub-consciously, he flexed his fingers. Bullet watched him but didn't know what to say. Curvis walked with his eyes fixed on the asphalt.

Across the fields, Bullet saw the odd figure in school uniform, heading for school. Fifty yards down the road, he watched a six-year-old play with a tennis ball outside a cottage. The young girl heard something, turned around and spotted a dark blue van motoring swiftly up the hill. She got off the road.

Bullet came to a halt. Curvis did likewise, finally lifting his head. Carlton veered on to the grass. 'This is it,' said Bullet. '*Stay* together.'

The van accelerated. Carlton sprinted into the field, leaving his bags behind. Bullet began to breathe heavily as Curvis stared blankly ahead, awaiting his fate. The van screeched to a halt a few feet away from Curvis and Bullet. Carlton was running with Olympic speed across the sloping field. Three men emerged from the van. The driver remained in his seat, looking at the two teenagers with disgust.

A man who weighed the better part of sixteen stone, wearing a Mickey Mouse T-shirt and fading blue denims, approached. Curvis recognised him. He was one of Mr Williams' assistants. 'Get in the fucking van!' he ordered.

The two other men watched Carlton disappear into the

bushes three hundred yards away. They wondered if they should take up the chase. 'What about the other nigger?' one of them asked.

'We'll get him later,' replied the fat man, his voice deep and brutal.

Curvis and Bullet silently entered the van and sat down together on a double seat. One of the men collected Carlton's bags. He joined his two acquaintances, sitting opposite the runaways. Two of them grinned. 'We knew you'd fucking come back,' one of them said.

The driver performed a three-point turn and steered the car towards the main office. The girl who was playing with the tennis ball looked on, not daring to stray on to the road. Curvis and Bullet wondered if they were returning to their respective cottages, or somewhere else.

Carlton, still sprinting as hard as his legs would allow, watched the van speed by the community centre from the fringes of the piggery. He bolted along a dried, mud path. In the heart of the thicket, he decided to take a rest. Blowing very hard, he bent down and placed his hands on his knees. The image of Thomas molesting him had grown strong in his brain. Fury seeped into his body. His adrenalin called up new reservoirs of strength, giving him the power to run.

He looked up and saw the flat roofs of the nursery. Not even checking to see if the blue van might be motoring up the hill, the sight of his home spurred him on. He galloped on and only slowed down when he arrived at the paved path that led to his front door. Someone observed him from a window. A nursery teacher, preparing for her day, watched Carlton from a classroom. She had never seen him like this before. She ran to find a phone.

His face full of intent, he tried to open his front door. It was locked. He smashed the letter box twice and started banging his fists on the door. Thomas stole a glance from an upstairs window next door.

241

The front door opened. Josephine, wearing a pair of oven gloves, glared at Carlton, not recognising the hateful face in front of her. 'Do you know how bloody worried I've been about you?' she stressed, trying to mask her relief that Carlton was safe. 'Mr Williams has just called and he'll be on his way soon. What *were* you thinking?'

'SHUT UP!' Carlton yelled, seizing Josephine by the arms. 'Now fucking listen, I ain't got a lot of time . . . I didn't run away 'cos of you, and secondly, that FUCKING BASTARD next door is a FUCKING PERVERT . . . And now he's gonna FUCKING PAY . . . Now you know . . . So get out of my FUCKING WAY!'

Carlton pushed Josephine with such force, she fell to the ground. Her head smashed into a wall. Female staff appeared in the hallway. Dazed, Josephine tried to haul herself up, rubbing her head.

'Is Glenroy home?' Carlton asked in a strange calm.

Josephine got to her feet and could barely dare to look at her charge. She glanced at him, trying to understand Carlton's sudden composure.

'IS GLENROY HOME!' he raged.

Someone went to dial a phone. Two other staff members backed away, not knowing what to do.

'No . . . He was very disturbed,' Josephine cried. 'He was blabbing. We had to get a doctor out. He wasn't making sense . . . I'm so sorry. We couldn't get any sense out of him. I know he was your best friend . . . I'm so sorry.'

'Where *is* he?'

'Hospital,' Josephine stuttered. 'A men— . . . It's just temporary.'

'What hospital? Where!'

Josephine took in a deep breath and closed her eyes. Tears were falling down her cheeks. 'A mental hospital,' she finally answered. 'They came for him an hour ago.'

Carlton's face became taut. His eyes were blazing. He

242

turned around and slammed the door, the frame resonating in his wake. He walked a few paces to Uncle Thomas's front door. Josephine, still dazed, scurried after him. 'Carlton! Carlton!'

Carlton ignored her and banged his right fist on the door. He tried the door handle and found it wasn't secure. He walked inside. Pairs of female feet were hastily trotting up the stairs. Three teachers were running towards the cottage from the nursery. The first spit of rain was in the air. Carlton slammed the door shut and heard someone shouting from outside. He paid it no mind. 'Thomas! Thomas, you fucking bastard!' Carlton tightened his fists.

Thomas emerged from his study with pen in hand. He had heard the shouting from next door and thought at the time if Carlton came to seek him, he would try and reason with him, attempt to calm him down. As he looked at Carlton, he knew that this was impossible. His hand trembled, he dropped the pen. For a moment he could not speak and fear swarmed inside him. 'Carlton . . . Now calm down . . . I know I should have apologised . . . I'm going to resign . . . Carlton . . . Now don't do anything stupid. You're already in a lot of trouble.'

Just then, Josephine stumbled into the house. Her face was red and full of panic.

'I'm gonna fucking kill you,' Carlton said quietly. Thomas backed away. Josephine scampered up the three steps that led to the hallway. She bear-hugged Carlton around his waist. Carlton stumbled, falling backwards. He landed on his side, shoving Josephine off him. Thomas saw his opportunity and made for the front door. Carlton quickly got up on his feet and set off in pursuit. Josephine was left at the foot of the staircase. 'Carlton! Carlton!'

The rain was now steadily falling. Thomas slipped and fell over near the nursery fence. A siren could be heard in the distance. The blue van, after dropping off Curvis and Bullet to a secure house within the grounds, had started its half-mile journey to Josephine's cottage to collect Carlton.

Carlton cornered his prey. Thomas raised his arms in an act of submission. 'Carlton, please calm down,' he pleaded.

There was a junior cricket bat, propped against the nursery fence about ten feet away from Carlton. He picked it up. 'How many!' he screamed. 'How fucking many! You sick bastard! Enjoy it, did ya? Who are you buying sweets for now? Well, enjoy this, you fucking nonce!'

Carlton hurtled towards Thomas. Thomas tried to leap over the fence, his right foot on top of the barrier, ready to push his weight over, when Carlton, swinging the bat in a full arc, smashed the side of Thomas's head. Instantly, his mouth began to ooze blood. Thomas lost his balance. He seemed to be moving in slow motion and his legs denied him co-ordination. He gasped for breath and his eyes dulled. He dropped to the ground.

Someone ran up to Carlton and tried to wrench the weapon from his grasp. In his rage he didn't even recognise Josephine. He cracked her square on the chin, and she fell to the grass as if shot by a mortar. Carlton turned around, his eyes blazing and beheld a whimpering Thomas, unable to move. He heard a voice in his head, an indistinct voice. *'Do it! Do it!'* He struck Thomas again, using the full power of his shoulders and following through like an ace baseball player. Then again. And again. A trail of blood trickled over Thomas's beard. His head was drowned in a pool of blood that stained the grass. Thomas lay perfectly still.

Suddenly, Carlton felt many hands grab him and wrestle him to the ground. He put up no resistance. He dropped the bloodied and dented cricket bat. He felt his head crack on the ground. His forehead started bleeding, adding to the spots of blood that covered his hands, arms and face. Blankly, he stared at Thomas's lifeless body. He looked at Thomas's crotch and wished he had saved a few blows. Carlton didn't

244

hear the sirens that were approaching fast. He kept his vacant eyes upon Thomas's dead body. He let out a scream of pain as his right arm broke. His vision became misty and his five senses suddenly left him, erasing the pain he was suffering. A moment before he blacked out, his brain conjured up the image of Thomas molesting him inside the swimming pool cubicle.

'Jesus Christ!' someone exclaimed, feeling nauseous at the sight of Thomas's body. 'Has someone called an ambulance?'

'It's on its way,' a woman replied from within Thomas's cottage.

Josephine was given first aid by members of her staff. She watched Carlton being carried away by three men who threw him inside the blue van, awaiting the arrival of the police.

'Where's Thomas's wife?' someone asked.

'She took one of the kids to school,' a female voice replied.

'Oh Christ!'

Within the next two minutes, three ambulances arrived and two police cars. Three policemen escorted Carlton to the hospital inside his ambulance. Josephine refused to travel in hers. Thomas's body was placed on a stretcher, a blanket covering his face. Other officers proceeded to seal off the whole area and kept the numerous spectators at bay. Staff were ordered to touch nothing and the blood-splattered, dented cricket bat lay on the grass near the nursery fence, awaiting expert examination.

Bullet and Curvis were seated in a room with no windows; it was small and badly ventilated. Book shelves and filing cabinets surrounded them along with boxes of council headed paper. Curvis guessed this place was some kind of storeroom. Three male staff kept a watch over the teenagers.

'Did you hear the sirens?' Curvis whispered to Bullet.

'Yeah. I hope Carlton hasn't done anything stupid.'

'*No* talking!' ordered one of the guards, who looked the

most intimidating, wearing a blue check lumberjack shirt with the sleeves rolled up. He was six foot three and his forearms were almost the size of Curvis's thighs. His leg muscles filled out his jeans with not a centimetre to spare. Colleagues called him 'Enery. 'You can save all that for when your social workers arrive. You have a lot of explaining to do.'

Curvis took offence. 'Who the fuck are you?' he challenged the guard. 'Telling us not to talk! It's a free fucking world!'

Bullet looked at Curvis in disbelief. Curvis stood up, defiantly lifting up his head. 'What the fuck you doing?' whispered Bullet.

Curvis didn't reply, watching 'Enery approach, his face full of menace. 'So we got a cocky one,' he said, grinning in contempt. 'I ain't having the likes of you address me like *that*.'

'So what are you gonna do about it?' snapped Curvis, his face daring the man for some kind of reaction. 'You lot are s'posed to be our fucking guardians! You're s'posed to do what's best for us! Well, that's a fucking joke!'

Bullet tugged Curvis's T-shirt in an attempt to make him sit down. Curvis didn't even look at his friend.

'You better shut your fucking mouth before I close it!'

Curvis laughed. 'That's real manly of you,' he grinned. 'I'm sure that's in the child carers' guidebook, it says beat up kids if they tell the *truth* . . . Well, *come* on then. You gonna shut my mouth? How *hard* are you?' Curvis pointed with his right index finger to his top lip. 'Come on, let's see how bad you are . . . You fucking waste of space!'

Bullet could hardly look. The other two guards stared at each other, wondering if their colleague would take the bait. Embarrassed, 'Enery stepped forward, ran his eyes over Curvis's lean body, and spat in the teenager's face.

Curvis did not wipe the saliva away. He stood his ground, returning 'Enery's fixed glare with interest. The spit ran down his right cheek, creeping over the corner of his mouth. He

246

could taste it. Behind Curvis, Bullet trembled, unable to say anything.

'Is that all you can do?' challenged Curvis, taking a step forward. His face was only six inches away from 'Enery's features. 'Some tough nut you are, you fucking ugly troglodyte! Spitting like a fucking girl. Do you fight like one as well? You're about as hard as dog shit! Do you always pick on boys? Do you *fuck* them as well?'

Bullet shuddered, his mouth agape. His anger overcoming his composure, 'Enery swung his right fist, connecting to the side of Curvis's head, knocking him to the ground. Bullet went to tend to his friend. '*What* the fuck you doing?' he asked under his breath. 'You wanna get us killed?'

Curvis acted as if he didn't hear the words. He got up and ambled towards his tormentor, the right side of his face reddened and swelling visibly. 'Feel better, do you?' he said, his tone still mocking. 'Will you tell your friends down the pub what you done today? You're a real fucking hero. Fuck me! You hit one of the kids you're s'posed to look after . . . Big fucking hero! What a fucking hard man! You smell like a pig's arse, you small-pricked wanker!'

'Enery hit Curvis with a right and a left, then another right, an uppercut that lifted Curvis off the floor. He kicked Curvis in the head. Bullet, tears hampering his sight, dashed to Curvis's aid, standing between him and 'Enery. The other two guards stepped in, knowing it had gone too far.

Curvis hauled himself up from the floor again. His nose was bleeding and the force of the uppercut had slammed his teeth against his tongue. He tasted his own blood and felt a tooth in his mouth. He spat it out on the floor. His left eye was bloodshot and now half the size of his right eye. He advanced again. He did not see 'Enery before him, he saw his own father. He wanted to distract his father from killing his mother, offering himself as a sacrifice. The vision was crystal clear, and he could smell the beer on his father's breath. The screams of his mother pierced his ears, and as Bullet tried to hold him back, Curvis thought it was his brother, Stanton, restraining him. 'Why don't you try me?' he provoked once more. 'You fucking bully. Is that all you can do? Hit people smaller than you? Why don't you fuck off and leave us alone. Go on! Fuck off and fuck a dog or something! You fucking animal! You ain't a fucking man, you're just a . . .'

'Enery leaped on Curvis. Bullet jumped to his friend's defence, sustaining blows to his body. 'Can't punch *that* hard,' Curvis yelled. 'You fucking wanker! You think you're hard? You fucking spastic brain!'

The two other guards went to restrain 'Enery again. Bullet shielded Curvis. Curvis's nose was broken in at least two places. One of his eyes was just about shut and his lips were grotesquely misshapen. The blood pouring from his mouth forced him to dangle out his split tongue. 'Enerly,' he stuttered. 'You'll al fucking walanker.'

One of the guards bundled 'Enery out of the room. With his palm, Bullet wiped away the blood from Curvis's face, cradling his head with his other hand. The other guard simply stared blankly at the teenagers.

An hour later. Feeling groggy and disorientated, Curvis heard a knock on the door. He turned his head and saw two suited men clutching briefcases, wearing expressions of superiority. They looked at Curvis's battered face. 'They were all fighting before we caught them,' said one of the guards.

Bullet heard the remark but didn't have the spirit to contest the allegation. Tears were falling down his cheeks as he wiped Curvis's face with his fingers, cleaning away the blood.

'Al! The Cavaly,' Curvis whimpered. 'Where youl takling us? Plison?'

The two suited men did not even acknowledge the runaways. One of them turned to a guard. 'Get them down to the car,' he ordered soberly.

Bullet, holding one of Curvis's arms around his shoulders

and helping him to walk, was led out of the building and into a waiting car, its engine still running. Incessant rain was bouncing off the windscreen. Standing on the pavement, holding an umbrella in his right hand, his eyes unforgiving, was Rodney. Bullet did not see him through his tears.

He laid Curvis down in the back seat gently. He felt the car pick up speed and was jolted as the vehicle went over the road-ramps. 'Four of us mighty are we,' he whispered. Being free ain't worth this, he thought. Look what it led to. Maybe we do need some kinda rules and discipline that Rodney keeps going on about . . . I can't believe what's happened to us. Poor Curvis. What come over him? I wish I was big enough to take on that fucking bully! And Lord knows what Carlton has done and where Glenroy is? What were those sirens for?

Disfigured and suffering, Curvis managed a smile. 'I weren't scared . . . Bullet . . . I weren't scared.'

PART FOUR

'Til Shiloh

8 July 1985

A lean, coffee-coloured man with dreadlocks stared studiously across the grassland before him. He glanced at his digital watch and saw it was just before 10.30 a.m. He heard, amongst the loud hum of the snarling traffic, the high-pitched tone of a skylark. He turned around and watched the vehicles inch by. Away to his right, the congestion on the A40 flyover had not relented since the rush hour.

Wearing black jeans that were now greying and a simple blue shirt over his black vest, the man scanned the drivers of the vehicles, expecting to recognise someone any moment. He gazed beyond the road and winced as he ran his eyes over the harsh brown exterior of Wormwood Scrubs prison.

It was a warm day. The sun attempted to steal a look through the stubborn cloud cover. The man could smell the over-heating engines and petrol fumes in the atmosphere. 'I hate London,' he whispered to himself. His diamond-shaped face had a goatish beard underlining it and his eyes seemed too vacant to belong to a city-dweller. He concentrated on the drivers again. Dangling from his right hand was a plastic bag, carrying a paperback and a broadsheet newspaper.

A car slowed down. The rasta ambled over to the car. In the back seat, a young woman, appearing tired but happy, was tending to a young child. She had straw-coloured hair and a freckled, pale face. Her chestnut-coloured eyes were round and kind. The man smiled and nodded in acknowledgement as the driver, his brown hair crudely cropped, stepped out of the car.

He went over to greet the dread, grinning widely. 'You wanna cut off those locks, Curvis,' Bullet hailed. 'You look like a nutter!'

The friends embraced, patting each other on the back. 'So you made it then,' resumed Bullet.

'As if I would miss this day! I would've hitch-hiked from John O'Groats!' Curvis said hello to Bullet's wife and produced a ridiculous grin for the baby. 'How's my little godson?' he cooed.

The baby gazed at Curvis's locks, wondering what to make of them. Curvis turned to Bullet again. 'So what was Live Aid like?' Bullet asked. 'I saw some of it on the telly.'

'Fantastic, especially U2.' Curvis laughed. 'My only problem was, everyone thought I was selling weed!'

Linda, Bullet's wife, joined in with the laughter. 'So, what time is Carlton being released?' she asked, swabbing her baby's mouth with a tissue.

'In twenty-five minutes,' replied Curvis.

Linda observed their faces and for a moment thought that their friendship was too close; too wrapped up in history and emotion, and sometimes she felt like an outsider. Since Bullet had been demobbed from the army, Linda had become the silent watcher as her husband and Curvis reminisced into the

254

nights and early mornings, talking of home-made trolleys, secret camps, hills, forests and adventure. She was troubled by the fact that Curvis knew more about her husband than she did.

Curvis climbed into the front passenger seat. Bullet pushed the car into gear and made the short journey up a side road to a small car park in front of the prison gates. He switched the engine off and Linda took this as a cue to question Curvis. 'So how is your brother Stanton?'

'Not too bad,' Curvis answered cheerfully, not letting anything deflate him on *this* day. 'He's a lot better than he was. Now and again he gets dizzy spells but he's started to do things for himself lately.'

Bullet glanced at his wife, both thinking that Curvis might be glossing over the facts and not revealing the full extent of Stanton's condition. Curvis resumed. 'When I collected him last year, I found that he was aware of things around him, you know. It's just that them bastards gave him all sorts of injections and shit to make him docile.'

Bullet's thoughts transferred to Carlton. 'You think Carlton will be alright? I spoke to him two weeks ago and he seemed OK. But I think he's a little scared of coming out. I hope he takes to it.'

Curvis glanced at the baby and then Linda. 'All of us are gonna have to help him to adjust . . . He's still angry. After all, the judge didn't believe Carlton about Thomas. And I'll never know why Elvin didn't testify . . . We'll have to keep a close watch on him. But Carlton's mentally strong. Probably stronger than all of us.'

'What are we gonna say when he asks about Glenroy,' interjected Linda.

There was silence for a few seconds. Bullet and Curvis watched the baby play with Linda's right index finger. 'Tell him the truth,' Curvis answered finally. 'We haven't found him, so what more can we do? I know he's told us we could've done more, but we've done our best. He'll just have to help us . . . We'll find him.'

'Yeah, we will,' concurred Linda, who had never met Glenroy but had heard so much. 'The system can't hide him for ever.'

The glorious day of Carlton's release was now flecked with a sadness Bullet or Curvis could not deny. Glenroy's smile was deep in their minds and when his name was mentioned, they had to relive that dreadful night back in the Pinewood Hills. For nine years they had been haunted by it and now could only speak of it with their eyes. They looked out of the car window and began to count down the minutes.

'So, what was it like in Northern Ireland when you left?' asked Curvis, turning his gaze to Bullet.

'It was rough,' replied Bullet. 'It's hard to take that most of the people over there hate you all because you're wearing an army uniform and have an English accent . . . I'm glad to get out of it . . . If it was left to me, I'd leave 'em to it. I mean, even a small kid would walk up to you as a dare from older kids and spit in your face. I used to wonder what the fuck I was doing over there. And on the other side, Protestants were glad to see us, offering to buy us drinks and introducing their daughters to us. And if you take up their offers, the Catholics look down on you even more . . . All the shit ain't worth it.'

Linda looked at her spouse curiously; he never answered her questions on Northern Ireland like this. Bullet continued. 'There's so much hate over there. You can just feel it walking the streets, going shopping, going for a drink. It makes me wonder whether the so-called Catholics and Protestants are really religious at all. They're just like two tit-for-tat gangs killing each other.'

'Seems like you've had enough,' remarked Curvis, still wondering why the hell Bullet had enlisted in the army in the first place; nine years ago they had almost come to blows about Bullet's decision. To this day Curvis could never understand why Bullet swapped one institution for another. 'You're out now and you can do what you like.'

'Well, I've served nine years and seen the world,' said Bullet. 'The army has been good to me. It bought me a house, taught me how to strip any engine, and I made some good friends . . . It was surprising how many guys from children's homes I met.'

While Curvis thought about Bullet's last sentence, Linda delved into her handbag and found a baby's bottle for her child. She lifted the baby onto her lap and the tot began sucking eagerly. Bullet, scanning the prison gates, asked, 'So what about you? You can't travel around so much now you have to look after Stanton.'

'Yeah, well. Stanton looked after me when I was a kid. You're right, I miss the travelling around; I loved working in the Lake District doing stuff for the Outward Bound Centre. But I'm getting by. Just the other day I was doing a private landscape job on this big house. Hopefully, when I make enough money, we'll move to the country somewhere.'

'Where would you go?' asked Bullet.

Curvis shrugged his shoulders, not feeling confident of his dream. 'I dunno . . . somewhere quiet with a lot of space. Maybe the New Forest. I done some work for a rich family down there; they treated me really good. They had a big stone house and they wanted me to do up their front and back gardens – there was enough space for two five-a-side pitches.'

'It's a pity you couldn't have taken Stanton down there with you,' sighed Linda.

'Yeah. I told the people who I worked for about Stanton and they used to give me the fare to go up and see him. But I felt guilty, you know. There was me enjoying life while my brother is banged up. Glenroy gets to me the same way, even though I don't know where he is.'

'Me too,' nodded Bullet. 'Sometimes I ask myself why did life work out for me? I feel *too* lucky. It's weird.'

'You two got nothing to feel guilty about,' stressed Linda. She had repeated this line many times before. 'Carlton and Glenroy wouldn't want you to feel guilty.'

Ten minutes later, Carlton emerged from the prison gates. Bullet watched him without moving a facial muscle, forgetting to climb out of his car. A rush of emotion overcame him, and without realising it, he began to cry. Curvis, disguising his feelings, quickly leaped out of the vehicle. 'Over here! Carlton, over here!'

Carlton was wearing an old, denim jacket. His blue, faded denims were struggling to contain his bulging thighs. His thick moustache and beard added five years to his real age. He was carrying a sports bag, draped over his square shoulders, and as he emerged from the shadows of the prison gates, walking very tall, he looked up to the heavens, tasting his freedom. He spotted a bird, fluttering to rest on the prison roof, and smiled. A car horn prompted him to snap his head to the right, realising he hadn't heard a sound like it for so long. I'm *out*, he thought.

Bullet got out of the car and sat on the bonnet. Curvis ran to greet his old friend. They hugged each other warmly, Curvis almost reduced to tears. 'Don't go all fucking soppy on me!' Carlton grinned. 'Fuck me, you only saw me three weeks ago!'

They walked together, almost bouncing with joy, towards Bullet's car. Curvis stood back so Bullet could receive Carlton's attention. 'You fucking nutter!' Carlton hailed, spreading his arms and enveloping Bullet in a bear hug, lifting him off his feet.

Linda sobbed and the baby didn't quite know what to make of it all. Carlton glanced at the infant. 'Bullet! Fuck me! I didn't know you was capable. Has he joined the cadets yet?'

As Bullet took hold of Carlton's bag and placed it inside the boot, Carlton climbed into the back seat beside Linda, and offered to hold the child. 'Linda, how the fuck could you let

Bullet call him Monty? Of all the names in the fucking world! Monty!'

Linda laughed, despite not liking the way Carlton swore in front of her son. 'It was his choice – but I call him Monny.'

Curvis filled the front passenger seat, and Bullet, unable to contain his joy, turned around and ruffled Carlton's hair before turning on the ignition.

'I can't fucking believe it,' said Carlton, peering through the window at the prison walls. 'I thought I'd never fucking get out of the place . . . I can't believe it.'

Two minutes later, Bullet was driving towards the Shepherd's Bush roundabout. 'So where're we gonna go? Carlton's gotta have a few beers.'

'Down my way, innit,' replied Curvis. 'Croydon. There's a good pub just up the road from my flat.'

Carlton shook his head, his face apologetic. 'Look, er, it's a nice thought, but I don't wanna spend my first day in a fucking pub.'

'How about we go to an off licence and buy a few cans,' offered Bullet.

'Yeah, that'll be better,' Carlton nodded.

'We'll pick up the drinks and head for my place,' said Curvis.

'Who won the tennis?' Carlton suddenly asked, catching his friends off-guard. 'Did Becker win? 'Cos of some fight in my block, we lost privileges.'

'Becker won,' answered Curvis. 'He's only seventeen. He wouldn't have won if McEnroe had been there.'

'They let us see the Barry McGuigan fight last month,' mentioned Carlton. 'Inside, one Paddy calls him the Nuclear Leprechaun.'

'Nuclear what?' asked Bullet, trying to read a road sign.

'Nuclear Leprechaun,' repeated Carlton. 'Leprechaun's Irish for midget, innit.'

'Yeah, he's good,' affirmed Bullet. 'But that Pedroza bloke looked like he was pushing forty.'

Later, as Bullet was driving alongside Streatham Common, Carlton gazed skywards, appreciating the brightening heavens. He looked at the field, which rose steadily before meeting a row of trees. It reminded him of the fields adjacent to Spurleigh. 'Hey, Bullet,' he called. 'Stop the car for a minute.'

Bullet braked and pulled over, his two left-sided wheels on the pavement. Carlton climbed out of the car while his friends exchanged curious glances. Carlton ambled onto the grass and performed an extravagant yawn, spreading his arms wide. 'YES!' he suddenly roared. 'YES!' He stooped down and plucked a blade of grass and inserted it into his mouth. He started to delicately chew, allowing his taste buds to savour the grass. He then returned to the car, only to find his friends laughing. He grinned widely and nodded. 'I feel free now.'

'Get in the car, you nutter!' Bullet mocked.

On the journey to Curvis's home, they passed a secondary school with the kids enjoying dinner break in the playground. The playful yelps and screams made Carlton realise he hadn't heard children playing for nine years. A sudden sense of loss swept over him. He turned his face away and looked at the car floor and momentarily covered his face with his palms.

Half an hour later, after Curvis and Bullet had bought canned lagers, crisps, peanuts, cigarettes, tobacco, cigarette papers and chocolate bars from an off-licence, they were pulling up beside Curvis's four-storey block of flats in South Croydon on a small council estate.

Curvis led the way to his third-floor flat, leaving Bullet to collect Carlton's bag. Linda winded Monty before carrying him out of the car. Arriving at his unpainted front door, Curvis turned to his friends. 'Stanton's probably asleep . . . He sleeps a lot . . .'

Curvis turned the key in the latch and stepped aside to usher his friends inside. The walls of the short hallway were painted a turquoise colour, and Curvis had fitted beige-coloured ceramic tiling on the floor. Leading off right of the hallway was the kitchen, where there was just enough room to walk around the four-seater pine dining table. Curvis turned right at the end of the passage and led his mates to the lounge, where the biggest feature was a rubber plant, its top leaves kissing the Artexed ceiling. The walls were painted in calm-sea green. Between the sofas was a rectangular, smoked-glass coffee table, supporting another green plant. A portable television set was placed on a wooden table at the far end of the room, where on either side of it Curvis had placed two more plants, their stems coiling around two sticks of bamboo.

Carlton surveyed the room. 'If you get any more plants, you'll start to breed fucking triffids!'

Linda filled one sofa, laying Monty down to sleep, and Carlton occupied the other, while watching Bullet set up the beers on the table. 'Carlton,' called Curvis. 'Grab a can then . . . Do you want a glass?'

'Nah, I wanna drink out of a can. Makes a change from drinking out of paper cups for so fucking long.'

Everyone picked up and opened their cans and Curvis offered a toast. 'To Carlton, and the muscles that grow on the big bastard. Cheers!'

'CHEERS!'

Curvis went to get something from the kitchen. Carlton watched Monty struggle to fall asleep and Bullet grabbed the peanuts. 'Couple of years ago,' Carlton started, 'I was sharing a cell with this guy who wouldn't accept any drink at meal-times. He never trusted anybody, not even other prisoners.'

Linda began rocking Monty to sleep. Bullet sat up, wanting Carlton to continue. 'Weird he was,' Carlton resumed. 'He was inside for beating up his mum. His mum was about seventy and this bloke was nearly fifty.'

'Sounds like a weirdo to me,' commented Linda.

'Yeah,' Carlton answered. 'Fuck knows why the fucking screws put him with me. One and a half years he was in my cell . . . When he got out he started to write me fucking letters, telling me I was his only mate.'

'Didn't you make any friends?' asked Bullet.

'Not really. Not real friends. You talk to people and get on, but I never got too close. I just kept myself to myself most of the time. If someone wanted to try it on, then I'd fuck 'em up. Doing the solitary was worth it 'cos when you come out, no one fucks with you . . . There was one guy I kinda liked. I felt sorry for the bastard. His name was Hilton Daniels and he came from up north; at first I couldn't understand a fucking word he said. His mum was a fucking smack addict, and she would do anything possible to get her fix; she was a total lost fucking cause. 'Cos she wanted Hilton to nick stuff so she could buy her smack, she got Hilton addicted to smack an' all. When he came to the Scrubs, he was going through cold fucking turkey. The screws didn't give a shit, taking the piss out of him and beating the fuck out of him when they felt like it. I'm telling ya, I've never seen a man sweat or spew up so much. He stank, the poor fucker.'

Curvis returned to the room and sat down on the brown carpeted floor, his back against the armrest of the sofa. He opened a bag of crisps and Carlton continued.

'When I first moved to the Scrubs, I had a fight on my second afternoon. This fucking guy thought he ruled the place and started to pick on me, trying to nick my tobacco and stuff. At games me and this guy had a roll. I fucked him up good and proper. Got fucking solitary again. But it didn't bother me 'cos of all the times I done solitary at Wandsworth. Funny enough, when I came out, me and this guy got on. We used to share our roll-ups. He got out but now he's back inside. He can't handle life outside. It fucks him up. Prison is like a fucking home from home for him.'

Listening intently, Bullet hardly recognised Carlton's voice.

To him it sounded cold and clinical, as if he had become quite immune to anybody's suffering. On his prison visits, Bullet had not detected this but now it was all too obvious. At the same time Curvis was telling himself that it might take Carlton another nine years to erase the institution of prison out of his system.

Carlton continued after swigging from his can, oblivious to the worried glances his friends were exchanging. 'After a few months in the Scrubs, it weren't that bad. Every Friday afternoon we were taken to a building in the middle of the grounds. They showed us films. Some guys used to wank if there was something sexy on. All it would take was a tart in a fucking bra and some of the pervs would have their hands inside their trousers going at it like they wanna pull their fucking dick off. None of them fuckers sat by me . . . You had to be careful what chair you sat on.'

By now, Linda had a look of disbelief on her face. Doesn't he know there is a woman in the room? she asked herself. Carlton went on. 'Bullet, thanks for reminding me if I wanted some Rizlas. You won't believe how precious those bits of paper are inside. Fucking precious.' Carlton lit a roll-up, pulled hard and reclined in the sofa, sighing pleasurably. 'Most of the time we had to use brown paper that we got from recreation. Some guys could roll up tobacco in anything. One guy could use shit paper. He was a fucking expert at it. No one picked on him 'cos he could roll you up tobacco in any shit. Very useful.'

Just then, a shuffling figure emerged from the hallway. Carlton was just about to recall another incident inside when he switched his eyes to take in the lumbering, giant figure of Stanton. Standing six feet five with the build of an A-list celebrity minder, Stanton slowly looked around the room, attempting to recognise the guests.

Stanton had a round, bald patch on the top of his head; the hair around it was thick and uncombed. Thick sleep matter stuck in the corners of his hound-dog vacant eyes, that blinked more than normal. His mouth was open, his breathing audible. He moved in slow motion. Finally his eyes located his brother. 'Alright, bru', bruv. Who's? Who's these people here? What? What are they doing here?'

Curvis stood up and walked towards his sibling, placing a reassuring hand on his left shoulder. 'You know Bullet and Carlton. Remember? From Pinewood Oaks? Bullet was here the other day.'

Bullet, Carlton and Linda could almost hear the slow whirring of Stanton's mind, trying desperately to remember. Bullet wanted to nudge his memory. 'Stanton! You know me. You should do 'cos you gave me a right beating a long time ago 'cos I was a bit cheeky.'

Stanton's face was in deep thought, but his eyes flickered into life and he nodded slightly. A quarter smile was developing as he searched Bullet's features.

Carlton laughed, not in amusement but to mask the pity he was feeling. He looked at Stanton's heavy frame. 'You've grown a fucking bit!' he chuckled. 'I thought I would've caught up with you by now.'

Stanton laughed freely, the deep sound emanating from his stomach. He turned to his brother. 'Yeah, bruv. I know 'em ... If they wanna start anything, let me know, bruv.' Stanton shuffled towards the sofa, staring at Bullet and Carlton cautiously. Linda made space for him, picking up Monty and placing him on her lap uneasily.

'What do you want to eat?' Curvis asked his brother. 'Egg on toast?'

'Yeah, bruv. Make it two eggs, not three.'

Curvis went into the kitchen, leaving his friends watching Monty being rocked to sleep once more. There was silence for a few seconds.

'I wish Elvin had come to visit me before he killed himself,' said Carlton. 'I might've stopped him from doing it ... When

264

I heard about it, I felt sick. I didn't talk to no one for fucking days.'

'Me too,' said Bullet. 'I couldn't understand why he didn't call one of us if he was feeling like shit . . . I still can't believe it. His wife is in a right state. I couldn't tell her nothing. Elvin didn't want her to know. It took him four years to finally tell her he spent his childhood in a children's home.'

'It's for the best,' concurred Carlton. 'It's enough for her that she lost him. No point adding distress to that by telling her about that fucking perv Thomas.'

Linda visibly shuddered, halting the rocking of her baby. She glanced at Bullet in such a way as to indicate her displeasure at the topic of conversation. Carlton glanced at Stanton, who was trying to remember who the hell Elvin was. 'You know,' Carlton began, 'sometimes I wish I'd never killed the fucking perv. If he'd lived I might've had a stronger fucking case. People might've believed me. In a way I done the fucking perv a favour. It still gets to me that all the other fucking staff in his house said he done nothing wrong. And it's a good thing I don't know where his fucking wife lives. She must know, 'cos he wasn't fucking her, he was trying to fuck the kids . . . I wouldn't hesitate to kick her ugly face in . . . She must've fucking known!' Carlton's voice had become bitter and vengeful.

'Hopefully, one day,' Bullet said, 'all the shit that happened in Pinewood Oaks will come out. I've heard stories that Thomas wasn't the only one. That guy he used to be friends with, he used to drive that red Mini with the blacked-out windows . . . Geoffrey's his name. He used to take kids up the top field for football practice. I've heard some disgusting things about him. There must have been some perv club or something.'

'Yeah, I remember him,' nodded Carlton, picking up another can of beer. 'He looked like a fucking hippy with his long hair and beard, and he was always taking the little kids in his car, packing them all in . . . It kind of gives me the shits just to think about it, 'cos back then, we didn't have a clue what he was up to.'

Curvis returned, carrying a tray with a plateful of toast and fried eggs and a mug of hot chocolate. He placed the food on Stanton's lap, his locks nearly falling into the breakfast. He then seated himself on the arm of a sofa. Carlton watched him. 'Do you know where Mellor is?' Carlton asked.

'Last time I heard, he was selling drugs,' Curvis replied, matter of fact. 'He moved to Liverpool where he's got two kids with a girl up there. Sonia went to visit him; he's got a big-time car and was wearing some expensive suit.'

'So what's Sonia doing with herself?' Bullet asked.

'Training to be a social worker,' Curvis replied. 'Can you believe it? Her son, who she had with Mellor, is seven now. I think she still has a soft spot for Mellor, but she's got her head screwed on.'

'Mellor lost a good thing there,' commented Carlton.

Curvis watched affectionately as his brother ate his breakfast. He turned to Carlton. 'So you'll be alright at Bullet's house?'

'Yeah, until I sort myself out . . . I learned about picture-framing inside. I'll have to have a look if I can put it to use.'

'As long as he don't snore, he can stay as long as he likes,' laughed Bullet. 'I hope you don't mind living in Sutton; nothing ever happens there.'

'Course I won't mind,' replied Carlton, placing his beer can on the table and lighting another cigarette. 'It's got a park with football pitches, ain't it? And now it's summer I wanna get into a cricket team. Take out my anger on a few suburban wanky batsmen . . . I really missed sport inside, especially as I was in isolation so much, and I don't want to see another fucking gym with weights again. I'm fucked off with doing weights.'

'Maybe you can take Monty out for walks in the park,' suggested Linda, glad that the topic of conversation had changed.

266

'Yeah, I'll be up for that,' Carlton smiled. 'I'll teach him to be the best sportsman ever. And I'll make sure he doesn't join the fucking army – any Action Men that Monty gets, I'll be burning 'em.'

Curvis laughed heartily, happy that Carlton hadn't lost his humour. Bullet nodded and smiled warmly. Assured of a receptive audience, Carlton turned to Curvis. 'So you've finally given up tramping around the countryside? I could never understand why you went off to Wales and Cornwall and fucked-up places like that where black people are as fucking rare as a fucking giraffe. I bet the people who saw you are still recovering from seeing ya. You'd never catch me going to mad places where there's more fucking cows and sheep than humans. I hope you ain't got addicted to eating fucking hay and sniffing pig shit.'

Even Linda joined in the laughter. Carlton continued. 'There was one guy in my block who sniffed some kind of paint. Sad bastard he was. I mean, of all the fucking things you can get addicted to. Fucking paint. Poor bastard wasn't allowed to go to art classes – screws wouldn't let him. Sad thing about it was, he was a bit tasty with his drawings and shit, so we heard.' He paused and thought of Glenroy. 'One day he paid for half a cup of turps with his tobacco. We used to call him Nasal Angelo.'

Bullet almost fell to the floor, overcome by mirth, and Curvis laughed harder than he had in a long time. Stanton grinned a ridiculous grin, still searching for the humour.

Carlton watched and waited until everybody had composed themselves while inhaling deeply on his roll-up. He eyed Curvis. 'So what are we gonna do about looking for Glenroy?'

Curvis felt the merriment being sucked out of him as he exchanged worried glances with Bullet. Stanton was still grinning as Linda dropped her head to gaze at Monty, not wanting to take part in this conversation.

'I've managed to get some mental hospital addresses,'

267

Curvis finally answered. 'Linda's got some as well. They're all in the Surrey area; we thought we'd start there first.'

'You should've started years ago . . . Well, when you're going to check them out, let me know . . . I promised myself that I'll see him again . . . And say sorry . . . I didn't get the chance at the time.'

'We'll find him,' nodded Bullet. 'As four mighty are we . . .'

On hearing these words, Carlton's eyes became misty and guilt crept up on him. He tried to suppress it but it was all too apparent. He dropped his head and looked at the floor. 'I have to say thanks to you lot,' he said in a quiet voice. 'You kept me going when I was going through all sorts of shit. And one of you was always visiting me when you had the chance.' Tears were now falling freely. 'Even Elvin saw me when I was in Wandsworth . . . Bless his poor soul . . . You lot kept me alive, man.' Carlton covered his face with his right palm, his sobbing just about audible. Curvis crossed the room and squeezed Carlton's left shoulder. 'You would've done the same for any of us, and even more.'

Bullet gazed at Carlton and was close to tears himself. As Carlton lifted his hand away from his face, Bullet caught him with a look and clenched his right fist. 'I wouldn't have survived what you went through,' he said. 'But you did 'cos you're the strongest.'

In acknowledgement, Carlton tightened his right fist.

Curvis stood up. 'I'm taking Stanton to the Pinewood Hills tomorrow,' he announced. 'Get some fresh air and get out of London for a bit. Why don't you come with us? It will bring back some memories.'

'How you getting there?' asked Bullet.

'This guy who I'm doing work for, I can borrow his car – he don't mind 'cos he thinks I'm doing up his garden a treat. I'll just say I need the car to get some supplies.'

'Yeah, I'm up for that,' responded Carlton keenly. 'As long as Curvis doesn't set up camp and fucking live up there, and have us tramping around the fucking hills like lost sheep.'

Bullet looked at Linda, making a silent request. 'Why not?' she said. 'Monty could do with some fresh air. It'll be a good day out . . . I'll make some sandwiches and stuff.'

Bullet smiled and nodded at Carlton. Carlton downed the last drop of his beer and got up to his feet. 'I don't want you lot to think I'm ungrateful, but to be honest, I can't wait to drop down on a decent bed.'

'It's all made up,' smiled Linda, slowly warming to Carlton. 'There's a little portable TV in your room as well, and Bullet bought some sports magazines that are on your bed.'

'And you still kept that Michael Holding poster?' Carlton asked urgently.

'Of course!' Bullet replied. 'You think I'd be here now if I'd lost it? Though I still reckon Jeff Thompson bowled faster than him.'

'Don't start that again, Bullet,' Carlton smiled.

Linda picked up a sleeping Monty and held him on her shoulder. Bullet and Carlton prepared to leave, saying good-byes to Curvis and Stanton. As Curvis watched his friends leave from the balcony, he glanced skywards. 'We'll see ya tomorrow, Mum.'

The next day

Bullet had to drive with his sun blind down to shield his eyes from the glare; the afternoon heat was nudging ninety degrees. On a country road, five miles out of Pinewood, he was following Curvis's borrowed Citroën. Carlton, his passenger window wound down fully and the tail wind refreshing his face, was staring out into the fields, remembering the past. As they passed sheep and cows grazing in the undulating fields, Carlton thought that the area hadn't changed much. Linda was in the back seat with a restless Monty, fascinated and eager to visit her husband's past. Bullet saw a road sign for Spurleigh, three miles away at the next right turning. Curvis palmed his horn in acknowledgement and Carlton smiled, recalling fondly their day out at the open-air swimming pool.

Curvis, who had Stanton in his passenger seat, was pointing out landmarks to his brother in an attempt to jog his memory. Stanton only reacted to his sibling's questions when they overtook a green country bus. He recollected more memories when the winding road began its climb uphill, passing large detached houses with individual name plaques on their gates. *The Hollies*, *Brambles*, *Ash Cottage*, *Laburnum Meadows*. Curvis knew them all, and reminisced about when he was a child, travelling to his uncle's place on the top of a green bus, reading these very names and wondering why they didn't have numbers.

Twenty minutes later, Curvis drove along a dirt track that led into the Pinewood Hills. The trees didn't seem as tall as before but the scent of the pines and the baked earth was invigorating. He inhaled deeply through his nose while closing his eyes for a second. Stanton was animated, looking here and there, knowing he had once been in this place.

The dirt track sharply inclined, cutting into the forest for one and a half miles, and then ceased at a natural plateau, where the renamed Seven Sisters Café stood. Resting outside the café, sipping cold drinks and wearing tight Lycra shorts and brightly coloured T-shirts, were a group of cyclists. Their tired features showing they had just completed riding their course. Carlton watched them out of his window and thought that none of them could beat him in a cycle race.

Curvis pulled up in a small, gravel car park that hadn't been there nine years ago. Bullet parked beside him and collected the picnic bags out of his boot. Linda, climbing out of the car and holding a fidgety Monty in her arms, circled around on the spot, observing her surroundings in awe. Looking south-west, she marvelled at the different shades of green fields that were bisected by the twinkling Crown Ash river that sliced through the lowest depths of the valley, giving life to the tall reeds and bushes that lined its route. It arched around the back of Spurleigh, beyond the hills. Bales of hay specked the green ocean and the isolated farm-houses appeared as if someone had painted them in. 'Wow!' she gasped.

Cows and sheep looked like Christmas cracker toys, and a lonesome tractor, its driver invisible, left in its wake a strip of parched brown field. The still black windmill, standing in a glade and surrounded by woodland, looked like a dark, misshapen crucifix. Linda thought of Elvin and Carlton and the suffering they had had to endure. She looked straight west and saw the best sight of them all: appearing like a golden Loch Ness monster, and with the barrow stones returning the sun's glare with interest, the Seven Sister hills dipped and rose as far as she could see, disappearing into an unguessable distance. The leaves in the trees caught the sunlight, reflecting a lucid green. Linda could just make out the faraway outlines of the South Down contours that shielded the Sussex border, underlining the brilliant blue sky, and crowned by a ripple of heat. 'It's beautiful here, innit.'

'Yeah,' Curvis answered, smiling at Linda's wonder and collecting an ice box full of soft drinks from the boot of his car. 'The scenery around here always made me calm. But at night it gives you the shits.'

'You can say that again,' said Carlton, seeing Bullet nod in agreement. 'It . . . It *changes*.'

Although wanting to return to the base camp that he had located nine years ago, Curvis thought it would be too far for Linda and her child, so he led his friends to a nearby isolated glade, surrounded by pines and bramble, where Bullet lay down a blanket. They all had a late afternoon tea underneath a still hot sun, washing it down with Coca-Cola and lemonade.

Curvis had spotted in the breezeless sky the perfect glide of a hobby bird that was searching for a smaller prey, and he followed its flight. He could hear the tuneful songs in the trees from warblers and skylarks, and he wished he could warn them of the peril above. His eyes returned to ground level and he pointed out to Linda the routes that he and his friends had taken nine years ago, while Stanton, becoming more animated and aware by the minute, challenged Carlton to an arm wrestle. Stanton won, leaving Carlton to curse under his breath. Bullet was playing with Monty, tickling his stomach, trying to teach him to say 'daddy'.

An hour later, when the sun was dipping under the branches – and although the Pinewood Oaks children's home had been closed for a year, making way for a proposed redevelopment of a private housing estate – the friends decided to visit the place in an attempt to recapture more memories. As Curvis turned into the complex, he noticed that the Lodge was now vacant and signs indicated that demolition was about to commence. For some reason he felt a sadness. Behind him, Bullet and Carlton felt the same melancholy, as if something had been uprooted from their souls. Curvis drove slowly. The deserted fields and unoccupied cottages and buildings troubled him. The sounds of shrieking children, gardeners mowing their lawns, barks of housemothers and housefathers, screams of foul during a football game, and the cry of tin-tam-tommy emitting from the piggery, were no more than sinking memories. In contrast, beside him Stanton was pointing out places, smiling, the environment refreshing his brain.

Curvis turned right as he came to the community centre, slowing to ten miles an hour. He almost expected a child to emerge from the bushes and pelt his car with acorns. But there was no one around.

Bullet tailed Curvis into the valley of the piggery, and Carlton felt a pang of guilt as they approached the cottage where he had spent his childhood. Auntie Josephine loomed large in his mind. I have to try and get in touch, he promised himself. The nursery was still there, its flat roof scorched by the sun. Curvis picked up speed. They veered left into a bend, approaching the swimming pool complex and the top field. A hundred yards away, Curvis saw the branches and leaves of the sycamore tree, standing in splendid isolation, their rendezvous point nine years ago. He smiled and decided to stop there.

Curvis and Bullet pulled up, and as everybody climbed out of the cars, they noticed that the gnats hadn't departed like everyone else. On their left was the southern tip of the orchard that seemed to be denser than ever before. To their right was the top field, and Carlton thought of cricket matches with the onlooking mayor sitting on his throne.

Just twenty yards from the hedges that formed the boundary to the top field, stood the sycamore tree, its stature imperious and its leaves like a browny-green crown; skylarks swooped in and out. The trunk was as straight as a Buckingham Palace guard, the inconsistent grooves in the bark visible from fifty yards away. Suddenly, Carlton ran for it. Bullet and Curvis quickly followed him, thinking Carlton had seen something. They caught up with him beneath the umbrella of the sycamore leaves.

'What is it?' asked Bullet.

'It's stupid really,' replied Carlton, his expression wistful.

'What's stupid?' asked Curvis, noticing that his brother was running freely into the field, singing something. Linda, with Monty hanging on her shoulder, was walking towards Bullet.

'For some crazy reason,' Carlton finally answered, 'I thought I might see Glenroy . . . Right here.' He dropped his head, staring at the grass. Tears were welling up in his eyes. Bullet and Curvis went to him. Bullet placed his hand on Carlton's left shoulder as Curvis wiped away a tear from Carlton's face with his left forefinger.

'We'll find him,' Curvis promised, his face filling up with resolve. 'Whatever it takes . . . We'll find him.'

Bullet nodded, his insides burning with determination.

Curvis lifted his head and closed his eyes as his gaze met the sun. He visualised his mother. Her face was unblemished and pretty. She was smiling. A small tear dropped onto his cheek and he knew now that to truly enjoy the most perfect happiness, you had to experience the lowest depths of pain. He had never been so convinced that a guardian angel had been watching over himself, Stanton and his friends. For some reason he sensed his mother's blessing on their joint search for Glenroy. 'Thank you, Mum,' he whispered. 'Thank you.'